He's the One

CARA COLTER
BARBARA HANNAY
JACKIE BRAUN

Published in Great Britain 2015
by Mills & Boon, an imprint of Harlequin (UK) Limited,
Eton House, 18-24 Paradise Road, Richmond, Surrey, TW9 1SR

HE'S THE ONE © 2015 Harlequin Books S.A.

Winning a Groom in 10 Dates, Molly Cooper's Dream Date and *Mr Right There All Along* were first published in Great Britain by Harlequin (UK) Limited.

Winning a Groom in 10 Dates © 2010 Cara Colter
Molly Cooper's Dream Date © 2011 Barbara Hannay
Mr Right There All Along © 2011 Jackie Braun Fridline

ISBN: 978-0-263-25206-4
eBook ISBN: 978-1-474-00385-8

05-0315

Harlequin (UK) Limited's policy is to use papers that are natural, renewable and recyclable products and made from wood grown in sustainable forests. The logging and manufacturing processes conform to the legal environmental regulations of the country of origin.

Printed and bound in Spain
by CPI, Barcelona

MOLLY COOPER'S DREAM DATE

BY
BARBARA HANNAY

Barbara Hannay was born in Sydney, educated in Brisbane, and has spent most of her adult life living in tropical North Queensland, where she and her husband have raised four children. While she has enjoyed many happy times camping and canoeing in the bush, she also delights in an urban lifestyle—chamber music, contemporary dance, movies and dining out. An English teacher, she has always loved writing, and now, by having her stories published, she is living her most cherished fantasy.

Visit www.barbarahannay.com

Special thanks to Jenny Haddon, whose wonderful
London hospitality inspired this story.

CHAPTER ONE

'THIS is my favourite part,' Molly whispered as the glamorous couple on her TV screen walked sadly but stoically to opposite ends of London's Westminster Bridge. 'He's going to turn back to her any minute now.'

Molly was curled on her couch in a tense ball. Karli, at the other end of the couch, helped herself to more popcorn.

'Don't miss this, Karli. I cry every time. Look. He hears Big Ben, and he stops, and—' Molly's voice broke on a sob. 'He turns.' She hugged her knees. 'See the look on his face?'

'Ohhh…' Karli let out a hushed breath. 'You can see he really, *really* loves her.'

'I know. It's so beautiful.' Molly reached for tissues as the gorgeous hero stood alone on the bridge, stricken-faced, shoulders squared, waiting for the woman in the long fur coat to turn back to him.

Karli grabbed a cushion and clutched it to her chest. 'He'll chase after her.'

'No. It's up to her now. If she doesn't turn back, he knows she doesn't love him.'

On the screen, a red double-decker London bus slowed to a stop and the movie's heroine, in her ankle-length, glamorous coat, hurried to catch it.

'No,' Karli moaned as the bus took off with the woman on board, and the camera switched to another close-up of the hero's grimly devastated face. 'Don't tell me it's a sad ending.'

Molly pressed her lips together to stop herself from speaking. The camera tracked upwards to a bird's eye view of London, showing the silvery River Thames curving below, and the Houses of Parliament, Big Ben…the solitary figure of the hero standing on Westminster Bridge…and the red bus driving away.

Karli was scowling. Molly hugged her knees tighter, gratified that her friend was hooked into the tension.

The camera climbed higher still, and the London bus was matchbox-size. The sounds of the city traffic were replaced by music—violins swelling with lush and aching beauty.

Molly had seen this movie more than a dozen times, but tears still rolled down her cheeks.

And then…at last…

At *last*…

The bus stopped.

The tiny figure of the heroine emerged…

The camera swooped down once more, zooming closer and closer as the lovers ran towards each other, arms outstretched, embracing at last.

The credits began to roll. Karli wrinkled her nose. 'OK. I admit that wasn't bad.'

'Not bad?' Molly sniffed. 'I suppose that's why you practically bit a piece out of my sofa cushion? Come on—admit it's amazing. The look on Christian's face when he thinks he's lost Vanessa is *the* most emotional moment in cinematic history.' She gave a dramatic sigh. 'And London has to be the most romantic city in the world.'

Shrugging, Karli reached for more popcorn. 'Isn't Paris supposed to be the most romantic city?'

'No way. Not for me. Paris is—Paris is… Oh, I don't know.'

Molly gave a helpless flap of her hands. 'Paris just…isn't London.'

'Admit it, Mozza. You have a thing for English guys. You're convinced that London is full of perfect gentlemen.'

It was best to ignore her friend's sarcasm. Molly wasn't going to admit that it held a grain—OK, maybe even more than a grain—of truth. Her love affair with London was deeply personal.

Pressing the remote to turn the set off, she went to the window and looked out into the night. The moon was almost full and it silvered the tall pines on the headland and the smooth, sparkling surface of the Coral Sea.

'One thing's for sure,' she said. 'Nothing romantic like that is ever going to happen to me. Not on this island.'

'Oh, I don't know. Our island might not have Big Ben or Westminster Bridge, but the moonlight on Picnic Bay's not bad. I wasn't complaining when Jimbo proposed.'

Molly smiled as she turned from the window. 'Sorry. I wasn't counting you and Jimbo. You guys are as romantic as it gets—best friends since kindergarten. Everyone here knew you'd end up together.'

'Well, to be honest, it's not exactly romantic when your husband spends half his life away on a fishing trawler.'

'I guess.' Molly moved to the kitchen and reached for a saucepan to make hot chocolate. 'I shouldn't keep watching that movie. It always makes me restless—makes me want to take off and live in London.'

'Does it have to be London? If you want to get off the island, why don't you try Sydney or Brisbane? Even Cairns?'

Molly rolled her eyes. As if any Australian city could live up to her vision of England's famous capital. For as long as she could remember, she'd been entranced by London—by its history, its buildings, its pageantry, its culture.

She loved all the names—like Portobello Road, the

Serpentine, Piccadilly Circus and Battersea. For her they had a thrilling, magical ring. Like poetry.

Karli shrugged. 'If I went overseas, I'd rather go to America. Jimbo's going to take me to Las Vegas.'

'Wow. When?'

'One day. *Ha-ha.* If either of us ever gets a job with better pay.'

'Money's my problem, too. The mortgage on this place uses up most of my savings. And the rent in London's horrendous. I've checked on the internet.'

'But you might be able to manage it if you rented out this place.'

Molly shuddered. Renting this cottage would mean a series of strangers living here, and it wouldn't seem right when it had been her gran's home for more than fifty years.

'Or,' said Karli, 'what about a house swap? That way you'd get to pick who lives here, and it would only be for a short time. My cousin in Cairns swapped with a couple from Denmark, and it worked out fine.'

'A house swap?' A tingling sensation danced down Molly's spine. 'How does that work?'

Patrick Knight glared at the towering pile of paperwork on his desk, and then he glared at his watch. Past eight already, and he would be here for hours yet.

Grimacing, he picked up his mobile phone and thumbed a hasty text message. Angela was *not* going to like this, but it couldn't be helped.

Ange, so sorry. Snowed under at work. Will have to bow out of tonight. Can we make a date for Friday instead? P

Snapping the phone closed, Patrick reached for the next folder in the pile. His stomach growled, and along with his hunger pangs he felt a surge of frustration.

The past years of global financial crisis had seen his job in London's banking world morph from an interesting and challenging career into a source of constant stress.

It was like working in a war zone. Too many of his colleagues had been fired, or had resigned. Some had even suffered nervous breakdowns. At times he'd felt like the last man standing.

Yes, it was true that he *had* saved a couple of major accounts, but he was doing the work of three people in his department, and the shower of commendations from his boss had rather lost their shine. He'd reached the point where he had to ask why he was slogging away, working ridiculous hours and giving everything he had to his job, when his life outside the office was—

Non-existent.

Truth was, he no longer *had* a life away from the bank. No time to enjoy the lovely house he'd bought in Chelsea, no time to go out with his latest girlfriend. How he'd managed to meet Angela in the first place was a miracle, but almost certainly she would give up on him soon—just as her predecessors had.

As for the crazy, *crazy* promise he'd once made to himself that he would balance his working life with writing a novel. In his spare time. Ha-ha.

Except for Patrick it was no longer a laughing matter. This was *his* life, or rather his *non*-life, and he was wasting it. One day he'd wake up and discover he was fifty—like his boss—pale, anxious, boring and only able to talk about one thing. Work.

His mobile phone pinged. It was Angela, as expected. Tight-jawed, he clicked on her reply.

Sorry. Not Friday. Not ever. One cancellation too many.
Goodbye, sweet P. Ange

Patrick cursed, but he couldn't really blame Ange. Tomorrow he'd send her two—no, three dozen roses. But he suspected they wouldn't do the trick. Not this time. If he was honest, he couldn't pretend that her rejection would break his heart—but it *was* symptomatic of the depths to which his life had sunk.

In a burst of anger, he pushed his chair back from his desk and began to prowl.

The office felt like a prison. It *was* a damn prison, and he felt a mad urge to break out of it.

Actually, it wasn't a mad urge. It was a highly reasonable and justified need. A must.

In mid-prowl, his eyes fell on the globe of the world that he'd salvaged from the old boardroom when it had been refurbished—in those giddy days before the financial world had gone belly up. Now it sat in the corner of his office, and lately he'd stared at it often, seized by a longing to be anywhere on that tiny sphere.

Anywhere except London.

Walking towards it now, Patrick spun the globe and watched the coloured shapes of the continents swirl. He touched it with his finger, feeling the friction as its pace slowed.

If I were free, I'd go anywhere. When this globe stops spinning, I'll go wherever my finger is pointing.

The globe stopped. Patrick laughed. He'd been thinking of somewhere exotic, like Tahiti or Rio de Janeiro, but his finger was resting on the east coast of Australia. A tiny dot. An island.

He leaned closer to read the fine print. Magnetic Island.
Never heard of it.

About to dismiss it, he paused. *I said I'd go anywhere—anywhere in the world. Why don't I at least look this place up?*

But why bother? It wasn't as if it could happen. He wouldn't be going anywhere. He was locked in here.

But what if I made it happen? Surely it's time?

Back at his desk, Patrick tried a quick internet search for Magnetic Island, and his eyebrows lifted as the first page of links scrolled down. The island was clearly a tourist destination, with palm trees and white sand and blue tropical seas. Not so different from Tahiti, perhaps?

The usual variety of accommodations was offered. Then two words leapt out at him from the bottom of the screen: *House Swap.*

Intrigued, Patrick hit the link.

House Swap: Magnetic Island, Queensland, Australia
2 bedroom cottage
Location Details: Nestled among trees on a headland, this home has ocean views and is only a three-minute walk through the national park to a string of beautiful bays. Close to the Great Barrier Reef, the island provides a water wonderland for sailing, canoeing, parasailing, fishing and diving.
Preferred Swap Dates: From 1st April—flexible
Preferred Swap Length: Three to four months
Preferred Destination: London, UK

Patrick grinned. For a heady moment he could picture himself there—in a different hemisphere, in a different world.
Free, free…

Swimming with coral fishes. Lying in a hammock beneath palm trees. Checking out bikini-clad Australian girls. Writing the fabulous thriller that resided only in his head. Typing it on his laptop while looking out at the sparkling blue sea.

OK, amusement over. Nose back to the grindstone.

With great reluctance, he lifted a folder of computer printouts from the pile and flipped it open.

But his concentration was shot to pieces. His mind couldn't

settle on spreadsheets and figures. He was composing a description of his house for a similar swapping advertisement.

Home Exchange: Desirable Chelsea, London, UK

3 bedroom house with garden
Close to public transport and amenities—two-minute walk.
* Television
* Fireplaces
* Balcony/patio
* Dining/shopping nearby
* Galleries/museums
Available for three-month exchange: April/May to June/July
Destination—Coastal Queensland, Australia

Two and a half hours later Patrick had closed the last folder, and he'd also reached a decision.

He would do it. He had to. He would get away. He would make an appointment with his boss. First thing in the morning.

CHAPTER TWO

To: Patrick Knight <patrick.knight@mymail.com>
From: Molly Cooper <molly.cooper@flowermail.com>
Subject: We're off—like a rotten egg

Hi Patrick

I can't believe I'll actually be in England in just over twenty-four hours. At last I'm packed (suitcases groaning), and my little house is shining clean and ready for you. Brand-new sheets on the bed—I hope you like navy blue.

I also hope you'll feel welcome here and, more importantly, comfortable. I considered leaving flowers in a vase, but I was worried they might droop and die and start to smell before you got here. I'll leave the key under the flowerpot beside the back door.

Now, I know that probably sounds incredibly reckless to you, but don't worry—the residents of Magnetic Island are very honest and extremely laid-back. No one locks their doors.

I don't want you to fret, though, so I've also left a spare key at Reception at the Sapphire Bay resort, where I used to work until yesterday.

Used to work.

That has such a nice ring, doesn't it? I've trained Jill, the owner's niece, to take my place while I'm away, and for now, at least, I'm giddily carefree and unemployed.

Yippee!!

You have no idea how much I've always wanted to live in London, even if it's only for three months. Thanks to you, Patrick, this really is my dream come true, and I'm beyond excited. I don't think I'll be able to sleep tonight.

Have you finished up at your work? Are you having a farewell party? Mine was last night. It was pretty rowdy, and I have no idea what to do with all the gifts people gave me. I can't fit as much as another peanut in my suitcases, so I'll probably have to stash these things in a box under my bed (your bed now). Sorry.

By the way, please feel free to use my car. It's not much more than a sardine can on wheels, but it gets you about. Don't worry that it's unregistered. Cars on the island don't need registration unless they're taken over to the mainland.

It was kind of you to mention that your car is garaged just around the corner from your place, but don't worry, I won't risk my shaky driving skills in London traffic.

Oh, and don't be upset if the ferry is running late. The boats here run on 'island time'.

Anyway, happy travels.

London, here I come!

Molly

PS I agree that we shouldn't phone each other except in the direst emergency. You're right—phone calls can be intrusive (especially with a ten-hour time difference).

And they're costly. E-mails are so handy—and I'll try to be diplomatic. No guarantees. I can rattle on when I'm excited.

M

To: Molly Cooper <molly.cooper@flowermail.com>
From: Patrick Knight <patrick.knight@mymail.com>
Subject: Re: We're off—like a rotten egg

Dear Molly

Thanks for your message. No time for a farewell party, I'm afraid. Had to work late to get my desk cleared. Rushing now to pack and get away. Cidalia (cleaning lady) will come in some time this week to explain everything about the house—how the oven works, etc.

The keys to the house are in a safety deposit box at the Chelsea branch of the bank I work for on the King's Road. It's a square brick building. My colleagues have instructions to hand the keys over to you—and I've left a map. You'll just need to show your passport. You shouldn't have any problems.

Have a good flight.

Best wishes

Patrick

To: Patrick Knight <patrick.knight@mymail.com>
From: Molly Cooper <molly.cooper@flowermail.com>
Subject: I'm in London!!!!!!!

Wow! Wow! Wow! Wow! Wow! Wow! Wow! Wow!

If I wasn't so tired I'd pinch myself, but I'm horribly jet-lagged and can hardly keep my eyes open. Insanely happy, though.

Your very gentlemanly colleague at the bank handed over the keys and wished me a pleasant stay at number thirty-four Alice Grove, and then I trundled my luggage around the corner and—

Patrick, your house is—

Indescribably

Lovely.

Divine will have to suffice for now, but the truth is that your home is more than divine.

Too tired to do it justice tonight. Will have my first English cup of tea and fall into bed. Your bed. Gosh, that sounds rather intimate, doesn't it? Will write tomorrow.

Blissfully

Molly

To: Patrick Knight <patrick.knight@mymail.com>
From: Molly Cooper <molly.cooper@flowermail.com>
Subject: Thank you

Hi Patrick

I've slept for ten hours in your lovely king-size bed and am feeling much better today, but my head is still buzzing with excitement! I've never left Australia before, so my first sight of England yesterday was the most amazing thrill. We flew in over the English Channel, and when I saw the green and misty fields, just the way I've always imagined them, I confess I became a tad weepy.

And then Heathrow. Oh, my God, what an experience. Now I know how cattle feel when they're being herded into the yards. For a moment there I wanted to turn tail and run back to my sleepy little island.

I soon got over that, thank heavens, and caught a taxi to Chelsea. Terribly extravagant, I know, but I wasn't quite ready to face the tube with all my luggage. I'm just a teensy bit scared of the London Underground.

The driver asked me what district I wanted to go to, and when I told him Chelsea, SW3, he didn't say anything but I could see by the way he blinked that he was impressed. When I got here I was pretty darned impressed, too.

But I'm worried, Patrick.

This isn't exactly an even house swap.

Your place is so gorgeous! Like a four-storey dolls' house. Sorry, I hope that's not offensive to a man. I love it all—the carpeted staircases and beautiful arched windows and marble fireplaces and the bedrooms with their own en suite bathrooms. There's even a bidet! *Blush*. It took me a while to work out what it was. I'd never seen one before.

Meanwhile, you'll be discovering the green tree frogs in my toilet. Gosh, Patrick, can you bear it?

I love the sitting room, with all your books—you're quite a reader, aren't you?—but I think my favourite room is the kitchen, right at the bottom of your house. I love the black and white tiles on the floor and the glass French doors opening onto a little courtyard at the back.

I had my morning cuppa out in the courtyard this morning, sitting in a little pool of pale English sunshine. And there was a tiny patch of daffodils at my feet! I've never seen daffodils growing before.

So many firsts!

After breakfast I went for a walk along the King's Road, and everyone looked so pink-cheeked and glamorous, with their long, double knotted scarves and boots. I bought myself a scarf (won't be able to afford boots). I so wanted to look like all the other girls, but I can't manage the pink cheeks.

I swear I saw a television actor. An older man, don't know his name, but my grandmother used to love him. But crikey, Patrick. I look around here and I have all this—I feel like I'm living in Buckingham Palace—and then I think about you on the other side of the world in my tiny Pandanus Cottage, which is—well, you'll have seen it for yourself by now. It's very basic, isn't it? Perhaps I should have warned you that I don't even have a flatscreen TV.

Do write and tell me how you are—hopefully not struck dumb with horror.

Cheers, as you Brits say

Molly

To: Patrick Knight <patrick.knight@mymail.com>
From: Molly Cooper <molly.cooper@flowermail.com>
Subject: Are you there yet?

Sorry to sound like your mother, Patrick, but could you just drop a quick line to let me know you've arrived and you're OK and the house is OK?

M

PS I'm still happy and excited, but I can't believe how cold it is here. Isn't it supposed to be spring?

To: Patrick Knight <patrick.knight@mymail.com>
From: Felicity Knight <flissK@mymail.com>
Subject: Touching base

Hello darling

I imagine you must be in Australia by now. I do hope you had a good flight. I promise I'm not going to bother you the whole time you're away, but I just needed to hear that you've arrived safely and all is well and to wish you good luck again with writing your novel.

Love from the proud mother of a future world-famous, bestselling author.

xx

To: Molly Cooper <molly.cooper@flowermail.com>
From: Patrick Knight <patrick.knight@mymail.com>
Subject: Re: Just checking

Dear Molly

Yes, I'm here, safe and sound, thank you, and everything's fine. It was well worth the twenty-hour flight and crossing the world's hemispheres just to get here. Don't worry. Your house suits my needs perfectly and the setting is beautiful. Everything's spotless, just as you promised, and the new sheets are splendid. Thank you for ironing them.

As I told you, I'm planning to write a book, so I don't need loads of luxury and I don't plan to watch much TV. What I need is a complete change of scenery and inspiration, and the view from your front window provides both.

I've already rearranged the furniture so that I can have a table at the window and take in the fabulous view across the bay to Cape Cleveland. All day long the sea keeps changing colour with the shifting patterns of the sun and the clouds. It's utterly gorgeous.

I'm pleased you've settled in and that you like what you've found, but don't worry about me. I'm enjoying the sunshine and I'm very happy.

Oh, and thanks also for your helpful notes about the

fish in the freezer and the pot plants and the washing machine's spin cycle and the geckos. All points duly noted.

Best wishes

Patrick

To: Felicity Knight <flissK@mymail.com>
From: Patrick Knight <patrick.knight@mymail.com>
Subject: Re: Touching base

Hi Mother

Everything's fine, thanks. I'm settled in here and all's well. Will keep in touch. It's paradise down here, so don't worry about me.

Love to you and to Jonathan

Patrick x

Private Writing Journal, Magnetic Island, April 10th

This feels very uncomfortable.

I've never kept any kind of diary, but apparently it's helpful for serious writers to keep a journal of 'free writing'. Any thoughts or ideas are grist for the mill, and the aim is to keep the 'writing muscle' exercised while waiting for divine inspiration.

I wasn't going to bother. I'm used to figures and spreadsheets, to getting results and getting them quickly, and it feels such a waste of effort to dredge up words that might never be used. But after spending an entire day at my laptop staring at 'Chapter One' at the top of a blank page, I feel moved to try something.

I can blame jet-lag for the lack of productivity. I'm sure my muse will kick in after a day or two, but rather than waste the next couple of days waiting for the words to flow, I'm trying this alternative.

So...what to say?

This isn't a test—no one else will be reading it—so I might as well start with the obvious.

It's an interesting experience to move into someone else's house on the other side of the world, and to be surrounded by a completely different landscape and soundtrack, even different smells.

As soon as I found notes from Molly scattered all over the house, I knew I'd arrived in an alien world. A few examples:

Note on a pot plant: Patrick, would you mind watering this twice a week? But don't leave water lying in the saucer, or mosquitoes will breed.

On the fridge door: Help yourself to the fish in the freezer. There's coral trout, queen fish, wahoo and nannygai. Don't be put off by the strange names, they're delicious. Try them on the barbecue. There's a great barbecue recipe book on the shelf beside the stove.

On the lounge wall, beside the light switch: Don't freak if you see small, cute lizards running on the walls. They're geckos—harmless, and great for keeping the insects down.

Beyond the cottage, the plants and trees are nothing like trees at home. Some are much wilder and stragglier, others lusher and thicker, and all seem to grow in the barest cracks of soil between the huge boulders on this headland.

The birds not only look different but they sound totally alien. There's a bright green parrot with a blue head and yellow throat that chatters and screeches. The kookaburra's laugh is hilarious. Another bird lets out a blood-curdling, mournful cry in the night.

Even the light here is a surprise. So bright it takes a bit of getting used to.

God, this is pathetic. I need red wine. I'm not a writer's toenail.

But I can't give up on the first day. Getting this leave was a miracle. I couldn't believe how generous old George Sims was. Such a surprise that he was worried about me 'burning out'.

But now...my writing. I'd always imagined that writing would be relaxing. I'm sure it is once the words really start to come. I'll plug on.

In spite of all the differences here, or perhaps because of them, Molly Cooper's little cottage feels good to me. It's simple, but it has loads of personality and it's almost as if she hasn't really left. It's bizarre, but I feel as if I've actually met her simply by being here and seeing all her things, touching them, using the soap she left (sandalwood, I believe), eating from her dishes, sleeping in her bed under a white mosquito net.

There's a photo of her stuck on the fridge with a magnet shaped like a slice of watermelon. She's with an elderly woman and it says on the back 'Molly and Gran'. It was taken about a year ago, and Gran looks very frail, but Molly has long, light brown curly hair, a pretty smile, friendly eyes, dimples and terrific legs.

Not that Molly's appearance or personality is in any way relevant. I'm never going to meet her in the flesh. Our houses are our only points of connection.

So...a bit more about her house.

I must admit that I was worried that it might be too girlie, a bit too cute with pastel shades, ribbons and bows. The sort of warm and fuzzy place that could lower a man's testosterone overnight. But it's fine. I especially like its rugged and spectacular setting.

The house itself is small—two bedrooms, one bathroom and one big open room for the kitchen, dining and lounge. It's all on one level and it feels strange not going upstairs to bed at night.

Lots of windows and shutters catch the breezes and the views. Loads of candles. You'd think there was no electricity, the way the candles are scattered everywhere, along with pieces of driftwood and shells, and decorative touches of blue.

I wouldn't normally notice colours, but for fear of sounding like a total dweeb I like all Molly's bits of blue—like echoes of the sea and the sky outside. Very restful.

When I leave the house, the island is hot and sultry, but inside it's cool and quiet and…soothing.

After these past years of financial crisis and endless overtime, this place has exactly the kind of vibe I need. I'm glad I told everyone I was going to be out of contact for the next three months. Apart from the odd e-mail from Molly or my mother, there'll be no phone calls. No text messages, no tweets, no business e-mails…

I think I might try the hammock in the mango tree.

To: Patrick Knight <patrick.knight@mymail.com>
From: Molly Cooper <molly.cooper@flowermail.com>
Subject: Update

Hi Patrick

How are you? I do hope the island is working its magic on you and that the book is flowing brilliantly.

I've begun to explore London (on foot, or riding in the gorgeous red double-decker buses—takes more time, but I still can't face the Tube), and I'm trying to do as much sightseeing as I can. Turns out most museums in the city of London don't charge any entrance fee, which is awesome.

To make the most of my time here, I've made a few rules for myself.

Rule 1: Avoid other Aussies. I don't want to spend my whole time talking about home. Just shoot me now.

Rule 2: Educate myself about the 'real' London— not just the tourist must-sees, like Buckingham Palace and Trafalgar Square.

Just as an example: yesterday I was walking the streets around here, and I stumbled upon the house where Oscar Wilde lived more than a hundred years ago. Can you imagine how amazing that is for a girl whose neighbours are wallabies and parrots?

I stood staring at Oscar's front window, all choked up, just thinking about the brilliant plays he wrote, and about him living here all through his trial, and having to go to prison simply for being gay.

You're not gay, are you, Patrick? I shouldn't think so, judging by the reading matter on your bookshelves— mostly sporting biographies and finance tomes or spy novels.

Sorry, your reading tastes and sexual preferences are none of my business, but it's hard not to be curious about you. You haven't even left a photo lying around, but I suppose blokes don't bother with photos.

Speaking of photos, I may go to see the Changing of the Guard, but I do not plan to have my picture taken with a man on horseback and an inverted mop on his head.

Rule 3: Fall in love with an Englishman. Actually, it would be helpful if you were gay, Patrick, because then I could have girly chats with you about my lack of a love-life. Now you've seen the island, you'll understand it's not exactly brimming with datable single men. Most of the bachelors are young backpackers passing through, or unambitious drifters.

My secret fantasy (here I go, telling you anyway) is to go out with a proper English gentleman. Let's get real, here—not Prince William or Colin Firth. I can lower my sights—but not too low. Colin Firth's little brother would be acceptable.

After a lifetime on an island where most of the young men spend their days barefoot and wearing holey T-shirts and board shorts, I hanker for a man in a smooth, sophisticated suit.

I'd love to date a nicely spoken Englishman who treats me like a lady and takes me somewhere cultured—to a concert or a play or an art gallery.

A girl can dream. By the way, I've done an internet search and did you know there are six hundred and seventy-three different shows on in London right now? I can't believe it. I'm gobsmacked. Our island has one amateur musical each year.

Patrick, I warned you I might rattle on. I've always tended to put the jigsaw puzzle of my thoughts on paper. For now, I'll leave you in peace.

M

To: Patrick Knight <patrick.knight@mymail.com>
From: Molly Cooper <molly.cooper@flowermail.com>
Subject: Cleaning

Cidalia came today. She's sweet, isn't she? And she speaks very good English. I've never met anyone from Brazil, so we sat at the kitchen table—I wasn't sure how Upstairs/Downstairs you were about entertaining employees in the sitting room—and over a cosy cuppa she told me all about her family and her childhood in San Paolo. So interesting!

But, gosh, Patrick, I didn't realise she was going to continue cleaning your house while I'm here. Apparently you've already paid her in advance. That's kind and thoughtful, and I realise Cidalia wouldn't want to lose her job here, but I haven't arranged for anyone to come and clean my house for you. It didn't even occur to me.

Magnetic Island must feel like a third world country to you.

If you would like a cleaner, I could contact Jodie Grimshaw in Horseshoe Bay. She's a single mum who does casual cleaning jobs, but I'm afraid you'd have to watch her, Patrick. I do feel rather protective of you, and Jodie's on the lookout for a rich husband. Added to that, her child is scarily prone to tantrums.

Do let me know if I can help. I could also try the Sapphire Bay resort. They could probably spare one of their cleaners for one morning a week.

Best
Molly

To: Molly Cooper <molly.cooper@flowermail.com>
From: Patrick Knight <patrick.knight@mymail.com>
Subject: Re: Cleaning

Dear Molly

Thanks for your warning about Jodie G. It came in handy when I met her at the supermarket this morning. She was rather...shall I say, proactive? Your tip-off was helpful.

Actually, I don't need a cleaner, thank you. I've worked

out the intricacies of the dustpan and broom, and your house is so compact I can clean it in a jiffy. No doubt you're surprised to hear that I can sweep, even though I'm not gay. ☺ I might even figure out how to plug in the vacuum cleaner soon.

To be honest, the lack of a cleaning woman doesn't bother me nearly as much as the fact that I can't go swimming. Who would have thought you can't swim on a tropical island? Apparently there are deadly jellyfish in the water, and a rogue saltwater crocodile cruising up and down the coastline. All the beaches are closed. And it's stinking hot!

That's my grumble.

For your part, I'm concerned that you're nervous about using the Tube. I can understand it might be intimidating when your main mode of transport has been the island's ferry service, but the Tube is fast and punctual, and Sloane Square station is very close by. Do give it a try.

Regards

Patrick

PS Someone called Boof rang and invited me down to the pub to watch a cane toad race. I looked on the internet and discovered that cane toads are poisonous South American frogs that can grow as big as dinner plates and breed like rabbits. So I guess the races aren't Ascot. Would appreciate any advice/warnings.

Private Writing Journal, Magnetic Island, April 16th

This journal isn't helping at all. I'm still staring at a blank page.

Any words I've put down are total rubbish. It's so distressing. The ideas for my novel are perfect in my head.

I can see the characters, the setting and the action, but when I try to put them on the page everything turns to garbage.

I'm beginning to think that Molly Cooper's a far better writer than I am and she isn't even trying. The words just flow from her. I'm feeling the first flutters of panic. I hate failure. How did I ever think I could write an entire novel? It's all in my head, but that's no use unless I can get it into a manuscript.

I'm going for a long hike. Walking is supposed to be very good for writer's block.

To: Patrick Knight <patrick.knight@mymail.com>
From: Molly Cooper <molly.cooper@flowermail.com>
Subject: Stingers, etc!

Hi Patrick

I'm sorry. I should have warned you about the marine stingers, and it's a shame about the crocodile. The good news is the National Park people will probably catch the croc and move it up the coast to somewhere safe and re-mote, and the stinger season finishes at the end of April, so it won't be long now before you're able to swim. You could try the stinger-proof enclosure over in Horseshoe Bay, but swimming inside a big net isn't the same, I sup-pose.

Just you wait—the island is paradise in late autumn and early winter. You'll be able to swim and skin dive to your heart's content.

I'll draw a map of the island and post it to you, showing you where all the best diving reefs are. And do check out the cane toad races. They sound grotesque, but they're actually fun. Listen to Boof. He catches the toads for the races, and maybe he can put you onto a sure thing to win a few dollars.

How's the writing going?

Molly x

To: Patrick Knight <patrick.knight@mymail.com>
From: Molly Cooper <molly.cooper@flowermail.com>
Subject: Thank you!

Patrick, you darling! Sorry if that sounds too intimate, when we've never actually met, but it's so, so sweet of you to send Discovering London's Secrets. It arrived this morning. You must have organised it over the internet. How thoughtful!

Believe me—I'm deeply, deeply grateful. I've looked at other travel books in the shops, but they only seem to cover all the popular sights, which are fabulous, of course—there's a reason they're popular—but once you've done Piccadilly Circus and Buck Palace, the Tower and Hyde Park you're hungry for more, aren't you?

Now I'm so well informed I can really explore properly, just the way I'd hoped to. This afternoon I went back to Hyde Park and found the hidden pet cemetery mentioned in this book. It was fascinating, with all those dear little mildewed headstones marking the final resting places of dogs, cats and birds, and even a monkey.

But to use the book you sent properly, I'm going to have to brave the Underground, and that still terrifies me. I hate to think that the whole of London is sitting on top of a network of tunnels and at any given moment there are thousands of people under there, whizzing back and forth in trains.

I do feel ashamed of myself for freaking out like this. I know avoidance only makes these things worse. I'm going to work at getting braver.

M x

To: Molly Cooper <molly.cooper@flowermail.com>
From: Patrick Knight <patrick.knight@mymail.com>
Subject: Re: Thank you!

Hi Molly

Thanks for offering to send a map of the diving spots on the island. It'll be very handy. I'll keep an eye out for the mail van.

So glad you like the book. My pleasure. But, Molly, it does sound as if you're getting yourself very worked up about using the Tube. Of course there are other ways to get around London, but if it's bothering you, and you feel slightly phobic, maybe you need a helping hand?

If you like, I could ask my mother to pop around to No. 34. I know she'd be only too happy to show you the ropes. That's not quite as alarming as it sounds. With me she's extremely bossy, but everyone else claims that she can be very calming.

Best wishes

Chin up!

Patrick

To: Patrick Knight <patrick.knight@mymail.com>
From: Molly Cooper <molly.cooper@flowermail.com>
Subject: Re: Thank you!

Dear Patrick

Yet again, thank you, but I'm afraid I can't accept your offer of a visit from your mother. I know it was kindly meant, but I couldn't impose on her like that.

From the way I rabbit on, you probably think I'm very young—but I'm actually twenty-four, and quite old enough to tackle the challenge of catching a train.

I've never liked to play damsel in distress, and, while this fear may be unreasonable, it's something I must conquer on my own.

Sincerely

Molly

PS You haven't mentioned your book. You must be very modest, Patrick. Or does your English reserve prevent you from confiding such personal information to a nosy Aussie?

CHAPTER THREE

Text message from Karli, April 19, 10.40 a.m.: *U never told us yr house swapper is seriously hot.*

To: Karli Henderson <hendo86@flowermail.com>
From: Molly Cooper <molly.cooper@flowermail.com>
Subject: House swap

Hi, Karli. Sorry—I can't afford to reply to an international text message, so I'm resorting to e-mail. I must say your text came as a surprise. After all, the whole house swap idea came from you, and you knew I was swapping with a guy called Patrick Knight. As you also know, I only ever saw pictures of his house. I still have no idea what he looks like, so I couldn't tell you anything about his appearance.

Actually, the lack of photos lying about here (not even an album that I can take a sneaky peek at) made me think that Patrick was shy about his appearance.

Is he seriously good-looking?

Honestly?

I'm having a ball here—not on the guy front (sigh), just exploring London. But I'm eventually going to have to get some work. The mortgage must be paid. As you know, Pandanus Cottage is my one and only asset, my key to getting ahead.

Have you spoken to Patrick? Does he have a sexy English accent? I've discovered that not many Londoners actually speak like Jeremy Irons or Colin Firth, which is a bit of a disappointment for me, but I suppose others wouldn't agree. Beauty is in the ear of the receiver, after all.

How's Jimbo?

Molly x

To: Molly Cooper <molly.cooper@flowermail.com>
From: Karli Henderson <hendo86@flowermail.com>
Subject: Re: House swap

Glad you're having a great time, Mozza, but I'm not sure that I should give you too many details about your swapper's looks. You might come racing home.

Be fair, girl. You're over there in London with millions of Englishmen and we have just one here. Not that your Patrick has shown any signs of wanting to mix with the locals. He's a bit aloof. Dare I say snooty? He brushed off Jodie Grimshaw. He was ever so polite, apparently, but even she got the message—and you know what that takes.

Our news is that Jimbo's applying for a job with a boat builder in Cairns, so it could turn out that we won't be on the island for much longer.

Have I told you lately that I'm very proud of you, Molly? I think you're so brave to be living in a huge city on the far side of the world. All alone.

You're my hero. Believe it.

Karli x

To: Karli Henderson <hendo86@flowermail.com>
From: Molly Cooper <molly.cooper@flowermail.com>
Subject: House swap

Karli, I'm sending positive thoughts to Jimbo for the job interview in Cairns, although I'm sure you know I'm going to really miss you guys if you leave the island. You've been my best friends my whole life!

But I can't be selfish. I know how much you'd like Jimbo to have a steady job that pays well, and you'll be able to start planning your future (including that trip to Vegas), so good luck!!

Re: Patrick Knight. I hope he's not being too standoffish and stuck up, or the islanders will give him a hard time.

I'm sure he's not really snooty. He and I have been swapping e-mails and he seems a bit reserved, but quite nice and helpful. Actually, he's probably keeping to himself because he simply hasn't time to socialise. He's very busy writing a book, and he only has three months off, so he'll have his head down, scribbling (or typing) madly.

Just the same, I think you're mean not telling me more about him. He's in my house, sleeping in my bed. Really, that's a terribly intimate relationship, and yet I have no idea what he looks like!

Why are you holding back? What are you hiding about him? Maybe you could find time to answer a few quick questions?

Is Patrick tall? Yes? No?

Dark? Yes? No?

Young? Like under 35? Yes? No?

Is he muscular? Yes? No?

Good teeth? Yes? No?

All of the above?

None of the above?

M x

To: Molly Cooper <molly.cooper@flowermail.com>
From: Karli Henderson <hendo86@flowermail.com>
Subject: Re: House swap
   Chillax, girlfriend.
   All of the above.
   K

To: Patrick Knight <patrick.knight@mymail.com>
From: Molly Cooper <molly.cooper@flowermail.com>
Subject: FYI

Progress report on the tube assault by Ms Molly Elizabeth Cooper:

A preliminary reconnaissance of Sloane Square Tube station was made this afternoon at 2.00 p.m.

• Thirty minutes were spent in the forecourt, perusing train timetables and observing Londoners purchasing tickets and passing through turnstiles

• Names of the main stations on the yellow Circle Line between Sloane Square and King's Cross were memorised—South Kensington, Gloucester Road, Notting Hill Gate, Paddington, Baker Street. Ms Cooper didn't cheat. She loved learning those names and letting them roll off her tongue!

• Ms Cooper acknowledged that people emerging from the Underground did not appear traumatised. Most looked bored, tired or in a dreadful hurry. A handful of passengers almost, but not quite, smiled. One was actually laughing into a mobile phone.

• Ms Cooper purchased a day pass, which she may use some time in the near future.

Ms Cooper's next challenge:

• To actually enter the Underground.

To: Molly Cooper <molly.cooper@flowermail.com>
From: Patrick Knight <patrick.knight@mymail.com>
Subject: Re: FYI

Dear Molly

Congratulations! I'm very proud of you for taking such positive steps. I feared you'd miss another great London experience. In no time you'll be dashing about on the Underground and reading racy novels to conquer your boredom instead of your fear.

Speaking of novels—you've expressed concern about the progress of mine, but I can assure you it is well in hand. It's a thriller, set in the banking world. It has an intricate plot, so I want to plan every twist and turn very carefully in advance. To this end, I've been taking long walks on the island. I walked from Alma Bay to The Forts and back yesterday. A group of Japanese tourists pointed out a lovely fat koala asleep in the fork of a gum tree.

While I'm walking, I think every aspect of my novel through in fine detail. The plotting is almost complete, and I plan to start the actual writing very soon.

Regards
P

To: Patrick Knight <patrick.knight@mymail.com>
From: Molly Cooper <molly.cooper@flowermail.com>
Subject: Re: FYI

That is such a brilliant idea—to set your novel in the banking world. Don't they always say you should write about what you know? And a thriller! Wow! I'd love to hear more.

Go, you!
M x

Private Writing Journal, April 27th.

Working hard or hardly working? Ha-ha-ha-ha-ha-ha.

I'm attacking the novel from a different angle (away from the window—views can be too distracting). I've gone about as far as I can with planning the plot, so I'm creating character charts now. A good story is all about the people in it, so once I have a firm grip on the lead characters the story will spring to life on the page.

Here goes...

Hero: Harry Shooter—*nearing forty, former intelligence officer with MI5, hired by the Bank of England specifically to hunt down spies who pose as bank employees then hack into the systems and siphon off funds. Harry's a tough guy—lean and stoic, hard-headed but immaculately dressed, with smooth, debonair manners. A modern James Bond.*

Female lead: Beth Harper—*mid-twenties. Innocent bank teller. Shoulder-length curly hair, lively smile, great legs, sparkling eyes... Mouthy—and nosy—yet smart...*

That's as far as I've got. For the past half-hour I've been staring out of the frigging window again.

This is hopeless. Writing down a few details hasn't helped. I'm no closer to actually starting my novel. I can't just dive into the fun bits, the action. What I need is to work out first what these characters would actually say to each other, how they'd think, how they'd feel! What I really need is a starting situation—something that will grab the reader.

It won't come.

I'm still blocked.

I have a sickening feeling that this whole house swapping venture has been a huge, hideous mistake. The

*strangeness and newness of everything here is distract-
ing rather than helpful. I can't concentrate and then I
procrastinate and the cycle continues.*

*I guess this is what happens when you're desper-
ate and you choose a holiday destination by spinning
the globe. Normally I would have given such a venture
much more thought. Thing is, apart from enjoying the
beautiful scenery on this island there's not a lot else to
do. That was supposed to be a plus.*

*If the writing was flowing everything would be
fine.*

*But if it's not, what have I got? There are a few cafés
and resorts, a pub or two, a gallery here and there, but
no cinema. Not even a proper library.*

*I spend far too much of my time thinking about Molly
in London, imagining the fun of showing her around,
helping her to explore the hidden secrets she's so keen
to discover.*

*Funny, how a stranger can make you take a second
look at your home town.*

I feel like a fraud.

To: Patrick Knight <patrick.knight@mymail.com>
From: Molly Cooper <molly.cooper@flowermail.com>
Subject: Rambling

Patrick, would you believe I actually woke up feeling homesick today? I can't believe it. I haven't been
here long enough to be homesick, but I looked out the
window at the grey skies and the sea of rooftops and
streams of people and streets and traffic and fumes and
I just longed for my tree-covered headland, where I can't
see another house, and to be able to breathe in fresh,
unpolluted air.

I stopped myself from moping by going to Wimbledon Common. It involved a bit of jumping on and off buses, but I got there—and it was perfect. Just what I needed with its leafy glades and tangled thickets and stretches of heath. I love that it still has a wild feel and hasn't been all tidied up—and yet it's right in the middle of London.

The minor crisis is over. I'm back in love with your city, Patrick.

Molly x

To: Patrick Knight <patrick.knight@mymail.com>
From: Molly Cooper <molly.cooper@flowermail.com>
Subject: Your mother...long!

You win, Patrick.

Your mother came, she saw, she conquered. In the nicest possible way, of course. I have now ventured into the bowels of the Underground, I've travelled all the way to Paddington Station and back, and it didn't hurt a bit.

Let me tell you how it happened.

WARNING: this will be a long read, but it's all of your making!

It started with a phone call this morning at about ten o'clock.

'Is that Molly?' a woman asked in a beautiful voice.

I said, tentatively, 'Yes.' I couldn't think who would know me.

'Oh, lovely,' she said. 'I'm so pleased to catch you at home, Molly. This is Felicity Knight. Patrick's mother.'

I responded—can't remember what I actually said. I was too busy hoping I didn't sound as suddenly nervous as I felt. Your mother's voice is so very refined and my accent is...well, very okker. (Australian!)

She said, 'I have some errands to run this afternoon, and I'll be just round the corner from Alice Grove, so I was hoping I could pop in to say hello.'

'Of course,' I said in my plummiest voice. 'That would be lovely.'

But I could smell a rat, Patrick. Don't think you can fool me. I knew you'd sent her to check up on me—maybe even to hold my hand on the Tube. However, I must admit that even though I told you not to speak to your mum about my little problem I am honestly very grateful that you ignored me.

'We could have afternoon tea,' your mother said.

I tried to picture myself presiding over a tea party. Thank heavens my grandmother taught me how to make proper loose-leaf tea in a teapot, but I've never been one for baking cakes. What else could we eat for afternoon tea?

I shouldn't have worried. Your mum was ten jumps ahead of me.

'There's the loveliest little teashop near you,' she said next. 'They do scrumptious high teas.'

And you know, Patrick, I had the most gorgeous afternoon.

Your mother arrived, looking beautiful. Doesn't she have the most enviable complexion and such elegant silver-grey hair? She was wearing a dove-grey suit, with a lavender fleck through it, and pearls. I was so pleased I'd brought a skirt with me. Somehow it would have been totally Philistine to go to high tea in Chelsea in jeans.

And, you know...normally, beautifully elegant women like your mother can make me feel self-conscious about my untidy curls. My hands and feet seem to grow to twice their usual size and I bump into and break things (like delicate, fine bone china), and I trip on steps, or the edges of carpet.

Somehow, magically, Felicity (she insisted that I mustn't call her Mrs Knight) put me so at ease that I felt quite ladylike. At least I didn't break or spill anything, and I didn't trip once.

We dined in fine style. The tea was served in a silver teapot and we drank from the finest porcelain cups—duck-egg-blue with gold rims and pink roses on the insides—and the dainty food was served on a three-tiered stand.

And, no, I didn't lift my pinkie finger when I drank my tea.

We stuffed ourselves (in the most delicate way) with cucumber sandwiches and scones with jam and clotted cream and the daintiest melt-in-your-mouth pastries.

And we talked. Oh, my, how we talked. Somehow your mother coaxed me to tell her all about myself—how my parents died when I was a baby and how I was raised on the island by my grandmother. I even confessed to my worry that living on an island has made me insular, not just geographically but in my outlook, which is why I'm so keen to travel. And that my first choice was London because my favourite childhood story was *101 Dalmatians*, and I've watched so many movies and read so many books set in London.

And because my father was born here.

I was very surprised when that little bit of info slipped out. It's honestly not something I dwell on. My parents died when I was eighteen months old, and I only have the teensiest memories of them...so wispy and fleeting

I'm not sure they're real. I think I can remember being at floor level, fascinated by my mother's painted toenails. And lying in a white cot, watching a yellow curtain flutter against a blue sky. My father's smiling face. My hand in his.

It's not a lot to go on. My gran was the most important person in my life, but she died just under a year ago, and if I think about my missing family too much I start to feel sorry for myself.

But, talking to your mother, I learned that your father lives somewhere up in Scotland now, and you don't see him very much. Why would any sane man divorce Felicity? I'm so glad Jonathan has arrived on the scene. Yes, her new man got a mention, too.

In the midst of our conversation it suddenly felt very important for me to find where my dad was born. I'd like to know something about him, even just one thing. So I'm adding his birthplace to my list of things I want to discover while I'm here, although I'm not quite sure where to start.

You'll be relieved to hear that I stopped myself from telling Felicity about my dream of dating a British gent. A girl has to have some secrets.

It's different talking to you, Patrick. I can tell you such things because we're not face-to-face. You're a safe twelve thousand miles away, so you get to hear everything. You're very tolerant and non-judgemental and I love you for it.

Felicity, of course, told me loads about you, but you know that already, so I won't repeat it. Anyway, you'd only get a swelled head. Your mother adores you—but you know that, too, don't you? And she's so proud that you're writing a novel. You wrote very clever essays at school, so she knows you'll be a huge success.

Anyway, as I was saying, we got on like the proverbial house on fire—so much so that I was shocked when I realised how late it was. Then, as we were leaving, Felicity told me she was catching the Tube home.

That was a shock, Patrick. I'd been lulled into a false sense of security and had totally forgotten the possibility that she might know about my Tube issues. Besides, your mother has such a sophisticated air I assumed she'd catch a taxi if she hadn't brought her own car.

But she said the Tube was fast and convenient, and so I walked with her to Sloane Square Station and we chatted all the way until we were right inside. And then it seemed like the right thing to do to wait with her till her train arrived. Which meant stepping onto the escalator and heading down, down into the black hole of the Underground!

That was a seriously freaking-out moment.

Honestly, I could feel the beginnings of a panic attack, and I was sure I couldn't breathe. But Felicity was so calm and smiling, telling me what a lovely afternoon she'd had, and suggesting that maybe we could have another afternoon together some time. She made me feel so OK I managed to start breathing again.

I must admit that once I was down there, standing on the platform, the station seemed so very big and solid and well-lit and I felt much better than I'd expected to. I actually told Felicity then that I'd been a tiny bit frightened, and she said she totally understood; she would be terrified if she was in the Australian Outback, and why didn't I travel with her to Paddington?

She had to change trains there, but if I felt OK I could travel back on my own, and I'd soon be a Tube veteran. She even gave me her mobile phone number in case I got into trouble. She wouldn't have reception until she was above ground again, but it didn't matter—I was over the worst by then, and actually sitting on the train was fine.

Everything went so well I was able to text her: *Thanks. This is a breeze!*

So I think I'm cured.

And I know that ultimately you're the person I should thank, Mr Patrick Knight-in-shining-armour. Because you arranged it, didn't you?

I wish there was some way I could help you, but I don't know the first thing about writing a novel.

Molly XXXXXXXXXXXXXXXXXXXXXXXXXXXX

PS Feel free to tell me to pull my head in, but I did wonder if it's possible to over-think the planning of a book. The way I over-thought the whole business of entering the Tube. Do you ever get the urge to just leap right in and let the words flow?

CHAPTER FOUR

To: Patrick Knight <patrick.knight@mymail.com>
From: Felicity Knight <flissK@mymail.com>
Subject: Mission accomplished

Dear Patrick

It's a pity you're on the other side of the world and unable to carry out your own rescue mission.

I only say this because Molly Cooper is charming, and I thoroughly enjoyed a highly entertaining afternoon with her. It seems to me that your taste in women improves considerably when you change your selection criteria. Perhaps you should try choosing your girlfriends by their houses.

Molly may not be a pint-size blonde, as most of your girlfriends are, but she can hold up her end of a conversation. She's very smart, Patrick, and you should see the way her blue eyes sparkle. They're breathtaking.

Darling, thank you for sending me on a very pleasant errand. I must say I was very curious about the girl you'd swapped houses with. Now that curiosity is happily satisfied.

I hope you're having as much fun with writing your novel as Molly seems to be having here in London.

Love

Mother xx

Private Writing Journal, Magnetic Island, April 30th

Note about character development: it might work quite well if I give my heroine a private fear that she must overcome.

To: Molly Cooper <molly.cooper@flowermail.com>
From: Patrick Knight <patrick.knight@mymail.com>
Subject: Re: Thank you!

Hi Molly

Your map of the island's reefs arrived today. Thanks so much. The information will be very helpful, and your request that I don't show the location of these reefs to too many tourists was duly noted. I'm honoured that you're sharing some of your island's secrets with me, a mere visitor.

I also enjoyed very much your drawings of the coral fish and the other weird and wonderful creatures that I'm likely to encounter when I finally enter the Pacific Ocean.

Your artistic efforts made me smile. Have you ever thought of a new career as a cartoonist?

I'm very keen to see a Chelmon rostratus (thank you for the helpful labels). Those fish are gorgeous, with their bright black, yellow and white stripes and their long snouts. And I'm fascinated by the anemone fish.

You were right about the crocodile. He was caught in Florence Bay—six brave fellows from the National Park manhandled him, trussed him up like a giant Christmas turkey and relocated him further north. Apparently he won't come back this way now that we're approaching the winter. Thank God.

So I can't wait to start diving. You've certainly whetted my appetite for discovering *what lies beneath*....

Molly, I'm very pleased to hear that you've got the Tube business sorted. I know my mother enjoyed meeting you. Well done.

It's getting a little cooler here at last. Today it's hard to believe it's autumn. The temperatures are almost down to those of an English summer's day.

If you'd like any help with looking for your father's birthplace, do sing out.

Best

Patrick

To: Molly Cooper <molly.cooper@flowermail.com>
From: Patrick Knight <patrick.knight@mymail.com>
Subject: PS

Molly, another thought. You might be surprised to know that you could quite possibly help me with this novel by sharing your reactions to London.

You were worried about sending me extra-long messages but I've enjoyed the descriptions in your e-mails... and I've found them helpful.

I'm still learning the ropes, so to speak, and it would be extremely useful to see my home town described through a fresh pair of eyes. In fact your reactions to life in general could be helpful, as it's hard for a fellow to get inside the female mind. In other words, feel free to continue sharing your discoveries and insights. Positive or negative—you won't hurt my feelings.

Just if the whim takes you.

Warmest wishes

Patrick

To: Patrick Knight <patrick.knight@mymail.com>
From: Molly Cooper <molly.cooper@flowermail.com>
Subject: My London eye

Dear Patrick

I'm more than happy to rattle on to you about my London adventures, and please feel free to use anything I say in your novel. Wow! What an honour.

I've been thinking that writing must be a lonely occupation, so I can imagine you'd enjoy getting e-mails at the end of a long day at the keyboard.

But if I get too carried away, flooding you with too much information, please tell me.

I had to laugh at a sign I saw today in a Tube station: *A penalty fare will be charged to any passenger who fails to hide true emotions fully or makes any attempt to engage with other passengers.*

That is so what it's like. I do love the way the British poke fun at themselves.

Yesterday I spent the loveliest morning checking out the Kensington Roof Gardens. They're gorgeous. Have you been there? It's amazing—one and a half acres of trees and plants growing thirty metres above Kensington High Street and divided into three lovely themed gardens.

There's an English woodland (which I think might be my favourite), with curving lawns and surprisingly large trees, a stream and little bridges, even a lake with ducks and pink flamingos. I'm so glad it's spring, because there were also lovely flowers everywhere, but unfortunately I don't know their names.

There's also a Tudor garden, with a courtyard and

creeper-covered walls and brick paths laid in a herring-bone pattern. It's filled with fragrant flowers—lilies, roses and lavender. And the Spanish garden is very dramatic, with its stunning white walls. Apparently it's inspired by the Alhambra in Spain.

By the way, thanks so much for offering to help with my family history research. My grandmother kept a box of papers that belonged to my parents, including their marriage certificate. When I was younger I used to take it out often and read every word. I haven't done that for ages, but I'm almost certain I remember that my father was born in Clapham. I used to want to call it Clap-ham. I know the year he was born was definitely 1956.

Molly

PS Would you like to send me a list of questions that might help you with getting inside your female charac-ter's head?

To: Molly Cooper <molly.cooper@flowermail.com>
From: Patrick Knight <patrick.knight@mymail.com>
Subject: Questions

It's very generous of you to offer to help with my female character. I hesitate to make these kinds of de-mands on your time, but authors do need to know an awful lot about what's going on inside their characters, and I'd truly appreciate your input.

My heroine is Beth Harper and she's a bank teller, about your age, and I'm supposed to know about her likes and dislikes—her favourite kinds of clothes and jewellery, favourite colour, music, animal, etc; her least favourite of these; her spending habits; her most prized possession; her talents (piano player, juggler, poet?); nervous habits. Any thoughts along those lines would be welcomed.

I'm hoping to create a girl who feels real and unique. So…whenever you have time…

Gratefully

Patrick

PS If you could tell me your father's full name, I just might have the right contacts to do a little research for you.

To: Patrick Knight <patrick.knight@mymail.com>
From: Molly Cooper <molly.cooper@flowermail.com>
Subject: Re: Questions

Patrick, I feel like I'm always thanking you, but the very thought of finding out more about my father makes me feel quite wobbly with excitement and emotion, so thank you so much for offering to help. His name was Charles Torrington Cooper, which I think sounds rather dignified, but I'm told that in Australia he was only ever known as Charlie Cooper.

You will no doubt already know what he looked like as there's a photo of him and my mother on my bedside table. You can see that he's to blame for my brown curly hair, but don't you think he has the nicest smile?

Now, about your book. I have to warn you, Patrick, that if you want your character to be unique, I may not be your woman. Truth is, I'm careful and conservative—as ordinary as oatmeal. And, whatever you do, don't give Beth Harper my hair.

Also, my favourite clothes—a bikini and a sarong— might not ring true for a teller in a bank in London.

So last night I sat down and tried to pretend I was Beth and to answer your questions as if I was her—and I suddenly understood your dilemma. It's really, really hard to just make someone up, isn't it? But it's fun, too.

So let's see. If I was Beth, working in a bank, I think I'd be super-prim like a librarian during the day, but I'd wear sexy lingerie underneath my work clothes (to remind the reader of my wild side and because it feels so lovely against my skin). And I'd wear wild colours on my weekends—rainbow-coloured leggings or knee-high red boots with micro-mini-skirts. And I'd be the queen of scarves—silk, crocheted, long, short. For when it's cold I'd have a coat with a big faux fur collar.

I'm getting carried away, aren't I? But it's so much fun to pretend to be English. I don't get to wear any of that sort of gear on the island.

Beth's favourite colour would change every week, and her spending habits would be a perfect balance between thriftiness and recklessness—because she wants to enjoy life, but she's also a sensible bank teller. Unlike me. I'm always the same about money—as penny-pinching as they come. I have to be.

Beth's most prized possession is the ridonkulously expensive little red (not black) dress that she bought for the one time she went to the Royal Opera House at Covent Garden with the man of her dreams. (My most prized possession is my house. As I'm sure yours must be for you, Patrick.)

In case you were wondering, my grandmother left Pandanus Cottage to me, but she left me a mortgage, too, because she had to refinance to keep me through the high school years. She sent me to a good private school she couldn't really afford, the darling.

I consider myself very lucky. My house is my ticket to a safe and steady future, so I pay my mortgage rather than splashing out on trendy fashions. That's where living on the island comes in handy. You must have noticed that it's a budget-friendly, fashion-free zone. Anything goes.

Not so for Beth.

Now for her talents. Could she be secretly brilliant at doing arithmetic in her head? (Again, that's the very opposite of me. The calculator on my mobile phone is my best friend.) Could Beth's cleverness be of huge save-the-day importance at some time in your plot?

As for nervous habits... Well, I tend to mess with my hair...as if it wasn't already messy enough. I don't think Beth should do that. I'm positive she has very sleek, flowing hair—the kind of shiny waterfall hair you see in shampoo advertisements. The kind of hair I used to pray for when I was twelve.

Could Beth be a stutterer instead? Could she have worked hard to overcome her stutter, and now it only breaks out when she's really, really nervous—like when your bad guy holds a gun to her head, or, to her huge embarrassment, when really, really gorgeous men speak to her?

Hmm... That's about all I can think of for now. Not sure how helpful any of this might be, but it was fun playing at being an author. There must be times when you feel like a god.

Molly x

PS Patrick, you do know Beth must have a tattoo,

don't you? Where it is on her body and what it looks like I'll leave to your fertile authorly imagination.

To: Patrick Knight <patrick.knight@mymail.com>
From: Molly Cooper <molly.cooper@flowermail.com>
Subject: Gainfully employed

You've been very quiet, Patrick. Is everything OK?

I have sad news. I landed a job yesterday and I have to start soon. I'll be serving drinks behind the bar in the Empty Bottle—which, as you know, is a newly renovated pub just around the corner. Four evenings a week. But that still leaves me with mornings free, and three full days each week for sightseeing.

I admit I'm not looking forward to working, but the coffers need bolstering, and at least this job should provide great opportunities to meet loads of new people (maybe even that dream man). I can't complain about a few shifts behind a bar when you're spending the whole time you're away slaving over a hot laptop.

I hope the novel is going really well for you.

Best wishes
Molly

To: Molly Cooper <molly.cooper@flowermail.com>
From: Patrick Knight <patrick.knight@mymail.com>
Subject: Re: Gainfully employed

Thanks for the description of your vision of Beth. I really like it. I think my hero's going to like her, too.

I'm very sorry you have to start work. Seems a pity when there's so much of London you want to see. I guess the extra cash will be helpful, though. Perhaps it will allow you to take a few trips out into the countryside as well? Rural England is very pretty at this time of year.

I've only been in the Empty Bottle on a couple of occasions (my usual is closer to work), but it seemed like a nice pub.

Please keep me informed. It could be a place frequented by the likes of Beth Harper, so keep a lookout for high-heeled red boots and micro-mini-skirts.

I've taken your advice and kitted my heroine out in sexy underwear and your recommended wardrobe.

I'm still giving deep thought to her (discreet) tattoo.

P.

To: Patrick Knight <patrick.knight@mymail.com>
From: Molly Cooper <molly.cooper@flowermail.com>
Subject: A bedtime story

Goldilocks Revisited

So I trudged home late last night, after a gruelling shift at the Empty Bottle. My head was aching from the pub's loud music and all the laughter and shouting of noisy drinkers. In fact my head hurt so much I thought the top might lift right off. As you might imagine, I wasn't in a very good mood.

My mood wasn't improved when I dragged my weary bones into my/your bedroom and switched on the light.

Someone was sleeping in my/your bed!

Someone blonde, naked and busty. And tipsy. Quite tipsy.

You remember Angela, don't you, Patrick?

She'd been at a party a few blocks away and she'd had too much to drink and needed somewhere to crash. She had a key to your house, and I don't think she had to go to a bank to get it from a safety deposit box.

I slept in the spare room, but the bed wasn't made up and I had to go hunting for sheets and blankets. I was so tired I might have slept on top of the satin quilt with only my denim jacket for warmth if satin wasn't so slippery.

Next day, a shade before midday, Angela came downstairs, wrapped in your port wine silk dressing gown and looking somewhat the worse for wear, and she asked about breakfast as if I was a servant.

Patrick, you asked for my reactions to your world, but I suppose I may be coming across as somewhat manipulative in this situation—as if I'm trying to make you feel awkward and maybe even sorry for me. Or you might even think it's the green-eyed monster raising its ugly head. But I'm not the type to get jealous of your former girlfriend when I haven't even met you.

I just don't do headaches well. That's all.

Anyway, I was determined to be generous, so I cooked up an enormous hangover breakfast for Angela and she wolfed it down. Bacon, eggs and tomatoes, with toast and expensive marmalade, plus several cups of strong coffee. It all disappeared with the speed of light. The colour came back into her face. She even managed to smile.

I do admit that Angela is exceptionally pretty when she smiles—a beautiful, delicate, silky blonde. I tried to dislike her, but once she understood my reasons for taking up residence in your house—that it was a fair swap and very temporary—she thawed a trillion degrees.

So then we poured ourselves another mug of coffee each and settled down to a lovely gossipy chat. About you.

I promise I didn't ask Angela to talk about you, Patrick, but your lovely kitchen is very chat-friendly, and she was the first English girl of my age that I'd had a chance to gossip with. I'd like to think of it more as a cross-cultural, deep and meaningful exchange.

Angela even flipped through the photos on her mobile phone to see if she still had one of you, but you've been deleted, I'm afraid. She told me that she's just one in a string of your neglected girlfriends, and that your work has always, *always* come first.

Case in point—the time you missed her birthday because you had to fly to Zurich (on a weekend). And there were apparently a lot of broken dates and times when you sent last-minute apologies via text messages because you had to work late, when she'd already spent a fortune on having her hair and nails done, and having her legs, and possibly other bits, waxed.

It's not for me to judge, of course.

Maybe Angela (and those other girls who preceded her) should have been more understanding and patient. Maybe you have a very ambitious and driven personality and you can't help working hard. After all, you're using your holidays to write a novel when most people lie on the beach and read novels that other people have written.

Or maybe, just maybe, you could be a teensy bit more thoughtful and considerate and take more care to nurture your personal relationships.

OK, that's more than enough from me. I'm ducking for cover now.

Cheerio!

Molly x

PS Angela was thoughtful enough to return your key.

To: Molly Cooper <molly.cooper@flowermail.com>
From: Patrick Knight <patrick.knight@mymail.com>
Subject: Re: A bedtime story

Dear Molly

I confess I'd completely overlooked the possibility that Angela Carstairs might still have a door key. I'm sorry you were inconvenienced by her unexpected visit, and thanks so much for going above and beyond. You're a good sport, Molly, and I'm very grateful. I'm sure Angela is too.

I suppose I should also thank you for your feedback and your advice regarding my previous and possible future relationships. As I said before, it's always helpful to receive a fresh perspective.

On the subject of unexpected visitors and questionable relationships, however, you've had a visitor, too. A young man called in here yesterday. A Hell's Angel look-alike with a long red beard and big beefy arms covered in tattoos. He asked ever so politely about some ladies' lingerie which you, apparently, are holding here for him.

I would have been happy to oblige your boyfriend. I might have asked a few pertinent questions. But he seemed very secretive, almost furtive, and I got the distinct impression that he would not welcome my curiosity. As you might imagine I was somewhat at a loss. I had no idea where I could lay my hands on lingerie in his size. I suggested he call back in a few days. Do you have any suggestions or instructions, Molly?

Kindest regards

Patrick

To: Patrick Knight <patrick.knight@mymail.com>
From: Molly Cooper <molly.cooper@flowermail.com>
Subject: Re: A bedtime story

Wipe that smirk off your face right now, Patrick Knight. I know what you're thinking, and stop it. That visitor was not my boyfriend, and he's certainly not a cross-dresser.

His name is David Howard and he's a butcher in Horseshoe Bay, married to a doting wife with three kids and as straight as a Roman road. But he also has a fabulous singing voice, and he's landed a major role in the local production of *The Rocky Horror Show*. It's all very top secret (and believe me, keeping a secret on Magnetic Island is a big call.) I organised his costume before I left, but I was so busy getting the house ready for you that I forgot to drop it off with the Amateur Players.

I'm sorry David had to disturb you. It's entirely my fault. I left the costume in a black plastic bag on the table next to my sewing machine in the back bedroom, so I'd be very grateful if you could pass it on to him, with my apologies.

Can you imagine the impact and the surprise when big David, covered in tattoos, steps onto the stage?

Thanks!

Molly

To: Molly Cooper <molly.cooper@flowermail.com>
From: Patrick Knight <patrick.knight@mymail.com>
Subject: One parcel of lingerie duly delivered.

Curiosity drove me to take a peek at the lingerie before I handed it over to David, and I must say you sew a very fine seam. The lace on the suspender belts is very fetching.

But while you wriggled off that hook quite neatly, Molly, I can't let you get away completely. You've had another visitor (dare I say admirer?) who turned up here late yesterday afternoon, expecting a massage. Probably the fittest looking character I've seen in a long while. He seemed very upset when I told him your services would not be available till the end of June.

Explain away that one, Miss Molly.

And while I'm on the subject of the men in your life, the strapping young ranger who supervised the crocodile capture last week was very keen to know when you'd be back.

Rest assured, I don't plan to sit down with these fellows for a 'cosy chat', so I won't be passing on any advice to you re: your previous or future relationships.

Patrick

To: Patrick Knight <patrick.knight@mymail.com>
From: Molly Cooper <molly.cooper@flowermail.com>
Subject: Re: One parcel of lingerie duly delivered

Patrick, I'm sorry. My friends do seem to be interrupting you lately. The guy who turned up for a massage was Josh. But honestly, it's not that kind of massage. He's a footballer—he plays for the local rugby league team and he has a problem with his shoulders. Like a lot of islanders he bucks the system and has no medical insurance, so he balks at handing over money for a professional massage from a physio.

That's why he comes to me.

I massage his shoulders. Only. He keeps me supplied with fish. Hence my well-stocked freezer. As for Max, the crocodile wrangler, I have no idea why he was asking about me. I should think that's nothing more than idle curiosity.

Anyway, as you know, it's not Australian men I'm interested in. I'm still on the lookout for my lovely Englishman. Any advice on where I should hang out to have the best chance of meeting my dream man would be deeply appreciated.

By the way, I've bought a Travelcard and I've done heaps of travelling on the Tube now. On my last day off I went to Piccadilly Circus, to explore the hidden courts and passages of St James's. I found the most amazing, ancient, hidden pub in Ely Street. It's so tiny and dark and dingy and old, and it has the stump of a cherry tree that Elizabeth I danced around!

I was rather overcome just trying to wrap my head around all the history contained in those tiny rooms.

Molly x

PS I'm such a traveller now. Last night, as I was drifting off to sleep, I kept hearing a voice saying, 'Mind the gap.'

To: Patrick Knight <patrick.knight@mymail.com>
From: Felicity Knight <flissK@mymail.com>
Subject: Surprise news
Dearest Patrick

I have the most amazing news. Jonathan has asked me (again) to marry him, and this time I've said yes.

Can you believe it? Your mother is getting married and she couldn't be happier.

As you know, it's taken me a very long time to get over the divorce. Actually, it's taken us both a long time, hasn't it? I know that's so, Patrick, even though you won't give in and talk about it.

I honestly thought I couldn't face another marriage after the way the last one ended, but Jonathan has been such a darling—so patient and understanding.

This time when he proposed I knew it was a case of saying yes or losing him. A man's pride can only take so many knock-backs.

Suddenly (thank heavens) the scales fell from my eyes and I understood without a shadow of a doubt that I couldn't bear to lose him. I simply couldn't let him go.

Now that decision's made such a weight has lifted from my heart. I'm giddy with happiness.

It's all happening in a frightful hurry, though. I think poor Jonathan is terrified that I might change my mind. I won't, of course. I know that as certainly as I know my own name.

So it's to be a May wedding, and then a honeymoon in Tuscany. Have you ever heard of anything more romantic?

Now, darling, I'm including your invitation as an attachment, but Jonathan and I know this writing time is precious to you. You've worked far too hard these past couple of years, and I'm so pleased you've taken this break, so we'll understand perfectly if you can't tear yourself away from your novel. The wedding will be a very small affair. We were lucky enough to book the church after a cancellation.

Even if you can't make it, I know you'll be happy for me.

Oceans of love

Your proud and very happy mother xxx

Patrick Knight
The pleasure of your company is requested
at the marriage of
Felicity Knight
and
Jonathan Langley
on Saturday 21st May
at St Paul's Church, Ealing
at 2.00 p.m.
and afterwards at 3 Laburnum Lane,
West Ealing

To: Felicity Knight <flissK@mymail.com>
From: Patrick Knight <patrick.knight@mymail.com>
Subject: Re: Surprise news

Wow! What fabulous and very welcome news! I'm thrilled, and I know you and Jonathan will be blissfully happy.

You deserve so much happiness, Mother. That's been my main concern ever since Dad left us.

I can just imagine Jonathan's relief. I know he's mad about you, and tying the knot will put him out of his agony.

Your plans sound wonderfully spontaneous and ro-mantic. I'm glad you're just getting on with it and not worrying too much about my presence. That said, I'd love to come back for a quick weekend to join the nuptial celebrations, so I'll give it serious thought and let you know very soon.

Don't fret about my attitude towards my father. I still can't forgive him for what he did to you, but Jonathan's made up for his behaviour in spades.

Love and best wishes to you both
Patrick

Private Writing Journal, Magnetic Island, May 3rd

This isn't about writing…but my mind's churning and it might help to get my thoughts down.

I hate myself for hesitating to jump on a plane and hurry back for my mother's wedding, especially as I wouldn't have stalled if the book had been falling into place.

I've tried to breathe life into the damn thing. I've even tried Molly's suggestion of leaping in and simply letting the writing flow. It worked for two days, then I made the mistake of re-reading what I'd written.

Utter drivel.

And now, of course, I can't stop thinking about my father and what a fool he was to leave my mother and take off with his secretary. His actions were a comical cliché to outsiders looking on, and a truly hurtful shock for us.

I was eighteen at the time, and I'll never forget how shattered my mother was. I wanted to help her, but I knew there was absolutely nothing I could say or do to heal her pain. I bought a plane ticket to Edinburgh, planning to go after my father and—

I never was quite sure what I'd do when I found him. Break his stupid, arrogant nose, I suppose. But Mother guessed what I'd planned and she begged me not to go. Begged me with tears streaming down her face.

So I gave up that scheme, but I was left with so many questions.

Along with everyone else who knew my parents, I could never understand why he did it—apart from the obvious mid-life crisis which had clearly fried his brains. Actually, I do know that my father worried about ageing more than most. He could never stand to waste time, and he hated the idea of his life rushing him towards its inevitable end. Perhaps it's not so very surprising that he started chasing after much younger women.

Fool. I still don't see how he could turn his back on Mother. Everyone loves her. Molly's response to meeting her was the typical reaction of anyone who meets her.

Of course the one thing in this that I've totally understood was my mother's reluctance to enter a second marriage. She didn't want to be hurt again, and my father is to be entirely blamed for that.

But her heart is safe in Jonathan Langley's hands. He's exactly like Molly Cooper's dream man—a charming Englishman, a gentleman to the core—and he and my mother share a deep affection that makes the rest of us envious....

I wonder if Mother wants me to write to tell Dad. She would never ask outright.

To be honest, I don't think I want him to know until Jonathan's ring is safely on her finger and she's away in Italy with him. Maybe I'm being overly cautious, but I'm not going to risk any chance that Dad might turn up and somehow spoil this for her.

To: Patrick Knight <patrick.knight@mymail.com>

From: Molly Cooper <molly.cooper@flowermail.com>
Subject: Impossible dreams

I assume from your silence that you're not going to pass on any wise advice about how I might find my dream Englishman.

Patrick, have you any idea how hard it is?

I don't mean it's hard to get myself asked out—that's happened quite a few times already—but the chaps haven't been my cup of tea. My question is—would you believe how hard it is to find the right style of man?

I've taken some comfort from reading that a clever academic has worked out that finding the perfect partner is only one hundred times more likely than finding an alien. I read it in the Daily Mail on the Tube. See how much progress I've made?

The thing is, I'm not looking for the perfect life partner—just the perfect date. One night is all I ask. But even that goal is depressingly difficult to achieve.

Some people—most people—would say I'm too picky, and of course they'd be right. My dream of dating an English gentleman is completely unrealistic. Mind you, my definition of 'gentleman' is elastic. He doesn't have to be from an upper class family.

I'm mainly talking about his manners and his clothes and—well, yes, his voice. I do adore a plummy English accent.

I know it's a lot to ask. I mean, if such a man existed why would he be interested in a very ordinary Australian girl?

I know my expectations are naive. I know I should lower my sights. This maths geek from the newspaper has worked out that of the thirty million women in the UK, only twenty-six would be suitable girlfriends for him. The odds would be even worse for me, a rank outsider.

Apparently, on any given night out in London, there is a 0.0000034 per cent chance of meeting the right person.

That's a 1 in 285,000 chance.

You'd have better odds if you went to the cane toad races, Patrick. Of winning some money, I mean, not finding the perfect date.

But then you're not looking for an island romance. Are you?

Molly

CHAPTER FIVE

To: Molly Cooper <molly.cooper@flowermail.com>
From: Patrick Knight <patrick.knight@mymail.com>
Subject: Re: Impossible dreams

Molly, I hesitate to offer advice on how to engineer a date with the kind of man you're looking for, because in truth I'm not sure it's a good idea. I hate to be a wet blanket, but I'm more inclined to offer warnings. The sad fact is that a public school accent and your idea of 'gentlemanly' manners may not coincide.

Of course there are always exceptions. And you might be lucky. But don't expect that any man who speaks with Received Pronunciation and wears an expensive three-piece suit will behave like a perfect gentleman. When you're alone with him, that is.

Sorry. I know that's a grim thing to say about my fellow countrymen, but I do feel responsible, and I'd hate you to be upset. All I can honestly say is take care!
Sincerely
Patrick

To: Molly Cooper <molly.cooper@flowermail.com>
From: Patrick Knight <patrick.knight@mymail.com>
Subject: Cane toad races

You've been unusually quiet lately, Molly, and I find myself worrying (like an anxious relative) that something's happened. I'd hate to think I've crushed your spirit. I suspect I knocked a ruddy great hole in your dating dreams, but I hope I haven't completely quelled your enthusiasm for adventure and romance.

I trust you're simply quiet because you're having a cracking good time and you're too busy to write e-mails.

However, in an effort to cheer you up (if indeed you are feeling low), I thought I'd tell you about my experiences at the toad races the night before last. Yes, I've been, and you were right—I enjoyed the evening. In fact, I had a hilarious time.

As you've no doubt guessed, I wasn't really looking forward to going, but I desperately needed a break from my own company and decided to give the cane toads a try.

I'd been curious about how these races were set up, and why they've become such a tourist draw. I'd read that the toads are considered a pest here. They were brought out to eat beetles in the sugar cane, but they completely ignored the beetles and killed all sorts of other wildlife instead. They ate anything smaller than themselves, and they poisoned the bigger creatures that tried to eat them.

I was a bit worried that if cane toads are considered a pest the races might be cruel, so I was relieved to discover that, apart from having a number stuck on their backs and being kept in a bucket until the race starts, the toads don't suffer at all.

The mighty steeds racing last night were:

1. Irish Rover
2. Prince Charles
3. Herman the German
4. Yankee Doodle
5. Italian Stallion
6. Little Aussie Battler

By the time all the toads were safely under a bucket in the centre of the dance floor, and the race was ready to start, there was quite a noisy and very international crowd gathered. Naturally I had to put my money on Prince Charles.

A huge cheer went up when the bucket was lifted and the toads took off.

At least the Italian Stallion took off. The other toads all seemed a bit stunned, and just sat there blinking in the light. I yelled and cheered along with the noisiest punters, but I'd completely given up hope for my Prince Charlie when he suddenly started taking giant leaps.

What a roar there was then (especially from me)! You have no idea. Well, actually, you probably do have a very good idea. As you know, the first toad off the dance floor wins the race, and good old Prince Charles beat the Italian Stallion by a whisker. No, make that a wart.

There'd been heavy betting on the Australian and American toads, so I won quite a haul—a hundred dollars—and the prize money was handed over with a surprising degree of ceremony. I was expected to make a speech.

I explained that I was a banker from London and, as a gesture, I wanted to compensate for the unsatisfactory exchange rate as quickly as possible by converting my winnings into cold beer.

That announcement brought a huge cheer.

The cheering was even louder when I added that if everyone would like to come up to my place (that is, Molly Cooper's place) there'd be a celebratory party starting very shortly.

Everyone came, Molly. I hope you don't mind. We all squeezed in to your place and had a fabulous night. I lit every single one of your candles and Pandanus Cottage looked sensational. It did you proud.

The party went on late.

Very.

I do hope you're having a good time, too.

Warmest wishes

Patrick x

To: Patrick Knight <patrick.knight@mymail.com>
From: Molly Cooper <molly.cooper@flowermail.com>
Subject: Re: Cane toad races

Dear Patrick

That's great news about the cane toad races and the party. I was worried that, working so much by yourself, you might have given the islanders the impression you were a bit aloof. Clearly that's not so.

I'm afraid I haven't been up to partying in recent days. I'm laid low with a heavy cold, so I've been curled up at home, sipping hot lemon drinks and watching daytime television. Cidalia's been a darling. She's come in every day to check on me and make these lemon drinks, and a divine chicken soup which she calls canja.

She said it was her grandmother's cure-all—which is interesting, because it's almost the same as the soup my gran used to make for me. Seems that chicken soup is an international cure-all.

But that's not all, Patrick. Your mother telephoned while my cold was at its thickest and croakiest, and when she heard how terrible I sounded she sent me a gift box from…

Harrods!

Can you believe it? I was so stunned. It's a collection of gorgeous teas—Silver Moon, English Breakfast, Earl Grey—all in individual cotton (note that: cotton, not paper) teabags. Such a luxury for me, and so kind of her. But how can I ever repay her?

As you can see, I've been very well looked after, and I'm on the mend again now, and cheered by your account of your adventures at the toad races. I'm trying to picture you cheering madly and delivering your tongue-in-cheek speech. Fantastic.

I'm more than happy that you hosted a party at my place. The candles do make the little cottage look quite romantic, don't they? And with all that beer, and with you as host, I'm not surprised people wanted to stay. I bet I can guess who crashed and was still there next morning.

And I'm also betting that you heard Jodie Grimshaw's entire life story at around 2.00 a.m. Looks like you're really settling in, Patrick. That's great.

Oh, thanks for your advice re: English gentlemen, but don't worry. Your warnings didn't upset me—although they weren't really necessary either. I might sound totally naive, but I did see the way Hugh Grant's character behaved in Bridget Jones, and I have good antennae. I can sense a jerk at fifty paces.

Best wishes

Molly

To: Felicity Knight <flissK@mymail.com>
From: Patrick Knight <patrick.knight@mymail.com>
Subject: Many thanks

Dear Mother

I'm sure Molly's already thanked you for sending a gift box when she was ill, but I want to thank you, too. As you know, Molly's totally on her own in the world. She puts on a brave face, but she was very touched by your thoughtfulness, and so was I.

Love

P

To: Molly Cooper <molly.cooper@flowermail.com>
From: Karli Henderson <hendo86@flowermail.com>
Subject: Your house swapper

Hi Molly

It's Jodie here, using Karli's e-mail. I'm helping her to pack because she and Jimbo are heading off to Cairns. I just thought you might be interested to know that your house swapper Patrick is totally hot and throws the best parties evah. Oh, man. That party last Saturday night was totally off the chain.

Bet you wish you were here.

Jodie G

To: Karli Henderson <hendo86@flowermail.com>
From: Molly Cooper <molly.cooper@flowermail.com>
Subject: Hands off, Jodie

Sorry, Jodie, I'm going to be blunt. Patrick Knight is not for you. He's—

The message Subject: Hands off, Jodie **has not been sent. It has been saved in your drafts folder.**

To: Molly Cooper <molly.cooper@flowermail.com>
From: Karli Henderson <hendo86@flowermail.com>
Subject: So long, farewell, auf wiedersehen, etc.
  Hi Molly
  I'm afraid this is going to be my last e-mail. What with the move and everything, Jimbo and I are a bit strapped for cash, so I've sold this computer, along with half our CDs, in a garage sale. This is my last e-mail to anyone, and I won't be back online for some time, but I'm sure things will improve once we're settled in our new jobs in Cairns. Will be thinking of you, girlfriend. Have a blast in London.
  Love
  Karli xxxxxxxxx

To: Molly Cooper <molly.cooper@flowermail.com>
From: Patrick Knight <patrick.knight@mymail.com>
Subject: An address in Clapham
  Molly, my (secret) contacts at the bank have found a Charles Torrington Cooper, born in 1956, who used to live at 16 Rosewater Terrace, Clapham.
  I can't guarantee that this is your father, but Torrington is an unusual middle name, and everything else matches, so chances are we're onto something.
  If you decide to go to Clapham by tube, don't get out at Clapham Junction. That's actually Battersea, not Clapham, and it confuses lots of visitors. You should use the Northern Line and get out at Clapham Common.
  Warmest
  Patrick

To: Patrick Knight <patrick.knight@mymail.com>
From: Molly Cooper <molly.cooper@flowermail.com>
Subject: Re: An address in Clapham

Bless you, Patrick, and bless your (secret) contacts at the bank. Please pass on my massive thanks. I'll head out to Clapham just as soon as I can.

I hope 16 Rosewater Terrace is still there.

Molly xx

To: Patrick Knight <patrick.knight@mymail.com>
From: Molly Cooper <molly.cooper@flowermail.com>
Subject: Re: An address in Clapham—another long e-mail

I've had the most unbelievably momentous day. A true Red Letter Day that I'll remember for the rest of my life.

Until today all I've ever known about my father was what my grandmother told me—that he was charming and handsome and he swept my mother off her feet, and that he didn't have a lot of money, but managed to make my mum very happy.

Oh, and she would also tell me how excited he was when I was born. How he walked the floor with me when I had colic and was so patient, etc.

I was quite content with these pictures, and because I never knew my parents I didn't really grieve for them. I had Gran, and she was warm and loving and doted on me, so I was fine.

But ever since I've been in London I've been thinking rather a lot about Charlie Cooper. I'd look at things like Nelson's Column or Marble Arch, or even just an ordinary shop window, and I'd wonder if my dad had ever stood there, looking at the exact same thing. I'd feel as if he was there with me, as if he was glad that I was seeing his home town.

The feeling was even stronger today when I arrived in Clapham. Every lamppost and shopfront felt significant. I found myself asking if the schoolboy Charlie had passed here on his way to school. Did he stop *here* to buy marbles or *there* to buy cream buns?

And then I found Rosewater Terrace and my heart started to pound madly.

It's a long narrow street, and it feels rather crowded in between rows of tall brick houses with tiled roofs and chimney pots, and there are cars parked along both sides of the street, adding to the crowded-in feeling. There are no front yards or gardens. Everyone's front door opens straight onto the footpath.

When I reached number 16 I felt very strange, as if tiny spiders were crawling inside me. I stood there on the footpath, staring at the house, at windows with sparkling glass and neat white frames, and at the panels on the front door, painted very tastefully in white and two shades of grey.

The doorknob was bright and shiny and very new, and there were fresh white lace curtains in the window and a lovely blue jug filled with pink and white lilies.

It was very inviting, and I longed to take a peek inside. I wondered what would happen if knocked on the door. If someone answered, could I tell them that my father and his family used to live there? How would they react?

I was still standing there dithering, trying to decide

what to do, when the door of the next house opened and a little old lady, wearing an apron and carrying a watering can, came shuffling out in her slippers.

'I was just watering my pot plants and I saw you standing there,' she said. 'Are you lost, dearie?'

She looked about a hundred years old, but she was so sweet and concerned I found myself telling her exactly why I was there. As soon as I said the words 'Charles Cooper', her eyes almost popped out of her head and her mouth dropped like a trap door. I thought I'd given her a heart attack.

It seemed to take ages before she got her breath back. 'So you're Charlie's little Australian daughter,' she said. 'Well, I never. Oh, my dear, of course. You look just like him.'

Daisy—that's her name, Daisy Groves—hugged me then, and invited me inside her house, and we had the loveliest nostalgic morning. She told me that she'd lived in Rosewater Terrace ever since she was married, almost sixty years ago, and she'd known my dad from the day he was born. Apparently he was born three days before her daughter Valerie and in the same hospital.

'Charlie and Valerie were always such great friends,' Daisy told me. 'All through their school years. Actually, I always thought—'

She didn't finish that sentence, just looked away with a wistful smile, but I'm guessing from the way she spoke that she'd had matchmaking dreams for my dad and Valerie. Except Charlie was one for adventure, and as soon as he'd saved enough he set off travelling around the world. Then he met my mum in Australia. End of story. Valerie married an electrician and now lives in Peterborough.

Daisy also told me that number 16 has exactly the same layout as her house, so she let me have a good look around her place, and I saw a little bedroom at the top with a sloping ceiling. My dad's bedroom was exactly the same.

But there are no Coopers left in Rosewater Terrace. At least three families have lived in number 16 since my grandparents died and the house has been 'done up' inside several times.

The best thing was that Daisy showed me photos of Charlie when he was a boy. Admittedly they were mainly photos of Valerie, with Charlie in the background, sometimes pulling silly faces, or sticking up his fingers behind Valerie's head to give her rabbit's ears.

But I felt so connected, Patrick, and I felt as if there'd been a reason I'd always wanted to come to London and now I no longer have such a big blank question mark inside me when I think about my father. In fact, I feel happy and content in a whole new way. That's a totally unexpected bonus.

So thank you, Patrick. Thank you a thousand times.

Oh, and I have to tell you the last thing Daisy said to me when I was leaving.

'Your father was a naughty little boy, but he grew up to be such a charming gentleman.' And she pressed her closed fist over her heart and sighed the way my friends sigh over George Clooney.

I floated on happiness all the way back to the Tube station.

Molly xx

To: Patrick Knight <patrick.knight@mymail.com>
From: Molly Cooper <molly.cooper@flowermail.com>
Subject: Re: An address in Clapham

Patrick, it's only just hit me—as I pressed 'send' on that last e-mail to you I had the most awfully revealing, jaw-dropping, lightbulb moment.

I'm in shock.

Because now when I think about my dreams of dating a perfect English gentleman, I have to ask if it's really some kind of deeply subconscious Freudian search for my father.

I felt quite *eeeeuuuwwww* when I tried to answer that. But where does my interest in gentlemen come from? I mean, it's pretty weird. Most girls are interested in dangerous bad boys.

And this leads to another question. Has becoming acquainted with so much about my father totally cured me of my desire for that impossible, unreachable dating dream? Can I strike the English gentleman off my wish list of 'Things to Do in London'?

I'm not sure. Right now I'm confused. It's something I'm going to have to think about. Or sleep on.

Molly, feeling muddled...

x

To: Molly Cooper <molly.cooper@flowermail.com>
From: Patrick Knight <patrick.knight@mymail.com>
Subject: Re: An address in Clapham

What fantastic news about your father!

I'm so pleased we found the right address and that you've had such a good result. Charles Torrington Cooper sounds as if he was a great guy (a gentleman, no less). Lucky you, Molly. Cherish that image.

I say that selfishly, perhaps, because my own father has caused me huge disappointment and I haven't forgiven him. It's not a nice place to be.

Don't get too hung up on trying to psychoanalyse yourself or your dating goals, Molly. I doubt we can ever understand how our attraction to the opposite sex works. And why would we want to? Wouldn't that take all the fun out of it?

Besides, you've only been in love with the idea of your perfect Englishman. Until you try the real thing you won't be able to test your true feelings.

Molly, you seem to me to be a woman with high ideals and fine instincts. Forget my warnings. I was being overly protective.

Take London by storm and have fun.

Patrick

To: Patrick Knight <patrick.knight@mymail.com>
From: Molly Cooper <molly.cooper@flowermail.com>
Subject: Surrender

Thanks for your kind and very supportive words, but I'm afraid they came almost too late. I've caved, Patrick. In one fell swoop I've wiped two of my goals from the board.

Rule 1: Avoid other Aussies.
Rule 3: Fall in love with an Englishman.

I've been out with an Aussie guy.

I know what I said about not mixing with Australians, but I realise now that I was limiting myself needlessly. It makes sense that I'd get along better with a fellow countryman. And besides, Brad's kinda cute—a really tall, sunburned Outback Aussie, a sheep farmer from New South Wales.

Brad may not take me to Ascot or to Covent Garden, but who did I think I was anyway—Eliza Doolittle?

When he came into the Empty Bottle the other night it was like something out of a movie. Heads turned to watch him, and he strode straight up to me at the bar with a big broad grin on his suntanned face.

'G'day,' he said, in a lazy Australian drawl and I have to say our accent had never sounded nicer. 'I remember you,' he said. 'You were on my plane coming over from Sydney. We said hi. Don't you remember?'

I hadn't remembered him (don't know why, because he's very attractive), but I mumbled something positive and I smiled.

'I sat on the other side of the aisle,' he said. 'I wanted to catch up with you when we landed, but I lost you in the crowds at Heathrow.'

Can you see why a girl might find that flattering, Patrick? We were on a plane together more than a month ago, and yet Brad recognised me as soon as he walked into a crowded London bar.

He doesn't want to sit around talking about home, and that's another reason to like him. He worked as crew on a yacht from Port Hamble to Cascais in Portugal, and then he crewed on a fishing boat back to England. You have to admire his sense of adventure.

I told him about the book of London's secrets that you sent me, and tomorrow we're going to go to Highgate Hill to find Dick Whittington's stone. I used to love the story about Dick and his cat, and the bells that made him turn around. Did you know that Dick really was Lord Mayor of London (four times), and that he gave money to St Thomas's hospital as a refuge for unmarried mothers? That's pretty amazing for way back in the 1300s.

So at least Rule 2—educate myself about the 'real' London—remains intact.

Don't feel sorry for me, Patrick. I'm happy. Brad's a nice bloke, and he seems pretty keen on me, so he's helped me to get over the whole silly idea of a dream date with an English gentleman.

I bet you're highly relieved that you've heard the last about that!

Best

Molly

CHAPTER SIX

To: Felicity Knight: <flissK@mymail.com>
From: Patrick Knight: <patrick.knight@mymail.com>
Subject: I'll be there to dance at your wedding.

Hi Mother

This is a quick note to let you know that I'm definitely flying over for the Big Day.

This morning I jumped straight onto the internet and made the bookings, so everything's all sorted and I'm really looking forward to seeing you both. I can't believe that I almost allowed this blasted writing project to get in the way of something so significant.

Nothing's as important as seeing you and Jonathan tie the knot.

I'll be there with bells on (or in this case in white tie and penguin suit).

Much love

Patrick

To: Molly Cooper <molly.cooper@flowermail.com>
From: Patrick Knight <patrick.knight@mymail.com>
Subject: Re: Surrender

Dear Molly

It appears that you're pleased with the latest turn

of events in Chelsea (i.e. your New South Wales sheep farmer), so I suppose your change of heart must be a good thing. But I can't help thinking it's a damn shame that none of my fellow countrymen have stepped up to the mark.

However, I do understand the appeal of someone from home when you're so far away, and I suppose there's no harm in breaking your own rules. If the rules have become outmoded they're not much use to you, are they?

From your e-mail, it sounds as if your new Australian escort is more than acceptable to you, and it sounds as if he's also very keen on you, so of course you must be flattered.

Just the same, I feel compelled to repeat the same advice I gave you once before—take care.

Regards
Patrick

Private Writing Journal, Magnetic Island, May 13th

Take care?

Did I really say that? Again?

If only there was a way to retract e-mails. How could I have told Molly to take care with her new Australian boyfriend? What an idiot.

It's not as if she's a helpless child. She's a grown woman—only four years younger than I. And she's on familiar ground now. She's dating the kind of fellow she's no doubt dated many, many times.

Who on earth do I think I am? Her big brother? Her priest?

OK, maybe she's all alone in the world, and in a completely new environment, but that doesn't mean I should try to stand in for her family. I have no inclination to be her father figure.

What's my excuse? Why am I so over-protective? And why did I try to warn her off this Brad character? It's crazy, but I find myself wishing he'd jump on another yacht and take off around Cape Horn, or go climb the North Pole—anything that would take him far away from Molly.

Anyone would think I was jealous of him, but that's impossible. I don't even know Molly. I've never met her and I have no plans to meet her.

Unless e-mails count.

I suppose e-mails are a form of meeting. They're certainly a very clear form of communication, and all over the globe friendships and relationships are forged via the World Wide Web. But it's not as if Molly and I are cyber-dating.

And yet, when I think about it, we are in rather unusual circumstances. We're exchanging very regular e-mails, and we're living in each other's houses. And if I'm honest I must admit that I do feel as if I know Molly incredibly well, even though we've never really met. In many ways I actually know more about her than I've known about the women I've dated.

I know her hopes and dreams and her fears, and to my surprise I find myself caring about them. I've even had my mother and colleagues from work involved in helping her. I can't ever recall doing anything like that for a girlfriend.

Each day I look out of the windows of Molly's cottage, at the view that has been her view for her whole life, and I think of her. I think of her when I switch on her kettle and use her coffee cups, when I boil an egg in her saucepan and use one of her crazy purple and pink striped egg cups. I even think of her when I drag out her damn vacuum cleaner and give the floors a once over.

Worse, I find myself leaping out of bed in the mornings (out of Molly's bed, as she likes to remind me) and racing to switch on the laptop, hoping that a message might have come from her during the night.

During the day, when I'm supposed to be writing, I find myself waiting to see the little envelope pop up in the bottom right-hand corner of my screen, telling me that I've got a message (as if she'd be writing to me in the middle of the UK night).

I've let myself become incredibly involved with her, and it's like she's become part of my life. I even find myself wishing she was here, wandering about this cottage in her bikini and a sarong.

Actually...there are a couple of beautiful isolated bays where locals tell me you can skinny-dip without being hassled. Now, that's an arresting thought...Molly, slipping starkers into the crystal-clear waters of Rocky Bay.

I've gone barking mad, haven't I? It must be this solitary lifestyle that's messing with my head.

Clearly I need to get out of this house.

Well, I'll achieve that when I go back to the UK for the wedding. A weekend of mixing with my family and some of my old crowd will soon clear my head.

Already, just the thought of seeing them makes me feel saner. And now I'm asking myself why I was so worried about writing two words in an e-mail. It's not as if Molly will take any notice of my 'take care' warning. She'll have the good sense to laugh at it.

To: Patrick Knight <patrick.knight@mymail.com>
From: Molly Cooper <molly.cooper@flowermail.com>
Subject: Having a good time

Hi Patrick

Unfortunately I can only fit in sightseeing jaunts around my work schedule, but Brad and I have still been getting around. Yesterday we investigated Cleopatra's Needle, which was rather impressive. It's hard to believe it's over three and a half thousand years old and was lying in the desert sands of Egypt until some English fellow dragged it back to London behind a steamer.

While I was at work Brad went off on his own to check out the Cabinet War Rooms Museum. They're leftovers from WW2, and still hidden away in tunnels and offices beneath Whitehall. Brad's interested because his grandad served over here as a fighter pilot, but I was quite pleased to miss that trip. I'm still a bit iffy about spending too much time underground.

All's well here. Hope you're fine, too.

Molly

To: Molly Cooper <molly.cooper@flowermail.com>
From: Patrick Knight <patrick.knight@mymail.com>
Subject: Re: Having a good time

Molly, I'm glad you're having such a fine time, and I'm pleased to report that I've made some exciting discoveries of my own. You're not the only one who can break rules, you know. I've taken entire days away from the laptop to go skin-diving. Now that the stinger season is well and truly over I feel as if I need to make up for lost time, so I bought myself a snorkel, goggles and flippers and headed down to Florence Bay.

Every day this week I've spent hours and hours in the sea. I'm surprised I haven't grown gills.

I'm hooked. It's amazing. Mere metres below the surface, I enter a different and fascinating world. The water is a perfect temperature, the visibility is excellent, and as you know it's like swimming in a huge aquarium, surrounded by millions of colourful fish.

Thanks to your fabulously helpful illustrations, I've been able to identify lionfish, trigger fish, blue spotted stingrays, clownfish—and of course our cheeky friend Chelmon rostratus.

I was so excited when I saw him poking his long stripy snout out from a piece of pink coral! I almost rang you just to tell you. I suppose I felt a bit the way you did the first time you spotted a film star on the King's Road.

Honestly, I've dived in the Mediterranean and the Red Sea, and I thought those reefs were beautiful, but I hadn't dreamed the reefs on this island would have so much diversity.

Using your map as my guide, I've now dived in all the main bays—Radical, Alma, Nelly, Geoffrey—and I've loved them all. Especially the range of corals in Geoffrey Bay.

The locals tell me that these are only fringing reefs. If I really want to see something spectacular I should head out to the main Great Barrier Reef. So, as you can imagine, that's on the agenda now as well.

I think I'll catch one of the big catamarans when they're passing through on their way to the reef. I can't wait. I might even head north to stay on one of the other Barrier Reef islands for a while.

Sorry, if I'm sounding carried away, Molly. I think I am.
Regards
Patrick

To: Patrick Knight <patrick.knight@mymail.com>
From: Molly Cooper <molly.cooper@flowermail.com>
Subject: Re: Having a good time

It seems we're both reaping the rewards of our daring decisions to break our own rules. I'm so pleased you're enjoying the island's reefs, Patrick. I got quite homesick reading your descriptions, and I found myself wishing I was there with you, sharing the excitement of your discoveries. Shows how greedy I am, because I wouldn't want to miss all the fun I'm having here.

Yes, I know I can't have my cake and eat it, too.

But, still…skin-diving with you would be so cool.

I hope you enjoy your trip to the Great Barrier Reef, or to other islands further north. Don't go if the weather's rough, though. I'd hate you to be horribly seasick.

Cheers!
Molly

To: Patrick Knight <patrick.knight@mymail.com>
From: Molly Cooper <molly.cooper@flowermail.com>
Subject: Quiet

You've been very quiet, Patrick, so I'm assuming you must have gone out to the Great Barrier Reef, or perhaps you're exploring further afield. Please don't tell me you've found another island you like more than Magnetic.

Molly

Private Writing Journal, Lodon, May 23rd

I almost didn't bring this journal back to London, but I threw it in my bag at the last minute because writing in it has become something of a habit. My thoughts (sometimes) become clearer when I put them on paper. So here I am, two days after my mother's wedding, pleased and relieved that it was the beautiful, emotional and happy event that both she and Jonathan wanted and deserved.

My duty phone call to my father in Scotland is behind me, so now I'm considering my options.

To see or not to see Molly.

To fly straight back to the island, or stay on here in London for a bit.

The thing is, I'm desperate to call on Molly while I'm here. I'll admit I'm utterly fascinated by her (and my mother could hardly stop talking about her), but I'm hesitating for a number of reasons.

1. The Australian boyfriend. It probably sounds churlish, but I don't think I could enjoy Molly's company if Brad the sheep farmer was hanging around in the wings.

2. Our house swapping agreement. I've handed over my house for three months in good faith, and if I suddenly turn up on Molly's doorstep in the middle of that time she'll be placed in a confusing situation—not sure if she's my hostess or my house guest. I guess this hurdle is one we could work our way around, but then there's—

3. The fantasy date with a gentleman. Here's the thing: I have the right accent and the right clothes to meet Molly's criteria, and if I was on my best behaviour I could probably pull off the role of an English gentle-

man. I could even take Molly on her dream date to the theatre. In fact, I'd love to.

But—

Maddeningly, I have a string of doubts...

• Does she still want that 'dream' date now that she has her Australian?

• Just how perfect does this Englishman have to be? A movie star I am not.

• What if I try to do the right thing by her, but she misinterprets my motives? Might she think I'm amusing myself at her expense? After all, she's spilled out her heart to me. She might feel horribly embarrassed if I turned up and tried to act out her fantasy.

So where does that leave me? I suppose I could arrange to meet her on neutral ground—in a little café somewhere. Or perhaps I should just phone her for a chat. But then I wouldn't see her, would I?

To: Patrick Knight <patrick.knight@mymail.com>
From: Molly Cooper <molly.cooper@flowermail.com>
Subject: You're never going to believe this, Patrick!

I don't know whether you're home from the reef yet, but I'm writing this at midnight because I just have to tell you. The most astonishing, amazing, incredible, miraculous thing.

He... Him... The man of my dreams has turned up on my doorstep.

The most gorgeous Englishman. In. The. World.

I hyperventilate just thinking about him, but I've got to calm down so I can tell you my news.

Patrick, I've met your colleague—Peter Kingston, who, as you know, has been working in South America for the same banking company you work for. Now he's back in London for a short break.

OK, I know you must be asking how I can gush about a new man when I'm supposed to be going out with Brad. No doubt you're thinking I'm the shallowest and ficklest woman in the entire universe.

First, let me explain that Brad left last Friday, heading off on another adventure, with no definite plans to come back this way. He's now somewhere at the top of Norway in the Arctic Circle, looking for the Midnight Sun.

He wanted me to go with him, but, while I'm sure the sun at midnight is well worth seeing, I didn't want to spend my hard-earned cash chasing off to another country when there's still so much of England that I haven't seen.

As you mentioned once in an e-mail, the rural parts of England are beautiful. I can't leave without seeing at least some parts beyond London, so other countries will have to come later.

Besides, Brad was fun to go out with here in London, but he was never the kind of guy I'd follow to the ends of the earth.

So, Brad had gone, and it was a Monday night—one of my nights off—and I was having a quiet night in. Oh, you have no idea, Patrick. I was at my dreckest, with no make-up and in old jeans, an ancient sweater and slippers (slippers—can you imagine anything more octogenarian?).

Worse, I was eating my dinner on my lap in front of the telly, and when the front doorbell rang I got such a surprise I spilled spaghetti Bolognese all down my front.

I was mopping bright red sauce from my pale grey

sweater as I headed for the door, and then I was stuffing tissues into my back pocket as I opened the door. And then, as they say all the time on American TV—Oh. My. God.

Patrick, let me give you a female perspective on your work colleague.

He's tall. He's dark. He's handsome. The nice, unself-conscious kind of handsome that goes with chocolate-brown eyes and a heart-stoppingly attractive smile.

And when he spoke—you know where this is going, don't you? Yes, he has a rich baritone voice, and a beautifully refined English accent, and I swear I almost swooned at his feet.

The only thing that stopped me from fainting dead away was my need to make sure he hadn't rung the wrong doorbell by mistake.

There was no mistake, thank heavens. Number 34 was Peter's destination. But, to be honest, our initial meeting was a teensy bit awkward. I was flustered. Of course I was. Can you blame me? And I guess my blushing confusion flustered Peter, too.

He seemed rather nervous and uncertain, and I couldn't help wondering if you'd given him orders to call on me. If you did, were you setting yourself up as a matchmaker?

Anyway... We both tried to talk at once, and then we stopped, and then he smiled again and said, ever so politely, 'You go first, Molly. You were saying...?'

Oh, he was the perfect gentleman. He kept his eyes averted from the sauce stains on my chest while I stumbled through my story of why you weren't here and why I was living in your house. Then he explained who he was.

Once that was sorted, and it was clear after a few more prudent questions that we were both at a bit of a loose end, Peter asked ever so casually if I'd like to go out for a drink. I'm afraid I had to wait for my heart to slide back to its normal place in my chest before I was able to accept his invitation.

In no time Peter was comfortably settled on your sofa and watching TV, while I scurried upstairs to change.

If there was ever a wardrobe crisis moment when a girl might wish for a fairy godmother, that was it. The jeans and T-shirts I'd worn on dates with Brad were totally unsuitable to wear out for a drink with Peter. He was in a suit! (No tie, admittedly, but still, a suit's a suit.)

I might have found it easier to think about clothes if my brain hadn't been swirling like a Category 5 cyclone. Here I was, with a chance to go out with my dream Englishman, and I was freaking out. I was very afraid I wasn't up to the challenge.

Panic attack!!

Thank heavens the possibility of failure snapped me out of it. How could I not go out with this man? Till the end of my days I would never forgive myself. And in a strange way I also felt I owed it to you, Patrick. You sounded rather disappointed that I'd given up on my Englishman.

So I fell on my camel suede skirt like an old friend—the same skirt I wore to afternoon tea with your mother—and the gods must have been smiling on me, for I found a clean silk shirt and tights with no ladders.

I can't do fancy make-up, so applying lipgloss and mascara didn't take long, and there's not a lot a girl can

do with my kind of curly hair, so Peter was pleasantly surprised when I was back downstairs inside ten minutes.

He gave me the warmest smile, as if he quite liked
how I looked, and off we went. Not to the Empty Bottle,
thank heavens. Peter quite understood about avoiding
my workplace.

We went to a bar that I hadn't even noticed before.
It's so discreet it just looks like someone's house from
the outside. (Another of London's secrets?) Inside, there
were people gathered in couples or small groups, and
everyone was comfortably seated on barstools or in
armchairs, which made a pleasant change from the noisy
Empty Bottle, which is usually standing room only.

After our awkward start, I was surprised to feel quite
quickly at ease. Sitting there with Peter in comfortable
chairs, sipping my Sloe gin fizz and gazing into his lovely
dark coffee eyes, I should have been dumbstruck with
awe, but he has the same easy way that your mother
has.

Is that something well-bred people learn? Are they
given lessons in how to put other people at their ease?

Anyway, I found myself chatting happily. I don't suppose that surprises you, considering the way I chat on
endlessly with you.

Peter asked what I'd seen of London, and I told
him about some of the things I'd discovered—like the
Kensington Roof Gardens and the tiny old pub in Ely
Street—and to my surprise he was really interested. He
said he'd lived here nearly all his life and hadn't known
about them. I told him about the book you'd so kindly
sent to me, and tomorrow we're going to do some more
exploring together.

Me and Peter Kingston. Can you believe it?

Patrick, I've just realised how long this e-mail is. Sorry, I've been carried away. But I'm sure you have the gist of my news, and I suppose I should try to get some beauty sleep. I'll tell you more after tomorrow (or you can tell me to shut up, if it's all a bit much).

Don't worry, Patrick. I won't do anything rash. I have a highly efficient built-in jerk-detector, and I just know deep in my bones that I'm safe with Peter. But I will try to follow your very sweet advice and *take care!*

Yours, bubbling with too much excitement

Molly x

CHAPTER SEVEN

To: Patrick Knight <patrick.knight@mymail.com>
From: Molly Cooper <molly.cooper@flowermail.com>
Subject: London explorations

Dear Patrick

I hope you're having as fabulous a time on the Great Barrier Reef as I'm having here. I could carry on about the way discovering London with Peter just keeps getting better and better, so that each discovery is more interesting and fascinating than the last. But you'll be relieved to hear that I'm going to save you from that kind of bombardment and give you a brief overview only.

I saw my last message to you on the screen and almost had a fit. Sorry I rambled on so much, but meeting Peter was all so unexpected and so exciting.

However, I would like to tell you about our excursion to Westminster Bridge. Now, I know it's not exactly a secret or hidden part of London, but have you ever seen the movie *A Westminster Affair*? It's one of the few movies I saw on the big screen when I was very young, and that day has always been a standout memory for me.

My gran and I caught the ferry over to Townsville on the mainland and we went to the big cinema complex. I can remember every detail, like eating the hugest choc-topped ice creams while we waited for the show to start, and then the movie was just the most beautiful sappy romance. (I won't bore you with the details.)

Afterwards we were both a bit weepy when we came out blinking in the late-afternoon light. Then, to cap things off, we went to a Chinese restaurant and ate big bowls of wonderful chicken soup with floating wontons.

Finally we caught the ferry home, and Gran and I sat out the back, watching the mainland slip away while a cool breeze blew in our faces, and we smelled the sea, and we watched the most gorgeous sunset colour the sky and the water. I've always thought of that day as one of the most perfect days of my life.

Which is probably why *A Westminster Affair* has remained my all-time favourite film, and you'll understand why it was incredibly special for me to be there on the bridge with a man like Peter.

We admired the magnificent Coade stone lion that guards one end of the bridge. (Did you know a woman invented the special cement that stone is made from?) And we walked across the Thames, and it was a beautiful morning, and it was just like those lines from Wordsworth's poem.

Ships, towers, domes, theatres, and temples lie
Open unto the fields, and to the sky;
All bright and glittering in the smokeless air.

Sorry if that looks like I'm showing off. I'm not really a poetry buff, but because of my soft spot for Westminster I looked up the poem years ago.

Peter and I didn't just walk on the bridge, though. We climbed Big Ben's clock tower. That was Peter's suggestion. I had no idea you could go up there.

'My father brought me here when I was five years old,' he told me as we started up the three hundred and thirty-four stairs.

It was rather fun, climbing all those stairs together, going past the cell where the famous suffragette Emily Pankhurst was held for some time, poor thing.

We walked behind the illuminated clock faces of Big Ben, and heard the tick-tick-ticking in the clock room.

As we watched the busy cogs and wheels, Peter told me that his father had made him stand in front of this machinery while he gave him a lecture about time marching on.

'He told me that this was my life ticking away,' Peter said. 'And that none of us knows how much time we've been allotted. Time's precious and we mustn't waste it.' 'That's rather a grim message for a little boy,' I suggested.

Peter smiled a little sadly. 'I guess it was. Considering I no longer respect the man, it's surprising that the message stuck.'

I didn't like to ask why he no longer respected his father. Instead I said, 'Does that mean you don't ever waste time?'

'I try not to.'

He reminded me of you, Patrick, and the way you've worked so hard at the bank and how you're still working hard when you're supposed to be on holiday. At least you were until recently. I'm glad you're taking a break now, on the Great Barrier Reef.

I told Peter that maybe he should try living on a tropical island.

One of his eyebrows shot up. 'Does time stand still on your island?'

'It can if you let it,' I said.

He smiled again, rather ambiguously, I thought. Then we went to the belfry and waited while the hammers struck the famous big bells.

Wow.

As you can imagine, there's a great booming sound. But it's not deafening, which was a relief. Just the same, the resonance penetrated all the way through me—rather like the way Peter's smile vibrates through me.

It was a very moving experience, actually, and Peter's eyes were extra shiny. As the gong faded he stared at me for ages, and then he reached for my hands and drew me closer and I knew he was going to kiss me.

My heart started booming louder than Big Ben. How utterly romantic to be kissed by my gorgeous Englishman high above the Thames and the London Eye and the thousands of rooftops and spires.

We shared a beat or two of delicious hesitation and then we inched closer. I was in heaven.

But just at the crucial moment a group of noisy tourists burst into the belfry and we lost our opportunity.

The beautiful moment when we might have kissed is now forever gone, which I suppose proves that his father was right about time and opportunity.

Gosh, Patrick, I'm sorry. I've rambled on, after all.

Molly x

The message Subject: London Explorations **has not been sent. It has been saved in your drafts folder.**

Molly's Diary, Chelsea, May 25th

I've decided a diary is a necessity right now. I couldn't send that e-mail to poor Patrick. The dear fellow has been very tolerant of my long-winded ramblings, and it's been wonderful to have him to talk to. But there are some things a girl shouldn't share—especially now that I've met one of his friends and I seem to be falling head over heels. That's too much information for any man.

I guess it's just as well that Patrick's away. I hope he's having a fabulous time, partying like mad at some luxurious Barrier Reef resort.

Actually, the person I really should be talking to now is Karli. She's been my best friend since we were born—or at least that's how it feels—but now that she and Jimbo have sold their computer and left for Cairns, she's out of touch.

Boy, is she going to be mad when she realises she's missed this golden opportunity. She's been waiting to discuss my love life since I was ten years old, but apart from one or two teenage crushes, and a couple of semi-serious boyfriends who eventually left the island, there's been nothing very exciting to report until now. We're both so over talking about her and Jimbo.

So…as I can't pour out my innermost feelings to Patrick or to Karli, I've turned to this diary. Which isn't a new phenomenon for me. When really big things happen in my life I've always felt an urge to write them down. I wrote scads when I was a teenager—especially when I first started at high school on the mainland and felt so lonely.

Then last year, after Gran died, I wrote in my diary

for weeks and weeks. It was as if I needed to get every sweet memory of her down on paper—the exact shape of her smile, her gentle hands and the blue sparkle in her eyes.

I wrote about all the feelings locked inside me, too. How I felt about losing her and why I loved her and how much I owed her, and how I knew she regretted that I hadn't gone to university. It was indeed a pity that I didn't get to extend the wonderful education she scrimped and saved to give me, but how could I have left her when she was so ill and doddery for the last few years? She needed me.

I cried oceans while I wrote, but in a weird way I think the writing helped to ease the painful knots of grief inside me. Eventually I was able to let some of it go.

So now that I've met someone as amazing as Peter Kingston, I have to get stuff down on paper or I'll simply explode.

But where do I start? With his dashing dark looks? His gorgeous smile? His sexy, sexy voice? It's just so amazing that this man is the incarnation of everything I ever dreamed of—good-looking and charming, with a divinely refined English accent that sends delicious shivers all the way through me. And on top of all of these assets he's just absolutely nice.

And he has perfect manners. In fact he's so perfectly lovely I could eat him.

I keep wondering if I've done something very good in a past life. Or perhaps the stars are perfectly aligned in my personal cosmos? Surely some special form of magic brought Peter to my doorstep?

I know I've never felt remotely like this before. This

is so much more than a crush. It's like I'm so constantly high I'm practically flying.

Should I be frightened? Might I fall?

I keep telling myself to calm down. I know Peter's only in London for a week, and I know he's only amusing himself in my company while he's here, and I know that he'll soon be back in South America. But he's persuaded me to ask for a few days off work from the Empty Bottle so that we can do lots together, and to my surprise they said yes—no problem.

And he does seem to be having a really good time. With me!

So for the moment I'm going with the flow (which feels a bit like a flash flood)—and I'm reminding myself every so often to breathe.

I haven't even mentioned my biggest piece of news yet.

This afternoon, after an expedition to elegant Hampstead and its many gorgeous, gorgeous houses, Peter and I were walking back from Sloane Square when he reached into his coat pocket and ever so casually produced two tickets.

'My cousin plays cello in the orchestra at the Royal Opera House and she gave me these,' he said, with his lovely, twinkling, careful smile. 'I've no idea if ballet's your cup of tea, but I wondered if you'd like to give it a try.'

I confess I squealed. I know, I know—I should have been more composed and ladylike. Thank heavens I didn't also give in to my impulse to leap on poor Peter and hug him to death.

But it just seemed too much to have the last part of my dream fall into place—an invitation from a lovely

Englishman to an evening of culture. Better still, I've been invited to something that's both cultured and romantic. The ballet is Romeo and Juliet and I know that story inside out. I can recite whole sections of Shakespeare's balcony scene. I adore it.

After I'd accepted (breathlessly, but politely, I hope) Peter told me that there's a restaurant at the Opera House and he suggested we should dine there, as well. We could have a starter and a main course before the show and then dessert at interval.

Be still my beating heart!

Eliza Doolittle, stand aside.

And I've made what is, for me, a hugely rash decision. I've been so cautious about spending money, but my bank balance is actually healthier than I expected, so I've decided that I can afford to pinch a portion of my savings to buy a new outfit (I really don't think my faithful camel suede skirt is quite right for dinner and the ballet at the Royal Opera House, Covent Garden).

I can afford a new dress. Maybe even a nice piece of jewellery to set it off. I've set tomorrow aside for shopping. Squee!

Maybe I should buy a lottery ticket before my good luck runs out.

To: Patrick Knight <patrick.knight@mymail.com>
From: Molly Cooper <molly.cooper@flowermail.com>
Subject: How are you?

Hi Patrick

I assume you're still exploring the wonders of the reef? I hope you're having a great time. All is going very well here.

Molly

Private Writing Journal, May 26th

I hesitate to admit on paper that I'm pretending to be someone I'm not. I've never thought of myself as an actor, but I must admit it's fun to take on a role. It all happened so spontaneously—as soon as I saw Molly. I suddenly wanted to become someone better than myself. The man she'd invented in her imagination.

As soon as she told me that Brad the Australian was no longer on the scene, I suppressed my impulse to cheer and instead interpreted his absence as a very clear green light.

So now Molly and I are having a great time. Molly's fabulous, so lively and engaging, and she's so incredibly excited about our planned date. I refuse to spoil this fun by worrying about when or if I should tell her the truth. For once in my life I'm having fantastic, incautious fun, and everything about this planned venture feels right.

Nothing ventured, nothing gained, etc.

Molly's Diary, May 27th

I know I have turned a corner tonight.

I've had the most wonderfully romantic and incredibly special evening, and I feel as if I'm a different person in some mysterious but vitally important way. (I'm wondering if I'm a late bloomer and I've finally grown up.)

I'm sure I can't still be the same overly excited twenty-four-year-old who wrote that rave in yesterday's diary entry. I feel calmer, safer, happier, surer.

Peter kissed me tonight, and I know I'll never be the same again.

But perhaps I should start at the beginning.

I had the most fabulous time shopping. It was a little overwhelming, of course, after living on the island, where there are just two dress shops both specialising in resortwear. Today I was shopping in London, which has thousands—yes, that's right—thousands of shops filled with dresses!

Instead of my usual experience of finding just one outfit that might do, for the first time in my life I had an endless range of clothes to choose from.

Did the vast array of choices do my head in?

Well, yes, I think I did get high from trying things on. I was like those women in movies who go on shopping sprees and try on scads and scads of dresses—whatever takes their fancy—except I didn't parade my dresses in front of anyone. I didn't even have a friend to consult, which was a pity.

But I'm pleased to report that I did not listen to the salesgirls, every one of whom told me that every single dress looked absolutely fabulous on me.

I took my time and I was careful, even though I wanted to be bold and reckless like Patrick's heroine, Beth Harper. It would have been scary but so exciting to have bought something like Beth's expensive little cocktail dress in show-stopping red. But I have to be so careful with my money, so I decided to play it safe. Even so, I'm happy.

I settled on a simple, sleek black cocktail dress that makes me feel beautiful and sexy. Honestly.

I love it! It fits me like it was made to measure and it feels so soft and sensuous against my skin. It's a truly feel-good, confidence-boosting dress. I teamed it with a lovely woven gold choker necklace, and I think the whole effect struck exactly the right note for this evening.

I also went to the make-up counter in one of the swishest department stores and had my face 'done'.

'Keep it subtle,' I pleaded, and the girl with brightly dyed hair surprised me by doing exactly that. She made my complexion look almost as soft and fine as an English girl's and she made my eyes look huge! Wow, I had no idea clever make-up could make such a difference. I have a new ambition. I'm determined to learn how to do that kind of make-up for myself—although I don't suppose I'll need it when I'm back home on the island.

(I don't want to think about that now.)

It was cool this evening, so I needed my coat, which meant that Peter didn't see my new dress until we got to the cloakroom. When I took the coat off I have to say the expression on his face was a perfect moment—exactly like something out of one of my favourite movies.

He told me I looked beautiful, and his voice was choked, and his throat rippled. And I almost cried.

I'm so glad I didn't. Think of the make-up disaster! And I would have hated to spoil such a lovely moment.

I'm sure that wearing my lovely, sophisticated black dress helped me to stay calm. No doubt the dress plus the fact that the most gorgeous man in the entire theatre was at my side. Have I mentioned how absolutely incredible Peter looked in his dark tux? And there he was, paying courteous and focused attention to me. Throughout the whole evening, I felt quietly, confidently, bone-deep happy.

Oh, and I loved the ballet. Thank heavens. I'd only ever been to the Christmas concerts put on by Karli's ballet teacher when we were kids, and I was always terribly bored by them.

There was no chance of being bored tonight. Before the show Peter and I ate—sorry—dined in the most

*elegant restaurant. We had goat's cheese and peppered
pear, followed by fillet of bream, and both these courses
were accompanied by proper French champagne.*

*Fortunately, Gran trained me well, and I had the
whole business of the cutlery sorted. Mind you, Peter
is so well-mannered he wouldn't have turned a hair if
I'd used the wrong knife or fork.*

*Then we went into the theatre which was even bigger
and grander and more gilded and sumptuous than I'd
imagined. There were chandeliers and velvet seats and
thick lush carpet and the flash of real diamonds among
the women in the audience.*

*As Peter guided me to my seat with a warm hand
protectively touching (and electrifying) the small of
my back, I did notice more than one feminine glance
directed his way, but he only seemed interested in me.*

*I can write that now without feeling a need to squeal.
The fact that Peter seems to really like me is a kind of
quiet truth that's settled happily inside me, keeping my
heart warm and light.*

*Of course everything about the ballet was fabulous.
I was so moved by the stirring music and the brilliant
dancing and the dramatic acting. As for the costumes,
the scenery, and have I mentioned the man sitting beside
me?—I was entranced.*

*At the interval we went back to the restaurant and
had a sinfully delicious champagne trifle for dessert.
And then we returned for the second half of* Romeo and
Juliet *and it was so emotional.*

*The performance was beautiful, exciting, heartbreak-
ing, intimate. I was spellbound. It was totally possible
to feel the pain of those tragic young lovers.*

But I managed not to cry.

I think I was still under some kind of spell.

Afterwards, I thought we might have met Peter's cello-playing cousin, but apparently she was triple-booked that evening, or something. So Peter brought me home, and it was time to say goodnight on my (Patrick's) doorstep, and I tried, rather inadequately, to thank Peter.

Then I saw the look in his beautiful dark eyes. Serious. Tender. Aching. All at the same time. My heart began a painful thumping. My skin burned. I knew what he wanted and I was almost certain it was the same thing I was willing to happen.

'Molly,' he whispered in his gorgeous deep voice. 'You know I'm going to have to kiss you.'

Oh, my.

I was trembling, but it wasn't from fear. I was trembling from very real, very hot desire.

I have to say, when it comes to seduction, gentlemen have it all over bad boys. Here was Peter, more or less asking permission to kiss me, and I had to restrain myself from screaming, 'Yes!'

As an aside, I should mention that I've always understood the general rule that a kiss is the litmus test of dating. I know the bottom line of any guy meets girl situation is chemistry. But, call me fussy, I've always wanted something more.

I've had quite a few kisses in my twenty-four years. I've had kisses from nice guys I've liked but who've left me thinking there's something missing. (Brad would be my most recent example.) And I've had kisses from dubious guys I wasn't too sure about that have really turned me on.

But now I realise I've never had the vital elements

coincide—a really nice guy that I liked a lot, and a really hot kiss.

Until tonight.

And here's the wonderful thing I discovered as Peter and I performed a slow, lip-locked two-step through the doorway and into the front hall. Peter Kingston doesn't just look and walk and talk like my dream man, and he isn't just a charming and amusing companion, he's my dream lover.

His lips were warm and sexy and persuasive, and he tasted absolutely, perfectly, fabulously right. He smelled so good I wanted to bury my nose in his neck and stay there till the next Ice Age.

Truth is, I did not behave with ladylike decorum. I wound myself closer than a strangler fig clinging to a tree in the rainforest. As for the rest of my response— let's just say my mouth had a mind of its own. And my hands weren't exactly shy.

But I was following his lead.

I don't think either Peter or I expected the fireworks to be quite so volatile, although I suspect that Karli might tell me my interest in gentlemen was always about getting to this point—discovering the bad boy behind the polite, genteel façade.

Right at that moment I would have been quite happy if he'd regressed all the way back to Cave Man.

Now, however, I'm sitting on my bed and recording the fact that Peter did not stay here tonight, even though I know we both wanted him to. I suppose I'm grateful that he remembered he's a gentleman and left before things got out of hand.

I mean, really, one of us had to be sensible. He's going back to South America in a couple of days, and I'm going back to Australia in a few weeks, so it wouldn't be wise for us to get too involved. It would create all kinds of complications.

Just the same…I have to say that Peter's kiss felt like a beginning rather than a farewell. He lingered over saying goodnight so sweetly, and he looked so torn about leaving that I just knew—as if I was tuned in to his thought waves—that the best was not over yet.

'I'll ring you first thing in the morning,' he promised, before he kissed me one last, deliciously sexy time.

It's a nice thought to sleep on.

Please let me wake up remembering my dreams.

Text message from Patrick Knight, May 27th, 11.55 p.m.:
Hi Simon, sorry to disturb you so late at night. Wonder if we could swap cars tomorrow? I'd like to run down to Cornwall and stay overnight. Yr sporty MG so impressive. P.

Text message from Simon Knight, May 27th, 11.59 p.m.:
No prob. Who's the lucky passenger? Any girl I know?

Text message from Patrick Knight, May 28th, 12.03 a.m.:
Huge thanks. Trust u to guess. She's special + new + Aussie.

Molly's Diary, May 28th

OMG. I've pinched myself black and blue to make sure I'm not still dreaming.

It's only early, but Peter has already phoned to ask me if I'd like to drive down to Cornwall with him. He's borrowed a cousin's sports car, and as it's a nice day he's suggested we can drive with the top down if I liked. We could see Somerset and Devon on the way, and stay overnight in a B&B on the Cornish coast.

I said yes, I'd love that. Thank you very much!

I think I sounded calm, but, honestly, Peter probably has no idea how big this is for me. I'm flashing hot and cold. The dream date—our night out at the Royal Ballet—which I saw as the pinnacle of glam, is peanuts compared with having this gorgeous man drive me down to Cornwall in a sports car (with the top down), even if the sports car is borrowed (especially when we're staying overnight in a B&B).

This is a biggie. I've never actually gone away for a weekend with a man before. Peter probably assumes that I have.

Actually, I'm not sure if Peter and I will be sleeping in the same room, but after last night's kiss I can't help thinking there's a good chance the option might arise, so I'm seriously wishing I'd spent some of my money on new underwear (just in case, you know). Oh, and a new nightdress would have been nice.

It's too late now. I really must dash and start packing. Somehow I think this weekend is going to be a huge turning point in my life. In the right direction!

CHAPTER EIGHT

Molly's Diary, May 28th

Disaster!

Of the very worst kind.

Instead of my life turning in a good direction, my whole world has come crashing down. Right now I'm wishing I'd never heard of London, that I'd never left my lovely, safe little island.

I'm heartbroken. Inconsolable. I feel foolish and miserable and conned, and my dreams are dust at my feet.

The Girl Who Thought She Could Fly...has fallen. Big-time.

If Shakespeare was still alive he would probably write a play about me. Molly Cooper: a comic tragedy in three acts.

Oh, help. I have to make myself write this down, even though my heart is bleeding and every word is killing me. I need to get every painful detail down accurately, because there just may be a time in the very dim and very distant future when I'll try to read it again, with a clearer head and in a calmer spirit than I'm experiencing right now.

First, let me say that I am not in Cornwall, nor on the way to Cornwall in a sports car, with or without the top down. I'm still in Chelsea.

And I'm alone.

My overnight bag is sitting on the floor beside me, still packed. I may just leave it that way as an eternal monument to my foolishness.

So what has happened?

Ouch. Gulp. Squirm. Here goes…

This morning, after my last diary entry, I packed in a flurry of enormous excitement—a change of clothes, nightdress, toothbrush, etc. I dressed carefully in my new, authentic slim jeans and a white T-shirt, and I added an elegant sage-green scarf (carefully looped and draped) in case it was cool in an open car. I imagined the trailing ends flapping glamorously in the breeze.

For once I was happy about my curly hair. The wind could do its worst and my curls would look much the same as they always did. Tangled.

The doorbell rang just before nine o'clock, and I flew downstairs.

Peter stood on the doorstep, looking mega-hunky in blue jeans and a black T-shirt. He mustn't have shaved this morning, and a hint of dark stubble outlined his jaw, and his hair was a little mussed, but the whole casual effect only made him look sexier than ever.

Behind him, parked at the kerb, was a very sleek and low and shiny and very British dark green sports car. The man and the car created a picture beyond my wildest dreams, and I knew I was going to be putty in Peter's hands.

I greeted him with a goofy, it's-so-fantastic-to-see-you grin. We hugged and exchanged an excited kiss.

At least I was excited. But it was about then that I noticed Peter wasn't grinning. He looked—to my complete surprise—nervous.

'Is everything OK?' I asked, already suspecting that it couldn't be.

When he tried to smile, he didn't quite pull it off.

He said, 'Molly, before we head off today there's something I need to explain.'

I didn't like the sound of that at all. My stomach took a very unpleasant dive.

'Can I come in?' he asked.

'Sure.'

My legs were shaking as I took him through to the lounge room. We sat in separate chairs—at least I sat, but Peter remained standing. At first I thought he was just being a gentleman, waiting for me to sit down, but then I realised he didn't plan to sit.

What was his problem?

My mind was galloping ahead, trying to guess what he could possibly need to tell me. Now. This morning. When we were planning to go away together for a lovely romantic weekend. Why did he look so nervous?

I prayed. Please, please don't let him tell me he has a wife back in Argentina. Or a fiancée. Or even a girlfriend.

I know my expectations of this English gentleman were way over the top, but I couldn't bear to have my lovely man sully his perfect image now.

I wished Patrick hadn't taken off, gallivanting around on the Great Barrier Reef or wherever. If he'd been answering his e-mails he might have warned me…I might have been ready for this.

'Before we head off—' Peter began.

I told myself I was agonising over nothing. Everything was OK. He was still planning to take me to Cornwall.

'*I need to explain exactly who I am,*' *he said, giving me a slightly awkward but utterly gorgeous lopsided smile.*

Who I am...?

What on earth could that mean?

In that moment something in his eyes...something about the tilt of his smile...reminded me of someone I'd met recently—since I'd moved to London...

And then in a flash of insight I knew.

It was Felicity Knight.

But how could Peter...?

My skin chilled, and fine hairs rose on the back of my neck a split-second before the truth dawned.

My throat closed over, but I managed to whisper, '*You're not Peter. You're Patrick, aren't you?*' *Trembling with shock, I fought back tears.* '*You're Patrick, pretending to be Peter. Peter doesn't exist. None of this is real.*'

CHAPTER NINE

'WHAT happened?' SIMON Knight frowned when he opened his front door and found his cousin on the doorstep. 'Don't tell me—'

His eyes flashed to the kerb.

'It's OK,' Patrick assured him. 'I haven't pranged your car. Not even a scratch.' He forced a weak smile as he held out the keys. 'The trip's off, that's all.'

'That's bad luck.' Simon's sympathy sounded genuine as he pocketed the keys, but his intelligent grey eyes blazed with curiosity. 'So is Cornwall actually off the agenda altogether, or simply postponed?'

'It's definitely off.' Patrick shrugged, hoping the gesture looked casual. 'It's no big deal. I think I'll try to change my flight. Might as well head back to Australia tomorrow.'

Simon gave a sympathetic shake of his head. 'I suppose I'd better fetch your car key. It's in the kitchen.' As he turned to go, he hesitated and looked back at Patrick again with a frown. 'You look like you could use a drink.'

The offer held distinct appeal. Although it was only mid-morning, Patrick had never felt more in need of a stiff drink, and he always enjoyed his cousin's company. They were almost as close as brothers, and without the strain of sibling rivalry. At the wedding Simon had been eager to hear every bit of news about Patrick's stay on the island.

Even so, Patrick was reluctant to offload his disappointment. Simon would never press him for insensitive details about his planned romantic getaway, but it was only reasonable that he would expect their chat to include at least some information about the girl Patrick had planned to take to Cornwall.

Talking about Molly wasn't an option. Patrick was feeling too raw, too devastated, too frustrated and mad with himself. Simon had been telling him for years that he needed to give more time to his women-friends, and to lavish them with his attention. He wasn't about to confess that he'd been willing and ready to do just that with Molly, but instead he'd single-handedly conducted the biggest stuff-up in dating history.

'Thanks, but no thanks,' he told Simon quietly. 'I'll say cheerio for now. I guess I'll see you again at the end of June.'

The men shook hands.

'Well, have a safe trip back. And I hope you have better luck with the rest of the Australian girls,' Simon said with an encouraging wink.

'Sure.'

There was only one Australian girl Patrick wanted to enjoy, and he'd stupidly wrecked his chances with her. It seemed crazy that he was flying back to her house.

Of course he'd phone Molly later, and he'd try again to explain what now seemed totally, ludicrously unexplainable.

The crazy thing was that he'd stuffed up relationships in the past, mainly through selfish neglect, and he'd taken the ensuing rejection on the chin. Female company had only ever been a form of pleasant entertainment. Since when had it become a vital mission?

What was different this time? How had he let one bright-eyed, mouthy Aussie get so deeply under his skin?

Of course he'd never stopped to ask himself why meaningful romance wasn't on his agenda. No doubt a shrink would try to tell him it was all tied up with his parents' messy divorce. He couldn't deny that memories of his mother's distress had upset him deeply, and he'd shied away from marriage and the whole happy-ever-after myth. He couldn't bear to hurt a woman the way his father had.

Was it possible that he'd chosen to meet Molly in disguise so he could avoid facing the uncomfortable truth that he really, *really* liked her?

As Patrick depressed the central locking system for his car he felt hollow and utterly miserable and confused. And completely empty of hope.

Molly's Diary, May 29th

I was too upset to keep writing yesterday. I've spent most of the past twenty-four hours crying, and now my eyes and nose and throat are so sore I feel as if I've been terribly ill.

I've taken the phone off the hook so Patrick can't ring me, and I haven't gone anywhere near my laptop. I don't want to know if he's sent me an e-mail. I'm not ready to talk to him. I don't know if I'll ever be ready.

But I owe it to myself to write down the rest of what happened yesterday. Maybe (vain hope) the act of writing will help somehow.

So…

At first when I guessed the terrible truth and blurted out that Peter was actually Patrick he looked relieved. He smiled and the tension left his shoulders.

Not for long.

Something had snapped inside me. I suppose it was my sense of trust. I'd been lied to. Here I was, on the brink of sleeping with this man in a romantic Cornish B&B, and I'd learned he was a fraud. It was all an act.

As I leapt to my feet, Patrick's smile died.

'What are you doing here?' I demanded. (OK, I might have yelled.) 'You're supposed to be in Australia. Somewhere on the Great Barrier Reef.'

His face seemed to pale, as if my anger really bothered him.

Too bad. He couldn't have been nearly as bothered as I was.

'My mother was married last weekend,' he said. 'It was all rather unexpected and a bit rushed, and I came over for the wedding.'

His mother's wedding? It took me a moment to digest this news. Then I remembered the way Felicity's eyes had shone when she'd talked about her 'friend' Jonathan.

So they were married, and that was nice. Really nice. But what did that have to do with Patrick (or Peter) and me? So what if he'd come home for a family wedding? Why did he have to keep it a secret from me? And how did it give him an excuse to ruin my life?

So many questions were rushing through my head.

'Where have you been staying?'

He shrugged. 'The Lime Tree Hotel.'

Un. Believable.

It was the most ridiculous thing I've ever heard. Why would Patrick Knight stay in a hotel when there were two spare bedrooms here in his house? I wanted to cry, but I knew I mustn't give in to such weakness. I needed all my strength to deal with this shattering of my dreams. I couldn't bear to think that I'd been part of a game—a source of amusement.

'How could you?' I shouted, and my voice was as shrill as the proverbial fishwife's. 'How could you go to so much trouble to trick me? How could you be so cruel?'

'I'm sorry, Molly.' Patrick spoke quietly but earnestly. 'I didn't want to hurt you. It seemed like a good plan at the time, but I had no idea—' He raised a hand, as if groping for words, then plunged both hands into his jeans pockets.

'What seemed like a good plan? To totally deceive me?'

'You were so keen to meet your Englishman.'

'Oh, right. I foolishly poured out my heart, and you thought it would be fun to play games with me after your mother's wedding.'

'No. I—' Again, he floundered.

'You felt sorry for me.'

'Well…you sounded so disappointed.'

'You thought I was desperate and you'd lend a hand.'

'I wanted you to be happy.'

'I was happy, thank you. Very happy, as a matter of fact.'

Patrick sighed heavily. His right hand rose again, and this time he ploughed frustrated fingers through his lovely dark hair.

I was frustrated, too. He wasn't making sense. How on earth did he think his deception could have made me happy? It was tearing me apart.

I'd believed in Peter. I'd fallen in love with Peter.

'Why did you have to pretend, Patrick? Why couldn't you have just turned up and said, "Hi, I'm Patrick and I'd like to stay for a few days. And while I'm here why don't we go out?"'

It could have been so perfect, so much fun...

He was so lovely...

Now he'd spoiled everything.

Patrick shook his head. 'I was worried you wouldn't be excited if you knew it was me. It wouldn't feel like a proper romantic date to you. After all those e-mails when you told me so much about your dreams, I was sure that if I simply asked you out you'd think I was just going through the motions because... Well...yes— because I felt sorry for you.'

'But you did feel sorry for me!'

I was so furious I stamped my foot. My eyes filled with tears. Patrick, the man I'd spilled my heart out to...the anchor at the other end of my e-mails...the thoughtful guy who'd warned me to 'take care'...had been pretending, having fun at my expense.

How could he? You idiot, Patrick, I wasn't that desperate.

How could he kill off my lovely, romantic Peter and leave me with...?

Nothing?

He was right about one thing. I didn't want a man who felt sorry for me. But now—

I was forced to accept that the dream man who'd turned up on my doorstep hadn't been surprised to see me at all. And he hadn't suddenly liked what he'd found when I opened the door. Our relationship wasn't spontaneous—not even romantic. He'd been planning it, and he'd arrived determined to ask me out regardless of what I was like.

Our lovely times together were nothing more than a goodwill gesture from a London banker to a poor, hopeless Aussie chick with delusions of grandeur.

I'm pleased to say I was queenly and dignified as I pointed to the door, but I knew that I couldn't hold it together for long. At any minute I was going to break down completely. 'I think you'd better go,' I said.

Patrick looked dismayed, and I think he was about to protest when he realised how serious I was.

He glanced briefly at my overnight bag, packed and ready by the door. 'So you won't—?'

'I couldn't possibly go to Cornwall with you,' I said, interrupting him. But I choked back a sob, because although I was very grateful that I hadn't gone away to Cornwall before I found out the truth, I was still bitterly disappointed that I was missing out on so much.

I hadn't just lost my dream man, I'd lost the promise of a lovely weekend.

Which just goes to show how contrary a female can be and still be right!

'Molly, I—'

'Don't say any more, Patrick. Just go, please.'

My old, romantic-movie-watching self might have imagined that Patrick looked stricken—rather like the way Christian looked when he watched Vanessa walk away from him on Westminster Bridge. But then, my old, romantic-movie-watching self had believed in her good radar for detecting jerks.

Huh.

In the fifteen minutes since Peter had become Patrick I'd grown a hundred times older and wiser. And boiling mad to boot.

I opened the door and made a grand sweeping gesture. And, no, I didn't feel awkward about turning Patrick out of his own home. After all, he deserved this, didn't he?

As he moved past me in the doorway, I caught a hint of his special scent. I don't know if that scent is just the way his skin smells naturally, or if it's the cologne he uses. If it is cologne, it's nicer than any male cologne I've ever smelled before. Whatever it is, it's fine-tuned to my senses and fills me with longing.

I sucked in my breath and gripped the door handle to stop myself from leaning in to him.

On the doorstep he turned to me. 'Molly, I'm very sorry I've hurt you. It's the last, the very last thing I wanted.'

Yeah, you and me both, I thought. But I couldn't respond. I was too busy concentrating on not leaning any closer.

'Yoo-hoo, Patrick!' a voice called suddenly.

It was Mrs Blake, Patrick's elderly neighbour, popping her head over the neatly clipped hedge that divided their front gardens.

'Oh, it is you, Patrick,' she gushed. 'I thought I saw you get out of that lovely sports car!'

In the outdoor light I could see that Patrick looked pale and upset, but I steeled my heart.

As always, he was unfailingly polite.

'Good morning, Eleanor.'

Honestly, the neighbour must be at least eighty, but she was ogling Patrick with all the shameless delight of a tweeny fan-girl.

'You're back earlier than we expected.' She beamed. 'How absolutely lovely to see you, my dear. How was Australia?'

As if that wasn't bad enough, from across the street another woman (middle aged and in a floral dress of pleated chiffon with strings of pearls) started waving madly.

'Halloo, there, Patrick,' she called.

Charming, lovable Patrick Knight. If only they knew how dangerous this adorable, two-faced man could be.

I shut the door very quickly. OK, yes—I confess I probably slammed it.

Molly's Diary, May 31st

I'm sorry to report that my life is not back to normal.

I was going to try to pretend that everything's fine now, but I can't do it. I've always hated pretence, and since the Patrick-Peter debacle I've developed a particular sensitivity to any whiff of falsehood.

So this diary is going to remain brutally honest. I am still hurt and devastated, and terribly, terribly angry. So, as you can imagine, I wasn't in the right frame of mind first thing yesterday morning, when a delivery guy from a florist's shop tried to deliver armfuls of roses, carnations, lilies and daffodils. Honestly, there were enough flowers to fill every bathtub in the house.

But how could I accept them?

Under any other circumstances (i.e. circumstances that did not involve my faith in men being ripped wide open) I would have been ecstatic, but I told the delivery man he had the wrong address.

He wouldn't believe me. He showed me the address on the docket, and he even offered to ring the store to double-check. So then I had to tell him that I simply couldn't accept the flowers.

I told him I was very sorry, but I was allergic to pollen. I asked him to take them to the hospital, or to give them to his girlfriend or his grandmother, or to anyone he knew who'd appreciate them.

I thought my pollen excuse sounded plausible, but he shrugged and said I wasn't the first young lady who'd refused a delivery of flowers.

'I understand, ducks,' he said as he carried the gorgeous armfuls back to the van. 'Some dimwits never get it through their thick heads that flowers can't make up for each and every sin.'

Too true.

I suppose Patrick expected that these over-the-top and gorgeous flowers would make amends for his deception. Hasn't he any idea how very real my pain is?

If only he knew that over the weekend I've toyed with some terribly wicked ideas for retribution. I've considered:

- *Repainting his bedroom hot pink with black polka dots*
- *Super-gluing his remote control to the top of his TV set*
- *Using a pair of pinking shears to cut out the crotch of the expensive Italian trousers in his wardrobe*
- *Sprinkling chilli powder on his toilet paper roll (just before I leave)*

These were actually the nicer possibilities, but unfortunately they've only given me a momentary glimmer of satisfaction. I suspect that revenge doesn't really suit my personality, because while I was dreaming up these evil schemes one corner of my mind was also busily wishing that there'd been no trickery and I'd gone off to Cornwall.

Duh.

Anyway, after the flowers had gone yesterday (and that was an incident that caused several curtains in Alice Grove to twitch) I decided to get out of the house. I've always preferred to sulk out of doors.

So I went for a long walk along the Chelsea Embankment and all over Battersea Park, trying to shake off my angry mood.

But wouldn't you know it? Everywhere I went there were happy couples. Old, young and every age in between. Jogging together, strolling arm-in-arm, walking his-and-her dogs, pushing babies in prams, sitting on park benches, lying on the grass and gazing into each other's eyes. I swear no matter where I walked I was surrounded by images of blissful, idyllic, dreamy romance!

And of course no matter how hard I tried I couldn't stop my mind from going over and over my own tragic non-romance. So many sweet memories—my first sight of Peter on the doorstep, our London explorations, Westminster and Big Ben, that fabulous night at Covent Garden.

That kiss! Quite possibly the most fabulous kiss in all of history—certainly in all of my history.

I put so much emotional energy into my time with Peter (alias Patrick), and ever since he left I've been fighting useless regrets for what might have/could have/ should have happened. How crazy is that? How can I wish for romance with him when I'm mad enough to wring his neck?

The thing is, a part of me can't help wishing he'd never told me the truth on Saturday morning. I was so poised for the thrill of a lifetime—the sports car, the beautiful rural English countryside, the night in a Cornish B&B with my dream man.

If only, if only…

The unrealised romantic potential of that lost weekend in Cornwall haunts me like a tune I can't get out of my head.

And so do all kinds of questions—endless questions that have no answers—questions I wish I'd put to Patrick before I showed him the door.

The biggie that's really bugging me is why he waited until we were leaving for Cornwall to tell me who he was. Why did he wait until after he'd already kissed me?

Come to think of it, why did he ask me to go to Cornwall at all?

He'd already taken me out on the so-called 'dream date'. The deception had been successfully accomplished and his role as my companion was over.

I suppose he'd been planning to exploit the situation. After our kiss, he knew I was ripe for the plucking. But then his conscience probably got the better of him.

!!

This anger isn't doing me or my diary any good. I just ripped a blooming great hole in the page with my pen.

I need to calm down. I need to be kind to myself.

I have to remember that I've had a lucky escape and should be celebrating. I should also remember that I was having a great time in London before a certain tall, dark and incredibly handsome man landed on the doorstep, and that I can have a great time again.

I just won't share my future great times with Patrick—the Knight whose armour is no longer shining but severely tarnished and dented.

I shudder when I think of all the things I've told him in my previous e-mails. I just opened my heart and let it all out. He knows so much about me (in particular my penchant for English gentlemen in three-piece suits with lovely plummy voices). I trusted him, and he betrayed that trust.

I think that's what's hurt me most.

The terrible thing is Patrick warned me that an expensive suit and well-bred accent did not turn a man into a gentleman, and I still fell into the trap.

Let's be honest—a true gentleman would never be deceitful.

Even if he was trying to do someone a good turn.

Would he?

Private Writing Journal, June 2nd

I've been back in Australia for three days now, and I still haven't written to Molly. It's more than possible that whatever I say will upset her. The pollen allergy excuse that the florist kindly passed on shows how per-sona non grata I am. That's why I've resorted to this journal again. If I'm going to try to make amends, it might be easier to get my thoughts clear on paper before I commit them to e-mail.

I'm pretty sure it's up to me (as the offender) to make the first move towards reconciliation, and I doubt that either Molly or I will enjoy the rest of our house swap if we continue in uncomfortable silence. But after the way we parted, what can I say to mollify her? (Oh, God, terrible pun.)

Can I offer yet another apology? Try to set things straight? Should I attempt to justify exactly why I start-ed the whole subterfuge fiasco?

Do I actually have a decent excuse for totally stuffing up a perfectly happy girl's life?

It's not the first time I've been accused of doing that, of course, but in the past I've mainly committed sins of omission (e.g. last-minute cancellations of dates). This time I went to the trouble of manufacturing a perfect date, only to have it turn into a perfect disaster.

Molly has every right to ask why. I only wish I knew the right answer, or rather I wish I had an answer that she'd find acceptable.

When I started out on the flight back to the UK my plan was simply to knock on Molly's door and to say hello (yes, as Patrick, not Peter) and to satisfy my curiosity. But as the time to meet Molly drew closer I kept thinking about her big dating dreams. At some hazy point the Peter Kingston scheme emerged, but it wasn't till I saw Molly that I seized on it.

Why?

I suspect I was trying to protect myself. I'd already been entranced by Molly's personality, even though I'd only met her in e-mails, but I was reluctant to get too personally involved. After all, we are house swappers from different worlds, almost different planets. We had no plans for a relationship.

The truth is, I honestly did want that night at Covent Garden to be perfect. Molly had such high expectations of her dream date, and I was sure that she couldn't possibly be happy with a compromise date with a house swapper who'd read all her self-revealing e-mails. I was sure she'd assume I had pegged her as desperate and dateless, that I'd taken pity on her.

So my original motives were chivalrous—or so I thought—but my mistake was to get in deeper, when a ten-year-old could have told me I was asking for trouble.

Of course I should never have kissed her. I should have known that those soft, pink, talkative lips would be my undoing. Of course I should have known that kissing Molly would be beyond amazing and that one kiss could never be enough.

Instead I let the kiss get out of hand (almost), and that led me to an even bigger mistake—the proposed weekend in Cornwall.

How do I explain that one?

I suppose I could claim a longing to share in Molly's enthusiasm for new discoveries, but who's going to believe me? Certainly not Molly. Not after that kiss.

The crazy thing was I trapped myself. I fell for her harder and faster than I would have believed possible. I became the one who was desperate, but I couldn't contemplate sleeping with her without telling her who I really was. I may be casual in my relationships, but I've never been a con man.

And yet telling the truth meant bursting Molly's fantasy bubble.

That was my Waterloo. Thanks to my poor handling of this, our dream date was reduced to a pity date in Molly's eyes. And I was forced to accept that I had fallen for a warm, lovely, real girl, who in turn was in love with a dream.

Molly didn't want reality. How else can I explain her horror at discovering the truth that Peter and I were one and the same?

How could I possibly tell her how I felt when she was looking at me as if I'd murdered someone? (And I suppose I had. I'd murdered her fantasy.)

Now Molly has sent me the strongest possible negative messages—not with words but through her actions. She showed me the door. She refused the flowers. She stopped writing e-mails.

A man doesn't expose himself and declare his feelings unless he's pretty damn sure he will be well received, so all things considered it's pretty clear that continued silence is my wisest option.

Molly's Diary, June 6th

I've kept myself deliberately busy this past week, especially over the weekend, taking on as many shifts at the Empty Bottle as they'll give me. It helps to have something else to think about besides you-know-who.

This morning I'm finally feeling strong enough (or at least I hope I am) to open my laptop and take a peek to see if any e-mails have arrived. I can't help being curious.

OK—I've looked. There's only one e-mail and it's from Karli. Yay! I'm so pleased to hear from her at last.

I think I'm relieved that there's no word from Patrick. I'm sure he's OK. Of course he is.

To: Molly Cooper <molly.cooper@flowermail.com>
From: Karli Henderson <hendo86@flowermail.com>
Subject: Back online!!

Hi Molly

Sorry I've taken so long to get back to you. Jimbo and I are at last settled in Cairns, but it's been a mad month, what with packing up and starting new jobs and finding somewhere to live. Yes, I've got a job, too—in the office at the same boatyard where Jimbo works as a shipwright. So we're set, but I haven't had time to scratch myself.

We have a nice flat, and wages coming in, so we're very happy. We bought a second-hand computer (it works most of the time), and we've already made a few new friends. (Although no one will ever replace you as my best friend, Mozza.)

How are you? How's London? Have you found your dream British gentleman? I've been thinking about you so much even though I couldn't write.

Actually, I've just been looking back over our old e-mails (saved on a USB stick), and I've realised that you probably still have no idea what your house swapper looks like. So, honey, I guess it's finally time to satisfy your curiosity. Let me tell you. You might want to come rushing home.

Patrick's tall and dark. (Not a bad start, huh?) His hair was short when he got here, but it quickly started to grow and curl on the ends. (Very cute.) He has dark chocolate eyes with extra-long lashes. Jodie G verified this when she got a close-up look at him at the party he held after the toad races. But, honestly, I was there, too, and she didn't get as close to him as she likes to make out.

He has a good jawline, and when I saw him there was just the right amount of stubble. (So, yes, your Patrick is smoking hot. Are you drooling yet?) Oh, and he has wide shoulders and a six-pack. (We've seen him walking on the beach with his shirt off.)

So I guess it's no surprise that he's also good at sports. You know how Jimbo always plays in the Bay of Origin rugby league competition? Well, because we were leaving the island, the Sapphire Bay team was one player short. Your Patrick has only played rugby union, not league, but he volunteered to fill in and managed to catch on very quickly.

So, despite our initial concern that he might be a bit aloof, he's turned out to be a great mixer. Actually, he must have been a real bonus to our team, because we won for the first time in about three seasons. Jimbo has his nose out of joint about that. Guys and their tender egos—you've gotta love 'em.

I haven't heard much news since we left. Do write back soon and fill me in with everything that's happened in your exciting world. I miss you heaps!

Lots of love,

Karli x

To: Karli Henderson <hendo86@flowermail.com>
From: Molly Cooper <molly.cooper@flowermail.com>
Subject: Re: Back online!!
Attachment: Molly's Diary (125KB)

Hi Karli

Thanks so much for your e-mail. You have *no idea* how good it is to hear from you again. I've missed you so much.

There's so much I have to tell you, but first I must say I'm really glad your move to Cairns has worked out so well for you. That's fab. Although I still hate thinking about going back to the island when you won't be there. I'll be so lonely without you.

Thanks also for the info about Patrick, but actually I've seen him now, so I know that your description is extremely accurate. Patrick came back to London for his mother's wedding, you see, and he called in here. Actually, it's a short story, but I've sent you the long version in an attachment to this e-mail.

You'll be mad when I tell you that you were out of reach at a highly crucial point in my life. (My love-life, that is.)

I've used Patrick's scanner and sent you the relevant

bits from my e-mails and diary in the attachment. Once you've read everything you'll understand why I needed you.

These pages are for your eyes only, of course. I know I can trust Jimbo, but still, could you please delete them as soon as you've read them?

Oh, and it goes without saying that I need you to write back and tell me what you think. About *everything*. Thanks in advance.

Loads of love to you both

Molly x

To: Molly Cooper <molly.cooper@flowermail.com>
From: Karli Henderson <hendo86@flowermail.com>
Subject: Re: Back online!!

Wow!! I turn my back on you for a few weeks and you turn into a dating diva. Thanks so much for trusting me with your diary pages, Molly. I can't believe Patrick went back to England and actually turned up on your door-step and took you to Big Ben and Covent Garden and everything.

That. Is. So. Amazing.

I can just imagine how gorgeous you looked in your beautiful new black dress. Can you send me a photo? And how fabulous to see *Romeo and Juliet*. I'd give anything for that. Remember when I was going to be the world's greatest ballerina?

Now, Molly, I know you're upset that Patrick was pretending to be Peter, and as your best friend I totally respect your right to be upset. But, honey, I'm sorry. I don't get it. I really don't understand why you're so angry. Colour me confused, and I apologise in advance, but I don't see what's so wrong with what Patrick did. He gave you your dream date—exactly what you wanted. In my book that's incredibly sweet. I break into a happy dance every time I think about you on that night.

As far as I can tell, reading between the lines, Patrick was rather smitten by how you looked in your sexy black dress, and by your talented kissing, and that's why he wanted to whisk you away to Cornwall. But he didn't want your relationship to become—ahem—intimate, unless you knew who he really was. That's honourable, isn't it?

Clearly I'm not seeing this situation in the same light as you, Molly. Admittedly I wasn't there, and I only have your diary to go on. Sorry if I'm not much help.

Would you like to phone me so we can talk this over properly?

Love
Karli

Molly's Diary, June 8th

I'm shocked. I can't believe Karli's not supporting me at the one point in my life when I need her most. Why doesn't she understand how I feel?

All my life, whenever I've been let down or disappointed, Karli has been there for me. She was so understanding and sympathetic when Gran first got sick and I had to cancel my plans to go to university.

Now she's on a totally different wavelength. How can she possibly claim that Patrick's deception was sweet?

Sweet?

In a pig's eye. Can't she get how foolish I felt? How I hated to be strung along? How my trust in Patrick was shaken? Surely it's painfully obvious that I have every right to be furious.

I think Karli's right about one thing—the need for a phone call. I'll ring her tomorrow morning, when it's evening in Australia, and we'll sort this out. I won't feel right until I have Karli firmly on my side.

Molly's Diary, June 9th

Can't sleep. Am up drinking hot milk and honey and eating buttered raisin toast. Comfort food. In the middle of the night. At least a midnight feast is better than lying in bed, tossing and turning and trying to work out what I'm going to say to Karli when I call her in the morning.

Just the same, conversations with her keep going round and round in my head.

Karli: Why are you so angry with Patrick?

Me: Because he lied and cheated.

Karli: That's a bit heavy. He was only trying to make your stay in London perfect. Admit it, Molly, you were having fabulous fun with Peter. The time of your life.

Me: Maybe I was, but it was all a sham. It wasn't real.

Karli: Why did it have to be real?

Me: Because…

Karli: What's that, Molly? I can't hear you.

Me: Because I needed it to be real. It was so wonderful. I fell in love with Patrick when he was pretending to be Peter, and then I lost him. I lost both of them, and I'm devastated because maybe…

Oh, my, gosh…

(Cue evasive mumbling)

Karli: Excuse me, Molly?

Me(whisper): Maybe…I'm still in love with him.

Karli: I'm having trouble with this line. Speak up. I can't hear you.

!!

Help! I think it's true. About still being in love with Patrick, I mean.

Is that the reason I can't stop being angry with him?

I fell totally, crazily, deeply in love with Peter, and I wanted him to be just as totally, crazily, deeply in love with me. But he was only pretending.

My turmoil is actually a mixture of anger and deepest despair. I couldn't bear to know that Patrick was putting on an act. I needed him to love me, really love me, but it was all pretence.

And buried beneath my boiling anger is my deep sense of loss.

I think about all those times I spent with Patrick while he was pretending to be Peter. If Patrick hadn't been so busy pretending we could have talked about real things. Things that mattered to both of us. Our houses, our friends, his mother, my dad, his novel, my island, his London. Even the Chelmon rostratus fish.

But, as things were, instead of conversing intelligently with a man who already felt like a good friend, I spent far too much time swooning over a fantasy! And now—

I don't know! I'm confused. But one thing's certain— the damage has been done. Deeply and permanently.

And I don't think I'm actually ready to talk about this with Karli. I thought I wanted to wallow in a pity party, but now I suspect that I should just get over myself and move on.

I guess the best way to move on is to send Patrick an e-mail—short and friendly, let bygones-be-bygones—with not a hint of how I'm really feeling. I'd hate him to know I'm still hurting. I only hope I can strike the right note and sound friendly and interested, but not too interested.

CHAPTER TEN

To: Patrick Knight <patrick.knight@mymail.com>
From: Molly Cooper <molly.cooper@flowermail.com>
Subject: Safely home?

Dear Patrick

I trust that you had a good flight back to Australia, and that you're now safely on Magnetic Island and all is well—including your writing.

I'm pleased to report that everything is fine here, although Cidalia is in a bit of a flap, which is the main reason for this e-mail. Did you know she's about to become a grandmother at any moment? She's been knitting all kinds of impossibly cute, tiny clothes (even though we're diving into summer here).

If the baby's a boy he will be called Rafael Felipe, and if it's a girl she will be Yasmin Cidalia.

As you can imagine, the telephone at 34 Alice Grove has become a very important instrument. Every time it rings we rush to its summons, hearts a-clanging.

By the way, I didn't mention your recent return to London to Cidalia, and she hasn't said anything to me, so I'm assuming she doesn't know you were here and that it's best to leave it that way.

Best wishes

Molly

Molly's Diary, June 10th

I hope I got the tone of that e-mail right. The last thing I want is to sound like I'm stalking Patrick. I almost reverted to type and carried on about how I love the name Rafael, and how I think Yasmin is beautiful for a baby girl, and how I'm really hoping I get to see the baby. As always, I felt an urge to tell Patrick everything, but I reined myself in, thank heavens.

Now it's time to climb out of my post-Peter/Patrick depression and get on with my exciting, adventurous and uplifting life in London. (Notice I left out romantic?) I think I've finally bitten the reality bullet. Hip, hip hooray.

To: Molly Cooper <molly.cooper@flowermail.com>
From: Patrick Knight <patrick.knight@mymail.com>
Subject: Re: Safely home?

Hi Molly

Thanks for your e-mail and, yes, I'm safely back on the island and ensconced once more in Pandanus Cottage.

Thanks for your news about the imminent arrival of Cidalia's grandchild. I'm afraid I've rarely had time to chat with her, and I didn't even know her daughter was expecting—although I do remember a lot of fuss and excitement over her wedding a couple of years ago.

I look forward to hearing news of the safe arrival of little Rafael or Yasmin.

I'm pleased to report that I do have good news about my writing. To my immense relief, it's finally taken off. I've had fresh inspiration, you see, and suddenly I have so many ideas clamouring to be written down that I can hardly type quickly enough. It's rather annoying that I wasted all those weeks when I first arrived here going down the wrong track, but I suppose it's never too late to start again.

If my communication seems minimal during the rest of my stay here it will be because I'm busily writing this book. At last.

Cheers
Patrick

To: Karli Henderson <hendo86@flowermail.com>
From: Molly Cooper <molly.cooper@flowermail.com>
Subject: Re: Back online!!

Hi Karli

Sorry I emoted all over you as soon as you got back online. It was just so good to know you were there at the other end of an e-mail. Thanks a million for your lovely offer to chat on the phone, but I actually think I have myself sorted.

I've taken on board your comments re: the Peter-Patrick blow-up, and I'm prepared to admit that I may have (slightly) overreacted. I can see now that I didn't handle my disappointment very maturely, but I can't go back and change anything, so...

Whatever.

I'm over it, and I'm moving on. I'd like to think I've learned from the experience.

I've written to Patrick—not to apologise—I don't think that's called for—but to reopen communication. He's back on Magnetic Island and we are now exchanging polite and friendly (enough) e-mails. We're house-swappers again. Nothing more. Drama over.

I may yet take myself down to Cornwall. Yes, I know

it could rub salt into my gradually healing wounds, but I really do want to see more of England before I have to leave, and time's running out.

Thanks for being the best friend a girl could ask for.

Love to you and to Jimbo

Molly

Dear Molly

Greetings from Bodo. I do hope you're well, and having as good a time as I've been having here in Norway. Actually, I've joined the crew of an Australian yacht and I'm about to leave port. We're heading for Madeira, and then across the Atlantic to Barbados, where this boat will be chartered for Caribbean cruises.

I'm planning to hitch a ride home on another boat, travelling through the Panama and across the Pacific. You wouldn't like to join me, would you? Think of all those gorgeous Pacific Islands we'd visit on the way home. I'm sending my mobile phone number, just in case.

Miss you, Molly.

Brad xxx

Molly's Diary, June 12th

If I had any common sense I would probably jump at Brad's offer. What an adventure to sail a yacht home across the Pacific—and with such a nice guy for company.

Problem is (apart from the time it would take), I've lived on an island in the Pacific all my life, so that trip doesn't sound nearly as exotic and exciting to me as it would to a New South Wales sheep farmer. And while Brad's nice…he…well, there are times when nice isn't quite enough. And yet it should be, shouldn't it? Nice is safe. Nice doesn't break your heart.

*I hope I'm not going to be one of those women who
always falls for the wrong guys.*

To: Patrick Knight <patrick.knight@mymail.com>
From: Molly Cooper <molly.cooper@flowermail.com>
Subject: It's a boy!

Dear Patrick

Rafael Felipe Azevedo was born last night at three minutes past midnight. This morning Cidalia insisted that I go with her to the hospital. (She's so proud. She wanted to show him off, and her daughter Julieta was very well and happy to receive visitors.)

I don't usually get too excited about babies—but, honestly, Patrick, have you ever seen a Brazilian baby? Truly, Rafael is so cute, with a cap of dark hair, the darkest, shiniest little black eyes, and the sturdiest, kicking limbs. He looks just like his father, and that's saying something. Now I know why Brazilian men have such a reputation for their good-looks.

By the way, I have made an executive decision and told Cidalia not to worry about cleaning your place this week. I can easily run around with a vacuum cleaner, and I'm sure you'll agree she deserves the time off.

Best wishes
Molly

To: Patrick Knight <patrick.knight@mymail.com>
From: Molly Cooper <molly.cooper@flowermail.com>
Subject: RE: It's a boy!

Dear Patrick

Cidalia has asked me to pass on her deepest thanks. She was absolutely thrilled with the beautiful flowers and the card you sent her. She said it's the first time a man has ever sent her flowers, and she was a little bit weepy. So thank you from me, too. It was very sweet of you, and I wish you could have seen the joy on her face.

Julieta, the proud new mother, is also thrilled with the baby boy gift hamper you sent. She can't believe you were so generous, and she asked me to thank you (although she will also write), and to tell you that she feels like a celebrity mum.

So you see, you're quite the man of the moment here, Patrick. I hope all's well with you, and that your new book idea is firing.

Best wishes
Molly

To: Patrick Knight: <patrick.knight@mymail.com>
From: Felicity Langley: <flissL@mymail.com>
Subject: Home again

Dear Patrick

How are you, darling? I hope you're enjoying the rest of your time on the island. It won't be all that long till you're back home again. The time seems to have gone very quickly, doesn't it?

As you can imagine, Jonathan and I had the most wonderful time in Italy, and we're now having fun planning to set up house. We've decided to sell both our old places and to start all over again with a home of our own. Honestly, we're having such a good time you'd think we were giddy young twenty-year-olds.

Speaking of houses, I called in at your place yesterday to see Molly, and I must say I was a little concerned. I thought she looked pale, and as if she'd lost weight. I don't suppose it's anything to worry about, just that her Australian tan has faded, and along with it some of her sparkle.

I'd assumed that you'd caught up with her while you were in London for the wedding, and I said something along those lines to Molly. Obviously I chose the wrong moment, or the wrong words. The poor girl had offered me a cup of tea, and she was reaching into a cupboard when I asked the question. Somehow I startled her, and she dropped two teacups and their saucers.

I know you won't be upset about the breakages. You tend to use coffee mugs anyhow. But poor Molly was very distressed. In a bid to calm her I suggested we forget tea and raid your drinks cabinet.

But, although Molly was almost her old self after a nice chat over a couple of gin and tonics, I noticed that she still avoided talking about you, Patrick. Apart from admitting that the two of you had met, she was strangely silent. If I didn't know you better I'd suggest that you might have blotted your copybook somehow.

As you know, I've been very impressed by the interesting young woman who's occupying your house. And I'm inordinately proud of you, darling, so I was hoping to hear positive comments about you from Molly.

Perhaps I'm being over-sensitive, but her reluctance to talk about you bothered me. I sensed unhappiness—which might have been caused by any number of things. I sincerely trust it's in no way connected to you.

Anyway, on a brighter note, Molly's planning a trip to Cornwall, which I think is a very good idea. Perhaps all she needs is to get out of London for a bit.

I look forward to hearing your news.
Love
Mother

To: Felicity Langley <flissL@mymail.com>
From: Patrick Knight: <patrick.knight@mymail.com>
Subject: Re: Home again

Dear Mother

Thanks for your e-mail. It was good to hear from you, and to know that you and Jonathan are both so happy. I wish you luck with the buying and selling of your houses. Do keep me posted.

As for Molly…you're as astute as ever, and you're quite right. She's a wonderful woman, and unfortunately I did make a hash of meeting her.

I promise my intentions were honourable—dare I say chivalrous?—but I'm afraid my delivery backfired.

I'll spare you the details. Knowing your tender heart, you'll want to go round there and try to smooth things over, but I don't think that's wise.

I know you're concerned, but please don't worry. Molly and I are still in contact. We're not bitter enemies or anything like that.

Concentrate on Jonathan. At least you two have got it right.

Loads of love
Patrick

Private Writing Journal, June 15th

I can't bear to think that Molly's pale and losing weight because of me. Ever since my mother's e-mail I haven't been able to think of anything else. I need to make amends with Molly, but how?

I think a phone call's necessary. The worst she can do is hang up on me.

Molly's Diary, June 15th

Cornwall is so quaint!

I'm having two days away (midweek—can't afford to give up any more of my weekend shifts), and I can't believe how beautiful it is down here.

I mean, I've seen pictures of the English countryside before, so I don't suppose I should be surprised, but I thought there might just be the occasional little patch of quaintness. I've found old-world, picturesque charm everywhere.

I never imagined that so many cute and pretty little cottages actually existed. On the train journey down from London (leaving from Paddington), I saw whole villages of cottages—cottages with window boxes filled with flowers, or with roses climbing over the door, and cottages with proper, steep thatched roofs and little white-framed windows peeping out like eyes from beneath a fringe of thick hair.

I've seen the greenest of green, green fields, divided by low drystone walls, and sheep that are actually white—not dusty brown like ours in Australia. And there are wildflowers blossoming everywhere—beside the roads, filling little woodsy valleys, and poking out from piles of rocks or from crannies in the walls.

I'm so glad I've come down to Cornwall, even though I didn't come here in a British racing-green sports car with a gorgeous man at the wheel. The countryside is divine, and I realise now that after the excitement and busyness of London I've missed fresh air and wide open spaces and the straightforward simplicity of the outdoors. Here there are mountains in the distance, and moors, and villages huddled on cliffs—and the sea! Even palm trees.

Gosh, it almost made me homesick to smell the briny, sharp scent of the sea and to see the straggly fronds of palm trees.

I also got a bit weepy thinking about the romantic weekend that never happened. As a matter of fact I'm thinking about it far too much as I nibble on a Cornish pasty while making my way up and down steep cobbled streets that cling to the edge of cliffs, or when I'm lying on the soft green grass of a cliff-top, looking down into the most astonishingly beautiful cove.

Yes, it's sad, but true—I'm wishing that Patrick was here beside me. Pathetic, isn't it? To be thinking so much about that wonderful weekend that I/we threw away?

I hope I don't sound as if I've changed my mind about Patrick. I haven't. I'm still super, super mad with him for pretending to be Peter. But in spite of all that I just know I would have loved our romantic weekend in Cornwall. It would have been something to remember for the rest of my life.

Even if I'm married at some time in the future, and have my own family, I'd still be able to look back on that memory of a happy, reckless, utterly romantic weekend in my youth.

Instead, I sit here on the bed in my B&B and look out through the window at a small sailing boat zipping briskly out across the bay, and I try so hard just to enjoy this moment—the beautiful view, the soft after-noon light, the scents of the sea, the familiar call of seagulls—but I feel dreadfully, horribly lonely.

I admit it. I'm deadbeat hopeless. Because now I'm actually imagining Patrick lying here on this bed beside me. I can see him…

He's lying on top of the white cotton bedspread and his shirt is undone, revealing his gorgeous, broad, manly chest and his tight, flat abs. (These last details are not just figments of my imagination. Thanks to Karli, who's seen him at the beach, I know they're true.) My wicked imagination adds a trail of dark hair disappearing beneath his jeans.

His dark brown eyes are watching me, and they're smoky and serious with desire. He reaches out and touches my arm, lightly, and I know exactly what's going to happen next. My skin flushes wherever he touches.

Then his fingertips touch my lips, and next minute I'm kissing his fingers, taking them into my mouth and grazing his nails with my teeth. I feel so turned on.

'Come here,' he whispers, and his voice is deep and husky and I'm wilting with longing.

I lean into him, and I smell him, and I can't hold back a soft, needy sigh. I'm so ready. I know we're about to make love. Beautiful, emotional, sensuous, love. Out-of-this world, amazing, mind-blowing love.

In the afternoon.

OK. OK. OK. OK. OK. OK.

Enough!

I can't believe I just wrote that fantasy into my diary. It proves I am now officially an idiot.

A certified idiot, filled with regrets. And anger.

Yes, I'm still red-hot angry. I'm mad with both Patrick and with myself. Why did he have to pretend to be someone he wasn't? And why did I have to over-react?

Why did we both have to throw everything away when it seemed pretty clear we had masses of potential for happiness?

Molly's Diary, June 17th

Oh, my God. Another disaster!

I am not exaggerating. This is The Very Worst Tragedy of My Entire Life!

I'm back in London and I'm curled in the foetal position in abject horror. The most terrible letter arrived in the mail while I was away. The postman must have slipped it through the front door slot on Saturday morning, and I found it lying on the mat in the hall—a letter addressed to me and forwarded by Patrick from Australia.

At first I thought it was no big deal, but now I've read the contents and I'm so sick.

Oh, help! I feel so stressed about this I think I might actually throw up.

ALC Assured Loans
Fieldstone House
George Street
Brisbane

Miss M.E. Cooper
32 Sapphire Bay Road
Magnetic Island
QLD 4819

Dear Miss Cooper

Following the purchase of the former Northern Home and Building Co-operative by our company,

ALC Assured Loans, we are now holders of the mortgage on a property at 32 Sapphire Bay Road, Magnetic
Island—Lot 216, Parish of Cook—which is listed in
your name.

We regret to inform you that the loan repayments on
this property are in arrears to the sum of $5,450.69.

As holders of the mortgage, our company, ALC
Assured Loans, has the right to foreclose on this loan
and recover the outstanding amount of $46,300 in
full.

To avoid this foreclosure you are required to make
full payment of the arrears by June 10th.

J P Swan
Client services and recovery manager

Molly's Diary, June 17th

It's June seventeenth.

And they were demanding payment by June tenth!

*Oh, help! I have no idea how this has happened, but
the letter must have arrived on the island while Patrick
was in England. When he got back he forwarded it to
me, but it's taken another week to reach this address,
and I've been in Cornwall.*

*I still can't believe it! I've always been so careful
with my money, and paying off the mortgage has always
been my top priority. I've already made one horrible
trip to the bathroom, but I'm still sick with terror. That's
why my handwriting is so shaky.*

I don't understand this.

*I can't cope with it. Pandanus Cottage isn't just
my ticket to a secure future; I love that house. My*

grandparents bought it soon after they were married and it's the only home I've ever known. It may be humble, but it has million dollar views. I couldn't bear to lose it.

Accck! I've just checked my bank account on the internet and now I can see that the money for the repayments hasn't been taken out. No wonder I've been managing so well in London.

But how did this happen? I arranged the monthly transfers before I left Australia. What's gone wrong?

And why hasn't Patrick contacted me about this? I need to know what's happened. Has a debt collector landed on his doorstep? Has he been thrown out of my home? Oh, help, could anything worse happen during a house swap? I can't stand not knowing what's going on. I'm going to have to ring him.

It's two in the afternoon, so it's midnight in Queensland. I should probably wait till this evening to ring Patrick, but I think there's every danger that I will have perished from fright by then. And I can't ring the finance company. There won't be anyone in their offices now. I have to ring Patrick. I hope he'll understand.

Oh, no. As soon as I went to the telephone I realised there were messages. From Patrick:

'Hi Molly. It's Patrick here. Could you ring me back when you get in?'

'Hi Molly. It's Patrick again. Obviously you're still not home. I'll try again later.'

I'm ashamed to admit that in spite of my overwhelming fear and terror I had the tiniest swoon when I heard Patrick's voice. He really does have the loveliest, most refined accent. And I know this sounds crazy, but just hearing his voice made me feel a little bit calmer.

And he was ringing from my home phone, so that's one good thing. At least when he left those messages yesterday he hadn't been kicked out.

CHAPTER ELEVEN

RING, ring...

Patrick fought to block out the telephone. It was dragging him from deep sleep and threatening his blissful dream.

He was in Cornwall with Molly, and there was no way he wanted to wake up.

Molly was standing at the edge of a cliff, drawing in deep breaths of sea air. Her hair was windblown and wonderfully tangled, and she was wearing a dark green skirt that hugged her neat hips, and a white blouse with long sleeves made from something soft, with ruffles at her throat and her wrists. A pirate's shirt.

The wind pressed the soft fabric against her body, outlining the slimness of her waist and the sweet, tempting roundness of her breasts.

She turned to him and smiled. Her cheeks were pink from the sea air and her eyes sparkled with warmth, like sudden sunshine. Her arms opened to him and he hurried forward, his heart light and floating with the most amazing happiness.

Ring, ring...

No, please no. Not now. Molly was almost in his arms.

Ring, ring.

The phone nagged at Patrick, but he refused to move. Hadn't he read somewhere that dreams vanished when you moved? Besides, who would call at this time of night?

The answer came in a flash.

Molly. She would be calling from London, worried about her house.

He sat up, heart racing, and snatched up the phone from the bedside table. 'Hello?'

'Patrick? It's Molly.'

'Hi. How are you?'

'I'm very relieved to hear your voice, actually.'

He smiled in the darkness, pleased she could say that in spite of everything that had gone wrong between them.

She said, 'I assume you can't have been kicked out of the cottage if you're answering this phone?'

'Of course I'm still here.'

'I was worried because of the letter you forwarded. Did you know it was from the loan company who hold my mortgage?'

'Yes. But don't worry, Molly.'

'I can't help worrying. Have they contacted you at all?'

'They sent someone round here yesterday. He tried to serve foreclosure papers.'

'Oh, God.' Her voice trembled with terror. 'So they really are going to take my house away from me?'

'No, they aren't. They can't. They haven't a chance. Don't panic. I've sorted it out.' Patrick spoke soothingly, anxious to allay her fears. He knew how much she loved this house, and after the major emotional problems he'd created for her he hated that this had happened as well.

Under any other circumstances he might have seized this chance to apologise for the hash he'd made of things in London, but her fears for her home were more important.

'Patrick, what do you mean you've sorted it out? How could you?'

'Very easily. I'm a banker, remember?'

'Well, yes, that's true. But how did you manage it?'

'As I said, the loan company sent someone round. An islander called Ross Fink. Apparently he knows you?'

'Oh, yes. Everyone knows everyone on the island. Ross delivers parcels from the ferry. Gosh, he's such a sweet guy. I had no idea he was a debt collector.'

'Actually he was worried, because he knew you were away. So I sat him down, and got his end of the story, and then I asked him to wait while I rang the loan company in Brisbane to get to the bottom of the problem.'

'Gosh, Patrick. That's—that's wonderful.'

'It's no big deal. It's the kind of thing I do all the time.' Just the same, he couldn't help being warmed by the awe and respect in Molly's voice. 'They put me through to Jason Swan, the recovery manager, and I told him I was acting on your behalf. I explained my background in banking, and that I know how the system works, and I urged him not to proceed.'

'Really?' She sounded astonished, as if he'd accomplished a miracle.

'I told him he'd find himself in a legal mess that would cost him more than it's worth. Then I explained that you were overseas, and there'd been delays with forwarding the mail. I assured him that if he gave me his firm's account details the money would be transferred immediately.'

'Immediately?' There was an audible gasp on the other end of the line. 'But—but I couldn't pay. I've been in Cornwall.'

'It's OK, Molly. As I said, it's all settled.'

'You don't mean you've paid my debt?'

'It was a simple matter.' Patrick tried to make light of it. He knew how fiercely independent Molly was, and he didn't want this to become a big issue.

'It's—it's very kind of you, Patrick. Amazing. Thank you so much. But it's hardly a simple matter. I owed over five thousand dollars.' Molly had sounded stunned, but now she sounded worried again. 'I'll pay you back straight away. If you tell me where you'd like the money deposited—'

'Don't worry about that now. The problem's over. We can sort out the details later.'

'How much later? I hate being in debt.'

Patrick suppressed a sigh. 'That's very commendable, Molly, but you should hang onto your money for the rest of your time in England. You never know when you might need it, and you only have a couple of weeks left to enjoy the sights. You should splash out and make sure you see all the things you really want to see.'

She tried several more times to protest, but he held her at bay. He even tried to make a joke of it. 'I don't mind having a short-term investment in a lovely place like Pandanus Cottage.'

'The thing is,' she said eventually, 'I don't understand how this happened. I set up an automatic transfer. The money should have been going through.'

Patrick assured her that this kind of hiccup wasn't unusual. Human error or computer glitches could cause unexpected problems. A form had been misplaced. Someone had left a digit off an account number.

'The ALC company's dodgy, though,' he said. 'They were far too quick to jump on you to foreclose. They didn't give you nearly enough warning.'

'I continued using my gran's mortgage company,' Molly said. 'But it looks as if they've been taken over by this new crowd.'

He suggested she should use a reputable bank, and she promised to look into it just as soon as she got home.

She thanked him. Effusively. And he realised with a thud of alarm that their conversation might end at any moment.

He was grappling to think of a suitable question when Molly asked, 'How's your book progressing?'

Surprised, Patrick answered honestly. 'Really well. I'm writing twelve, fourteen, sometimes seventeen hours a day.'

'Wow. You're really burning the midnight oil.'

Patrick grinned ruefully. 'I guess I'm crazy to be working so hard when I'm on holiday on this beautiful island, but I want to have a rough draft finished before I leave.'

'Well, good for you.' Her voice was warm and genuine. Almost the old Molly. 'So what's the new story about now that you've dropped Beth Harper and the MI5?'

'You'll never believe this.'

'Why? You're not writing a novel about two people who swap houses, are you?'

'No, no—nothing like that. It's perfectly safe non-fiction. A step-by-step guide for Generation Y on how to manage their finances.'

'Oh, dear.'

Patrick's mind whirred as he searched for a fresh conversation topic. The last thing he wanted was to waste precious time talking about himself.

'How was your trip to Cornwall?' he asked quickly, but as soon as the question was out he was drenched with ridiculous memories of his dream. Of Molly's bright smile and her open arms, the deep ruffles on her white blouse, the soft fabric clinging to her perfect shape.

To make matters worse, his question was met by silence.

'Molly?' He wondered if he'd been so distracted by his fantasy that he'd missed her reply. 'Are you still there?'

'Yes.' Her answer was scarcely more than a tiny bleat.

'Did you like Cornwall?'

'Y-yes. It—it was l-lovely.'

Hell. He'd upset her. He'd raised a touchy subject and no doubt made her angry again.

Idiot, idiot, idiot.

'Um—while we're on the phone,' she said quickly, as if she couldn't wait to change the subject, 'I suppose we should talk about our return dates. Are your plans still firm? Will you be leaving Australia on the thirtieth?'

'Oh.' He struggled to drag his mind away from totally inappropriate images of himself and Molly in a cosy B&B in Cornwall. 'I—I haven't checked with the airlines, but I don't imagine anything's changed.'

'Good. I don't plan to make any changes either. So I guess we'll pass each other somewhere over the Indian Ocean?'

He felt a sinking feeling of cold despair. 'I dare say we shall.'

'But right now I'm keeping you up in the middle of the night,' she said matter-of-factly, 'so I'd better let you get back to bed.'

'Well, OK,' Patrick agreed, reluctantly accepting that Molly was anxious to get off the line. 'It's been great to talk to you, Molly.' He added this with heartfelt sincerity.

The phone call ended and Patrick sat in the dark, on the edge of Molly's bed, wide awake, listening to the silence of the house and the distant soft slap of waves on the beach.

Once again Molly was giving out loud and clear signals. She wasn't giving him *any* chance to resume or restore their relationship.

For the first time since he'd arrived on the island he felt desperately lonely.

Molly's Diary, June 17th

I'm feeling quite a bit calmer now. I've spoken to Patrick in person, and I'm still shaken and stirred, but definitely calmer.

I must say that I couldn't have chosen a better person to swap houses with than a banking expert and financial diplomat.

My phone call woke him up, of course, and he sound-ed understandably sleepy. I think he was yawning when he picked up the phone, but as soon as he realised I was the caller he woke up properly. And then I couldn't believe how kind and calm and take-charge he was.

He spoke with such quiet authority I began to breathe more easily straight away, and I felt safer. In truth I was awestruck by this very in-control banker side of Patrick.

Perhaps it's just as well he's in Australia, because if he'd been within arm's length of me I would have hugged him and kissed him—which is hardly wise after the way we parted.

The one bad thing was the way he wouldn't let me clear my debt immediately. He kept insisting there was no hurry. But I owe him five thousand, four hundred and fifty dollars and sixty-nine cents!

Perhaps he wasn't keen to give his banking details over the phone. In the end I gave up. For now. It was either that or have another argument with him, and I didn't want to fight when he'd been so kind and helpful.

But then he asked me about Cornwall, and I couldn't believe how stupidly tongue-tied I suddenly became. It should have been so easy to talk about two days in southwest England—like reciting a travelogue—but I was swamped with all kinds of emotions.

I couldn't help thinking about what might have been.

And, heaven help me, I started blushing, as if Patrick could read my mind and knew I'd been thinking about the silly fantasy I recorded in my diary—of him stretched out on the white bed in the Cornish B&B.

What would he have thought if he'd known that I was picturing his shirt falling temptingly open to reveal the dark breadth of his chest? Or that I was feeling his hand touching me, his fingers tracing the shape of my lips? And more.

Thank heavens fantasies are private affairs.

We got over that awkward moment, and I thanked him again profusely. But, honestly, I must be a terrible ingrate.

There I was, incredibly indebted to Patrick—he'd saved my home and lifted an enormous worry from my shoulders—and yet I still felt unsettled and vaguely unhappy as I hung up the phone.

Molly's Diary, June 18th

Today I've stopped angsting about the money I owe Patrick, because I'm beginning to see that he might be right. It's certainly nice to have plenty of funds for my last week and a bit in London. I've made a list of all the things I'd like to do before I go home, and unfortunately many of them involve spending money.

Things to do before I leave London:

1. Buy two replacement fine bone china teacups and matching saucers (NB not flowery ones).
2. Buy souvenir gifts for my friends on the island—especially for Karli and Jimbo. And for Jill, who's been filling in for me at the Sapphire Bay resort. OK, something small for Jodie G and her progeny.
3. Buy a thank-you/house-warming present for Patrick's mother, who's been so very kind.
4. Buy a round or two of farewell drinks for my work-mates at the Empty Bottle.

*5. Visit the National Portrait Gallery one more time.
I've already been there twice, but I need another chance
to take in the faces of all those famous people—everyone from Richard III to the Beatles.*

*6. Splash out on a haircut and styling at a really good
London salon. After living in trendy London for so long,
I want to go home looking* fabulous!

*I think that's all. Thing is, I'm out and about so much
now, using every moment of my spare time, that I hardly
have a moment to write in my diary. Which is a very
good thing, of course. If I stop to think too much my
thoughts head down a dead-end street straight towards
a certain Englishman...*

*I remember how close he is to my ideal English-
man...and how hard it is to accept that the only way
I've ever known the real Patrick is through e-mails.
The man I met was acting a part, but he knew me so
well through my e-mails that he knew what buttons to
press.*

*Put on a suit, play the gentleman, take her to Covent
Garden.*

*I think about the fun we might have had if Patrick
had been up-front and open—the fun we never could
have now.*

*But here's the thing that's been worrying me most...
keeping me awake at night and stealing my appetite.
Now that Patrick's saved my house, I can't help seeing
it as one deliberately kind act in a series of acts of
deliberate kindness.*

*Right from the very start Patrick Knight has been
kind and thoughtful. He sent me the book about
London's secrets. He sent his mother round to help me
get over my fear of the Underground. He sent lovely*

gifts to Cidalia and Julieta. And—most importantly, perhaps—he effectively rescued my cottage.

It seems that whenever I've needed something Patrick's been there for me. And when I think about that I can't help seeing that the whole Peter debacle was almost certainly Patrick again, trying to be kind.

Now that I have a little distance and perspective, and when I consider all the other ways he's helped me, I can see that it makes perfect sense that he would try to help me with the one thing I claimed to want more than anything else—my dream date with an English gentleman.

If that's true, the angry way I behaved must have come across as terribly rude and ungrateful to Patrick.

Then I remember his kiss, which could not by any stretch of the imagination be described as an act of kindness. That kiss was all about hot-blooded lust. No doubt about it. I was introduced to Patrick's inner cave man—and it was incredibly exciting, thrilling, intoxicating...

Until he remembered he was playing the role of a gentleman. And he retreated. Only to ring the next morning with the Cornwall plan.

Thinking about all of this, I'm overcome with shame for my rash and angry response. I'm drowning in if-onlys...

Not just if only we'd gone to Cornwall. But if only I'd been just a little more sympathetic when Patrick was offering his explanation.... If only I hadn't jumped in with guns blazing, slamming the door and sending back his flowers and refusing to phone him.

All that time I was smugly thinking I was in the right.

> *If only I could tell him I've shifted in my thinking and I'd like to apologise.*
>
> *If only I could see him one more time.*
>
> *But it's not going to happen, and I can't live my life weighed down by if-onlys and what-ifs.*

To: Molly Cooper <molly.cooper@flowermail.com>
From: Karli Henderson <hendo86@flowermail.com>
Subject: Your Patrick!

Hi Molly

I hope you're making the most of your final days in London. Hasn't the time flown? I wish I was going to be on the island to welcome you home.

I hear that the islanders are planning a huge farewell party for your house swapper, so it seems that for a quiet man Patrick's become a big hit.

I understand Jodie G is going to make the most of this party, and will have one last stab at trying to win Patrick's attention/heart/body. (Take your pick. She's not fussy.) You have to hand it to that girl—she never gives up. I don't suppose you'll mind what happens between them now, so that's one good thing.

I wonder if you've developed a taste for travel? Maybe you'll decide to keep house swapping. I can see you in Tuscany, or on a Greek Island. Let me know if you decide to swap with someone from Las Vegas.

Seriously, Mozza, have a safe journey home. I'll try to get back to the island as soon as I can—or you're very welcome to visit us here, if you don't mind sleeping on the sofa. You must know I'm dying to see you.

Love you heaps

Karli

Molly's Diary, June 24th

OK, I've made a decision. A very big decision. Huge.

It all came from thinking constantly about my unfinished business with Patrick. Not just my financial debt, which is bad enough, but my feeling of being out on an emotional limb with no safe place to settle.

The last time I saw Patrick I was confused and disappointed, and I never gave him a chance to explain his behaviour. We didn't talk, which is crazy, because I love to talk. Now, if I want to make amends, I think it's up to me.

My plan, therefore, (quite brilliant, actually) will allow me to kill two birds with one stone.

Instead of going back to Australia without seeing Patrick again I'm going to change my flight, delaying it by four hours, so I'll still be here in London when he arrives. Then I propose to talk to him about everything, and make peace with him, and hand over a cheque for the money I owe him. Thus all debts and issues will be settled.

NB This has nothing to do with Karli's suggestion that Jodie Grimshaw might win Patrick's attention at the farewell party on the island. If he was going to fall for Jodie it would have happened ages ago.

I'll meet Patrick at Heathrow, and I'll be calm and polite and ladylike and mature (and hopefully I'll also look ravishing, with my new hairstyle from Edgar's in Soho), and Patrick and I will be able to have the conversation we should have had weeks ago.

I know it's too late to change the past, or to try to revisit it. We won't take off for Cornwall or anything wonderfully crazy like that. But at least my conscience will be clear and...

I don't know...

I guess I'll be able to get on with the rest of my life.

Now the decision is made I feel so much better.

Private Writing Journal, June 29th

I can't believe my time here is over.

There are so many, many things about this island that I'm going to miss—the views through the trees to the bright sparkling blue sea, the towering, scrub-covered mountains and the rocky bays, the palm trees and the sandy beaches, so white and gold. I'll miss the little rock wallabies scampering about, even in the backyards and public places, and the bright, squabbling parrots that come to my balcony to be fed.

I've also grown so used to the silence here that I'm sure I'm going to miss it. I've become accustomed to the occasional sounds of nature—the bird-calls at sunrise and the buzzing of cicadas in the gum trees at sunset, the chattering of fruit bats in the mango tree... There are almost no man-made sounds.

Now, too late, I wish I'd explored more, taken more photographs, learned more about the trees, the plants and the original inhabitants...

I know I'll miss the friendly locals, with their laconic good humour and their laidback manner and their smiling, shoulder-shrugging reaction to everything.

When I get back to work at the bank (shudder) and old George Sims throws the first of his fits, I plan to simply turn to him with a slow grin and tell him, 'No worries, mate.'

The thing is, this is the worst time to leave a tropical island—in the middle of the glorious winter days. Molly was so right—this time of year is magical. Out of this world. The air is as clear and crisp as champagne, and although the temperature is cooler it's so sunny I long to abandon my desk and go for long walks, or to swim from one end of the bay to the other.

Each evening at dusk the sky and the sea and the tops of the hills are tinged with a magenta blush.

It's another world.

If Molly was here with me...

It would be Paradise.

Molly's Diary, June 30th

I've been through such a seesaw of emotions during this past week. I'm so sad about leaving London and leaving the friends that I've made here—all the people at work, as well as Cidalia and her lovely family, and Patrick's wonderful mum.

But now my suitcases are packed and groaning once again, and I've said my goodbyes to my favourite London people and to my favourite London places. I've given and received gifts. I've eaten farewell dinners and downed farewell drinks. I've returned Patrick's key to the safety deposit box at the bank around the corner on the King's Road. And I've wept.

OK, I'm not going to write about how often I've wept, because I might come across as a complete watering pot, or I might get teary again, and I need to be dry-eyed and smiling today. I'm already at Heathrow, you see.

This evening I travelled to the airport in a square black London taxi through the rain. The roads were shiny and wet, reflecting all the streetlights and the neon signs. It was quite magical, really, to see all that shiny black bitumen streaked with shimmering splashes of yellow, red, green and blue. I think there's some-thing extraordinarily beautiful but sad about a city on a rainy night—especially when you're dry in the back of a comfortable taxi cab and you're leaving, and you know you will almost certainly never be coming back.

In a few hours' time I'll be flying home.

But right now I don't want to think about that. I'm in the Arrivals lounge, and I can see on the huge screen above the doorway that Patrick's plane has just—at this very moment—landed.

Squee! Just writing that he's here makes my heart leap like a nervous kitten. His plane is somewhere out there on the Heathrow tarmac, taxiing into its gate, and I'm practically exploding with excitement.

I know I'm taking a big risk by surprising him like this, but I've practised what I have to say a thousand times and I really feel it needs to be said. Face to face.

Oh, help. Now I just have to get it right.

Of course it's going to be ages yet before I see Patrick. First he has to get through Customs and Immigration, and then he has to collect his baggage, and he's going to be tired and jet-lagged, and he won't be expecting me, so the whole situation is fraught. I'm trying to stay calm, but it's very hard.

I thought writing in my diary might help.

It's not helping.

I've been to the Ladies' twice already to check my clothes and to touch-up my make-up, and—yes, I should be honest—to admire my new hairstyle. Edgar's in Soho has given me an amazing new look. Now, instead of tight brown corkscrews, I have soft, silky curls that bounce.

'It's all about using the right products,' Edgar explained.

So I'm going home to Australia armed with vitamin-enriched lotions, deep conditioners and a daily spritz. Although once I'm back on Magnetic Island the tropical humidity will have its wicked way, and before long I'll probably give up trying to look glamorous....

OK, it's now half an hour since Patrick's plane landed, so he should be moving through the tedious lines of travellers, gradually making his way towards this lounge. The place is teeming with people of every race and every age and in every kind of dress. There are people in Middle Eastern robes and Indian saris, and in pinstriped business suits and ripped jeans and T-shirts.

I have no idea what Patrick will be wearing. I'm suddenly terrified I might miss him.

I didn't think it would be possible to miss seeing Patrick. Apart from the fact that he's so tall and dark and stand-out handsome, I was sure I'd have some kind of inbuilt sensor that would zero in on him and pick him out of millions. But now that I'm here in this vast sea of humanity I'm having doubts. I'm thinking that I should have warned him and arranged a proper meeting.

I have no choice but to stand as close as possible to the door that he has to come through. Surely I can't miss him there.

Still at Heathrow...

Another hour has passed and there's still no sign of Patrick. I know he hasn't walked through this door, and I think it's the only way he could have entered. I heard Aussie accents some time back, and so I asked a man what flight he was on and it was Patrick's flight. I did *my best to remain calm after that. I stood by the door in eager anticipation, but Patrick hasn't appeared.*

I can't have missed him. Not when I'm standing here, more or less on guard by the door. Unless there are other doors.

Oh, God, I have no idea where he is, and very soon I have to leave or I'll miss my plane. I've already paid an extra fee because I've changed my flight once. I can't afford to change it again.

I'm worried. What can have happened? I refuse to consider the possibility that Jodie Grimshaw got her claws into Patrick at the farewell party and convinced him to stay with her and her hyperactive child. I can rise above such thoughts. I can. I can.

Just the same, I've forgotten every word of my rehearsed speech. I'm so sick with nerves that if I saw Patrick now I'd be a stammering mess. But I guess it doesn't really matter because I have to go.

My plan has failed. I have to pack up this diary and trudge over to Departures. I'm fighting tears.

My heart is a stone in my chest.

I know it's silly, but I can't help thinking about that scene in A Westminster Affair, when Vanessa was riding off on a red double-decker bus, about to zoom out of Christian's life, but then she realised she was making a terrible mistake and that she would never see him again if she didn't act immediately.

That's how I feel. I can't get on that plane until I've seen Patrick. But—

Where is he?

CHAPTER TWELVE

THE ferry bumped against the wharf at Nelly Bay, and the movement woke Molly.

Disorientated, she sat up, and when she peered through the window of the lower deck she saw barnacle-encrusted pylons and aqua-green water. Her nose wrinkled as she smelled the sharp salt of the sea mingled with the dank mustiness of seasoned timbers.

Lifting her gaze, she saw the familiar glass-fronted ferry terminal and a row of palm trees in giant pots. Beyond the terminal hills towered, studded with gumtrees and huge, smooth boulders, and arching above everything the bright blue sky was turning soft mauve as the afternoon slipped towards dusk.

She was home.

Safe on the island—*her* island.

She knew she should be happy, but this was the first time she'd come home to the island when neither her gran nor Karli was there to welcome her. And this homecoming was so much worse, because she'd left England without sighting Patrick. Her worry over where he might be had eaten at her like a nasty disease throughout the long flight back.

She still had no idea. At Brisbane airport she'd rung his home in Chelsea, but she'd only heard his answering machine, so she still didn't know if he'd missed his plane, if he'd been detained in transit, or if he was ill.

On top of those concerns her head ached and her neck had developed a crick from sleeping sitting up. Her limbs were leaden as she tried to stand.

After twenty-four hours of travelling, all she wanted was to crawl into bed and sleep for a week. No, a month.

She disembarked via a ramp which was steeper than usual because it was very low tide. Phil, one the ferry's attendants, had dumped her luggage on the wharf.

'How was London?' he asked.

'Fabulous.' She managed a weak smile, then wheeled her suitcases to the car park, where her old rust-bucket was waiting in the sun like a faithful puppy—exactly where Patrick had said he would leave it, with its key tucked inside the exhaust pipe.

Molly hefted her luggage into the boot and slammed the lid. Yawning deeply, she sagged behind the steering wheel and turned on the ignition, surprised that the motor didn't cough or splutter.

Winding down the window, she steered the car gently forward. The sea breeze played havoc with her hair as the ancient rattletrap chugged over the hill to Geoffrey Bay, then on through Arcadia and over the next hill to the bay after that.

From the crests of the hills Molly saw the tropical sea stretching out to the curving horizon. As always, the water at this time of day was silver-grey and tinged with lavender and pink—serene and cool and endless.

Looking at it, Molly felt her spirits lift. Momentarily. They quickly drooped again.

Perhaps in time…in a very long time…she would begin to feel like her old self. Or perhaps not.

Right now she was too tired and too emotionally flattened to feel anything close to happiness. She felt as limp as a balloon, forgotten in a corner after everyone had left the party.

At last she saw her little white cottage through the trees. She turned down the short dirt track that wound through the scrub and pulled into her carport. Then she struggled with her luggage, dragging it to the front door.

The key was under the flower pot, and as she retrieved it she couldn't help thinking that not so long ago Patrick's hand had placed it there.

Fool. I've got to stop thinking about him.

The front door opened on unexpectedly silent hinges. Molly stepped inside, drew a deep breath, and looked about her. Her house was tidy, and it smelled clean. For a moment she fancied she could almost catch of whiff of Patrick's special scent.

How silly.

She drank in details. Amazingly, Patrick had put everything back in its right place, so that her house was exactly as she'd left it three months ago. He'd even left little handwritten notes dotted about the furniture.

Abandoning her bags on the doorstep, she hurried forward, eager to snatch up the nearest note propped against a pot plant in the middle of the dining table. She stared at Patrick's distinctive, spiky handwriting.

I've watered this plant and it's still alive. Note new growth—three new leaves and a bud. No water in saucer and no mossies.

Molly's mouth curved into a smile. She couldn't help it. She clutched the note against her suddenly thumping heart.

She turned to another note, stuck on the wall near the light switch.

Gecko lizard has had babies and they live behind the painting on this wall. Their names are Leonard, Zac and Elizabeth.

Molly's smile broadened, then wobbled as she felt a painful lump filling her throat. She went on to the next note in the kitchen.

This tap no longer leaks.

'Amazing,' she announced to the empty room. 'Patrick not only takes care of pot plants and geckos, he's also a plumber. The man's a legend.'

She was trying to sound sarcastic, to prove she wasn't moved, but she found herself stifling a sob. Dismayed, she whirled around, only to find yet another note stuck on the fridge.

Champagne and chocolates in here.

'Oh, Patrick, no.'

He was being kind. Again. Still. And she wasn't sure she could bear it. Not when she hadn't been able to see him, or speak to him, or say any of the things she'd wanted to tell him.

She opened the fridge and saw proper French Champagne and Belgian chocolate truffles. How on earth had Patrick found such exotic luxuries on this island? Molly's emotions threatened to overwhelm her.

It's just jet-lag, she decided as her mouth pulled out of shape. She pressed a fist against her lips. *I mustn't cry. Not tonight.*

If she started she might never stop.

Blinking hard, she retrieved her luggage from the doorstep and carried it purposefully through to her bedroom. Golden sunlight slanted into the darkened room through the bamboo blinds, tiger-striping the straw matting and her neatly made double bed—the bed Patrick had slept in until very recently.

There were two small squares of paper—two more notes—one on each pillow.

The first note said: *We need to talk, Molly.*

The other: *I have so much to tell you.*

Her heart leapt, beating hard and fast, like wings trying to hold her up in the air, but her knees were distinctly wobbly and she sank helplessly onto the edge of the bed.

What did the notes mean? Where could they talk? When? How?

Where *was* Patrick?

Her weariness had vanished, washed away by shock and by wonder and by the teensiest flicker of hope.

She couldn't help wondering if Patrick was as keen as she was to set things straight between them.

But that didn't mean…

That he…

Felt…

Oh, help. Molly's heart thrashed as she scanned the room, searching for more notes…

There was nothing that looked out of place, but the light was dim. Jumping to her feet she flicked the light switch.

No more messages.

Perhaps he'll send an e-mail, she thought. I mustn't get too worked up about a few Post-it notes. I should unpack. Be sensible. Make a cup of tea.

Instead she went to the white louvred French doors that led to the bathroom and pushed them open.

There was a note stuck on the mirror. It was longer than the others. In fact it looked like a list.

Almost afraid to read it, Molly stepped closer and her eyes flew down the page.

10 Reasons Why I Must See Molly Again
1. To tell her how sorry I am for stuffing things up in London.
2. To try to explain that I would *never* willingly hurt her.
3. To tell her that her e-mails have brightened my days.
4. And my nights.
5. To tell her that meeting her in person has changed me.
6. That she's changed my life in vitally important ways.
7. To tell her I need to kiss her again.
8. And again.
9. And again.
10. And again.

Now Molly was smiling and weeping at the same time.

The phone beside the bed began to ring, and she spun round, a hand pressed against the leaping pulse at her throat.

If the caller was one of the islanders she didn't think she could talk. She couldn't drum up cheery chatter about her holiday. Not tonight.

But if it was Patrick...

Could it be Patrick?

She picked up the phone carefully, as if it were a bomb about to explode. As she held it to her ear her insides danced as if she'd swallowed fireflies. 'Hello?'

'Oh, you're home at last.' His voice was deep and beautifully English. 'Welcome back.'

'Patrick?'

'How are you, Molly?'

He sounded as if he was smiling, and it was ridiculous but Molly felt instantly happy. Just hearing his lovely voice soothed her and excited her.

'I'm fine, thanks.' She was grinning from ear to ear.

'I thought you'd be home earlier.'

'I changed to a later flight.'

'Oh, I see. Have you settled in?'

'Not yet. I've only just arrived.' Feeling suddenly emboldened, she said, 'I've been busy tidying up all the mess here.'

'Mess?'

'Yes. Someone was staying here, you see, and he's left bits of paper all over the house.'

'Oh. How thoughtless… Some chaps are dashed untidy.'

'Aren't they just?'

An awkward silence fell, and Molly wondered if her little attempt at humour had fallen flat. Her confidence faltered.

'Patrick?'

'Yes?'

'I—I've seen the bathroom.'

'Oh, right,' he replied cautiously. 'Was it tidy?'

'It was particularly *un*tidy.'

After a beat, he said, 'Sounds like the fellow who's been staying at your place might need to apologise.'

'No apology necessary.' Molly swallowed. 'I—I loved the note.'

There was a shaky laugh and a huff of relief.

Molly's curiosity got the better of her. 'Where are you? I waited for you at Heathrow and you weren't on your flight.'

'You waited?'

'Yes, I wanted to talk to you. There was so much I wanted to tell you.'

'Oh, Molly.'

'What happened, Patrick? I couldn't find you.'

'I didn't catch the plane.'

'Really?' Shock riffled through her like a lightning strike. 'Why not?'

'I wanted to be here when you got back.'

'Here?'

'On the island. I'm on the beach right now, and I'm looking up through the trees to your house. I can see the light in your bedroom window.'

It was almost dusk, and the light was fading fast, but Molly fairly flew down the track to the beach. The path was steep, and at times rocky, and twice she almost tripped over tangled tree roots.

She reached the lower section quite quickly, and could see the smooth white sand ahead. And the darkening sea. And the tall, shadowy outline of a man.

Patrick.

He was coming across the sand towards her.

She began to run.

Now they were both running. Running towards each other. Arms outstretched.

And at last—

At last Patrick swept her into his arms. He was looking earnest and worried and yet extraordinarily relieved. She wanted to tell him all the things she had planned to say, but before she could speak he kissed her.

And so she kissed him back.

And it took a very long time.

They sat on the warm sand, watching the full moon rise out of the sea, a great golden disc of molten brilliance. Molly's head rested on Patrick's shoulder, and he knew his heart had never been fuller.

'I've made so many mistakes,' he said. 'But I think now

that they were all preparation for this.' He brushed a corner of her brow with his lips. 'Have you any idea how long I've been in love with you?'

She appeared to give the question serious thought. 'Could it have started when you saw me in my black dress at Covent Garden?'

Patrick laughed.

'What's so funny? That's as glamorous as I get.'

'You looked beautiful that night, but I'd fallen long before then.'

'Tell me about it,' she said with an unabashed smile. 'I'm all ears.'

'Let me see…' Reaching an arm around her shoulders, he hugged her. 'I think it more or less dawned on me when I was so ridiculously excited about going back to London for my mother's wedding. I mean, I was thrilled and happy for her and Jonathan, but I think I knew that a lot of my excitement was about wanting to meet you. Your e-mails were so open and honest. I loved your zest for life and your thirst for adventure and I wanted to share it.'

'So it had nothing to do with the way I looked?'

'Are you joking, Molly?'

'Tell me. A girl likes to hear these things.'

Patrick was aware that he'd never been very forthcoming with compliments, but with Molly it was incredibly easy. 'Actually, I was in lust with the photo you left on your fridge,' he confessed. 'I spent hours and hours, when I was supposed to be writing, staring at your legs, or trying to work out the colour of your eyes. And then I met the real thing and I was a lost man.'

Molly grinned, and her blue eyes sparkled, and she leaned in and rewarded him with another lovely kiss. 'So I'm to blame for ruining your novel?'

'Not really. That fault was all mine. I'm not very good at fiction.' Patrick frowned, aware that he needed to broach a very important subject. 'Molly, can you forgive me for pulling the Peter Kingston stunt?'

'Of course,' she said, surprisingly calm. 'I'm sorry I made such a stink. That's the big thing I waited at Heathrow to tell you. I realised you were just being kind.' She turned to look at him with a direct and clear gaze. 'That's right, isn't it?'

'It was partly that—about trying to give you your fantasy.' Patrick looked at the rising moon, which had cast a silver path across the sea almost to their feet. 'But you had such high expectations, and I wasn't sure I'd measure up on my own. It seemed safer, somehow, to hide behind a mask. I foolishly assumed that you'd understand.'

'I understand now.' She laid a gentle hand on his arm. 'But you shouldn't have worried. Patrick Knight has so much more going for him than Peter Kingston.'

'Tell me why,' he said, smiling with relief. 'I'm all ears.'

'Well, to start with, Patrick Knight lives in my favourite city in the whole world.'

'There's that, I guess.'

'And he has a wonderful mother—someone I already look on as a friend.'

'She adores you.'

'And he likes my island.'

'He does. He loves it.'

'I should possibly also mention the fireworks in my veins every time I look at him.'

'Molly…'

'And the fact that he's so sweet.'

'*Sweet?*'

Molly smiled. 'Don't look so surprised. Patrick Knight is very kind and thoughtful. He sent me a book about London, and ever since he's gone out of his way to make me happy.

I've learned so much from him about the world beyond this little island, about my father, about myself.' She pressed her nose against his neck. 'And then there's the way he smells. It drives me wild.' Her lips grazed his jaw seductively. 'Would you like to know the best thing?'

He gave a choked little laugh. 'Sure.'

'Patrick's not always a perfect English gentleman. I have the distinct impression that I'm going to love his inner cave man.'

With a cry somewhere between laughter and longing, Patrick jumped to his feet, reached down and scooped Molly into his arms.

'You can't carry me,' she gasped. 'Not all the way to the cottage.'

'I can try.'

'No need. Put me down and let's run.'

EPILOGUE

To: Patrick Knight <patrick.knight@mymail.com>
From: Molly Cooper <molly.cooper@flowermail.com>
Subject: My first love letter

Dearest Patrick

By now you will be safely home in Chelsea. I hope you had a comfortable journey and that everything was just as it should be at 34 Alice Grove.

I'm sure you can guess that I'm missing you already, but I'm determined not to moan. How can I complain when I've had you all to myself for two whole, perfectly blissful weeks?

I'm thrilled that you broke your lifelong habit of hard work so you could devote all that time just to me. It was two weeks of heaven, and I'm honoured to know that this was one of the vitally important changes you wanted to make in your life—taking time out, not working, not writing a book. Just being.

With me.

I must admit that when you handed me your journal with that cute, shy smile of yours and said you'd like me to read it, I was a bit stunned. That's a pretty big step for a guy, and I was very nervous about letting you read everything I'd written in my diary (especially about my trip to Cornwall).

But it was actually very liberating to share such complete and intimate honesty, wasn't it? No wonder we felt so wonderfully close by the end of our two weeks—as if we'd known each other all our lives.

Now that you're home again, Patrick, it's time for me to get busy with planning for September. It was so sweet of you to insist on having our wedding here on the island.

I couldn't think of anything more perfect than to be married to you on the beach at sunset. But to be honest, my darling, I would have married you anywhere—even in a Tube station. As for our honeymoon in Cornwall—you know how over the moon I am about that.

Next week I'm heading up to Cairns, to spend a few days with Karli and Jimbo. Of course I want to show off my gorgeous engagement ring, but Karli and I will also have huge fun hunting in the lovely Cairns shops for our dresses. She's thrilled to be my bridesmaid.

So that's my news.

I'm pleased that you're going up to Scotland to visit your father, and that you're going to invite him to our wedding. I'm looking forward to meeting him.

Good luck with finishing your book. I have my fingers crossed for you, but, honest to God, I'm your target audience and I think it's absolutely brilliant. Even I could end up wealthy if I followed your advice.

I'm sure every publisher who sees your manuscript will want to buy it. There'll be a bidding war, and very soon you'll be a famous author and the backs of your books will announce that you divide your time between London and a tropical island.

Your readers will think that sounds wonderfully romantic, and they'll be right. I'm sure they'll also think that your wife is the luckiest woman in the world—and they'll be right about that, too.

All my love, my kind, brilliant, sexy Englishman.

Until tomorrow, and all our tomorrows…

Molly xxxxxxxxx

MR RIGHT THERE
ALL ALONG

BY
JACKIE BRAUN

Jackie Braun is the author of more than two dozen romance novels. She is a three-time RITA® Award finalist, a four-time National Readers' Choice Awards finalist, the winner of a Rising Star Award in traditional romantic fiction and was nominated for Series Storyteller of the Year by *RT Book Reviews* in 2008. She lives in Michigan with her husband and two sons, and can be reached through her website at www.jackiebraun.com.

For my husband, Mark.
We've had lots of reasons to cry.
We've chosen to laugh instead.
That—and you—have made all the
difference in my life.
I love you.

CHAPTER ONE

High School History 101

WHEN SHE SPIED the invitation amid the pile of bills and junk mail, Chloe McDaniels's lips pulled back in a sneer. She'd been expecting it, but that didn't make her reaction any less visceral.

Tillman High School's Class of 2001 was set to celebrate its ten-year reunion.

Chloe did not have fond memories of her New Jersey high school. In fact, she'd spent her four years at Tillman ducking into bathroom stalls and janitors' broom closets to avoid the unholy trinity of Natasha Bradford, Faith Ellerman and Tamara Kingsley.

She'd known the girls since grade school. They'd never been friends, but neither had they been enemies… until the start of their freshman year when, for reasons that had never been terribly clear to Chloe, she'd become their favorite target.

Literally.

Somehow on that first, already awkward day of high school, they managed to attach a "Kick Me" sign to the back of her shirt just before the start of first period. It was the last time Chloe ever accepted a friendly back slap without taking a gander over her shoulder afterward. As cruel pranks went, it wasn't terribly original, but it was effective. She'd taken enough sneakers to the seat of her favorite jeans to feel like a soccer ball.

Then, between third period and lunch, Simon Ford had happened along.

"You might not want to wear this," he'd said simply, removing the sign and handing it to Chloe. That was his way. Understated.

Good old Simon. He always had her back. Or backside, as the case had been. They'd been friends since his family had moved into her family's apartment building at the start of third grade and their friendship continued to this day. Thinking of him now, Chloe picked up the phone before realizing the time. It was well after five on a Friday. He was probably out with his girlfriend.

Chloe realized she was sneering again. Well, it couldn't be helped. She didn't like Sara. The long-limbed and lithe blonde was too…too…perfect.

She glanced down at the invitation. Perfect Sara would never find herself in this position. Perfect Sara would have been the homecoming queen and the prom queen and the every other kind of queen at her high school. Unlike Chloe, whose only class recognition had come in the form of "curliest hair" and "most freckles."

Yeah, that was what a girl wanted to be remembered for, all right.

Her gut told her to ball up the invitation in a wad, spit

on it and, with expletives she knew in four languages, send it whizzing into the trash can. Her heart was a different matter. It was telling her to reach for a spoon and the pint of mint chocolate chip ice cream in her freezer.

Diet in mind, she went with her gut.

Sort of.

She lavished the invitation with every foreign epithet she could think of before heaving it in the trash. But, while she bypassed the ice cream, she booted up her computer and downloaded a recipe from her favorite cable cooking show, *Susie Kay's Comfort Foods*. If it was all but guaranteed to clog the arteries and contribute to heart disease, Susie Kay made it.

Tonight's dinner selection was a case in point. Macaroni and cheese with not one, but four kinds of cheese and enough butter and calories that Chloe swore her clothes fit tighter just reading the ingredients. Not good considering she was already wearing her fat pants.

Actually, the pants were elastic-waist exercise gear that she didn't exercise in but instead reserved for days when she felt particularly bloated. Today was just such a day. Strap a few cables to her and she would be right at home gliding down Sixth Avenue like one of those huge helium balloons in the annual Thanksgiving Day parade. Even so, that didn't keep her from making the mac and cheese and eating half of the six servings.

The wine she poured for herself was an afterthought. She'd been saving the pricey bottle of cabernet sauvignon for a special occasion. This definitely was not it, but three glasses later, she didn't care.

Chloe set the wine aside and went to her stereo. Music. That's what she needed now. Something with a wicked beat and a lot of bass. Something she could dance to with reckless abandon and maybe work off a few extra calories in the process. She chose…Céline Dion.

As one weepy ballad after another filled Chloe's Lower East Side studio apartment, her willpower wilted like the water-deprived basil plant on her kitchen windowsill. Again muttering foreign curses, this time aimed at herself, she fished the crumpled invitation out of the trash. When the telephone rang, she was still sitting on the kitchen floor smoothing out the wrinkles.

It was Simon.

"Hey, Chloe. What are you doing?"

Anyone else—her older and über-chic sister, Frannie, for instance—and Chloe would have felt compelled to come up with some elaborate reason why she could be found home alone on the official start of the weekend.

Since it was Simon, she confessed, "Drinking wine, wearing Lycra and listening to the soundtrack from *Titanic*."

"No ice cream?"

How well he knew her. Despite her best intentions, the mint chocolate chip was next on her list. "Not yet."

"Want some company?" he asked.

Did she ever. She and Simon always had a good time together, whether it involved going out or just hanging out. Still, his question surprised her. Wasn't he supposed to be with his girlfriend tonight? She liked thinking he'd throw over Perfect Sara to be with Comfortable Chloe. Liked it so much that she immediately felt guilty. She was a terrible friend. To make up for it, she would share her ice cream and what was left of the wine.

"When can I expect you?"

"Right now. I'm standing on the other side of your apartment door."

If he were a boyfriend—not that Chloe had had one of *those* in several months—this news would have sent her into a panic. Her apartment was a mess. For that matter, so was she. Her red hair was a riot of curls thanks to the day's high humidity. And what little makeup she'd applied that morning was long gone. But this was Simon. *Simon,* she reminded herself, after a glance down at her unflattering attire had her wanting to flee to her bedroom and change.

It was sad to admit, but he'd seen her looking worse. Much worse. Such as when she came down with the chicken pox in the sixth grade or the time in high school when she'd succumbed to salmonella after her cousin Ellen's bridal shower. Aunt Myrtle made the chicken salad, which was why, henceforth, the woman was only allowed to bring paper products or plastic cutlery to family gatherings. The coup de grâce, of course, was last December. Three days shy of Christmas, the guy Chloe had been dating for the previous six months dumped her.

Via text message.

And she'd already bought him a gift, a Rolex watch, which she couldn't return since the street vendor who'd sold her the incredibly authentic-looking knockoff had moved to a new location.

So, now, she flung open the door, feeling only mildly embarrassed by what her hair was doing, by the mac-and-cheese stains on her shirt or the fact that her lips had probably turned a slightly clownish shade of purple from the wine she'd enjoyed.

"Hey, Simon."

As usual, his smile made her feel as if seeing her was the highlight of his day.

"Hey, gorgeous." He kissed her cheek as he always did before waving a slim, square box beneath her nose. "I've got pizza. Thin crust with extra cheese from that new Italian place just shy of Fourteenth."

Any other time, the aroma of pepperoni and melted mozzarella would have had her salivating. Right now, it reminded her of how full she felt. "Thanks, but I just finishing eating."

His gaze took in the stained shirt. The sides of his mouth lifted. "So I see. What was on today's menu and why?"

Yes, he knew her way too well.

"Mac and cheese."

"Ah." He nodded sagely. "Comfort food."

She touched an index finger to the tip of her nose. "You got it in one."

He smiled in return. Simon had a great smile. She'd always thought so. With perfectly proportioned lips in a face that wasn't drop-dead gorgeous but handsome and pleasingly male. Over the years, his cheeks had gotten leaner and more sculpted-looking, but his ready smile kept him from ever looking hard.

"How much did you eat?" he asked.

"Too much."

"Save me any?" He glanced in the direction of the stove.

"Enough." She tapped the box he held. "What about your pizza?"

He shrugged. "You know pizza. It's even better cold." Then, with the pad of his thumb, he pressed down on her lower lip. She ignored the sensation his touch sent coursing up her spine. "And what about the wine? Did you save me any of that?"

Chloe laughed. How did other women manage to drink a few glasses of cab and not wind up with stained lips? For that matter, how did other women manage to eat a meal's worth of carbs and not have to do deep knee bends so they could breathe in their jeans?

"There's almost half a bottle," she told him.

"Pour me a glass and tell me about your day."

He set the pizza box on the kitchen counter and shrugged out of his trench coat. He was wearing his usual business attire—crisp white shirt and tailored suit with a perfectly folded handkerchief peeking from its breast pocket. The matching silk tie, however, was pulled askew. It struck Chloe then. "Did you just come from work?"

It was nearly eight o'clock.

"The merger with that other software company I mentioned is eating up a lot of my spare time." He dropped heavily into one of the kitchen chairs.

How had she missed how tired he looked? She wanted to go to him, wrap him in her arms. Friends hugged. But she held back. More and more lately, she found herself doing that. She blamed Perfect Sara and the bevy of beauties that had come before her.

"Sorry to hear that." She switched on the stove to reheat the mac and cheese, and poured him a glass of wine. After handing it to him, she stood behind his chair and began kneading the knotted muscles in his neck and shoulders.

His moan of pleasure nearly made her stop. Instead, she kept at it and asked, "So, how does Sara feel about the long hours you're keeping?"

"Not happy," he admitted. His tone was rueful when he said, "We were supposed to go to a Broadway show tonight."

"You stood her up?" That wasn't like him. Simon was the kindest, most considerate man Chloe knew... even if he had really lousy taste in women.

"Ouch!"

Apparently, she'd massaged a little too vigorously.

"Sorry."

"Actually, when I called to tell her I was running late and we'd have to skip dinner beforehand, she told me to go... Never mind." He shook his head. "It doesn't matter. The relationship wasn't heading anywhere anyway."

Jubilation.

Before Chloe could help it, the feeling bubbled up inside her with all of the effervescence of champagne. Maybe this day didn't totally stink after all.

However, because she knew a friend wasn't supposed to feel happy upon hearing such news, she kept her expression sympathetic when she slid into the chair opposite his.

"Ooh. Dumped. Sorry."

"It was mutual," he muttered, reaching for his wine. "Sara just said it first."

"Okaaaay."

"My heart's not broken, Chloe. Hell, it's not even dented or mildly scratched." He sipped his wine and sighed heavily before squinting at her. "That's not right, is it? I should feel…a little sad, shouldn't I?"

"You don't?"

Jubilation made another appearance, but she carefully tucked it behind a bland expression.

"Not one bit." He studied his wine a moment before his gaze lifted to hers. "I guess we weren't suited."

No kidding. It had taken him nearly a year to figure that out? Chloe had concluded as much within mere minutes of meeting Sara for the first time.

"But that's neither here nor there," Simon was saying. He rallied with a smile. "We were going to talk about your day."

Her day. *Ick!*

Chloe rose and went to the stove to plate his dinner. She opened the fridge and got out a sprig of fresh parsley to add to the mac and cheese before bringing it to the table. Simon's eyebrows rose.

"Appearances are everything," she said, setting the plate before him with a flourish.

He picked up his fork and pointed the tines in her direction. "That's exactly your problem, Chloe."

It was an old observation. Under normal circumstances, it wouldn't have bothered her. Tonight, however, she snapped in exasperation, "Do you want to analyze me or do you want me to tell you about my day?"

"Actually, I want you to tell me about *that*." Again, he used the tines of his fork to point, this time toward the class reunion invitation that, somewhere between belting out "My Heart Will Go On" and hearing about Simon's newly single status, Chloe had forgotten all about.

She shrugged, striving for nonchalance. "It seems our ten-year reunion is right around the corner."

"I know. My invitation arrived in the mail last week."

"Last week? Are you kidding? We live in the same city, practically in the same zip code. I bet the unholy trio had something to do with that," she alleged.

So much for nonchalance.

"Chloe, really. It's been ten years." Simon said it in that patient way of his that usually served to talk her down from whatever ledge she was on.

Not on this day. Nope. She was poised to jump, ushered to the edge of reason by the wine and some very unhappy memories.

"Seems like yesterday to me," she muttered.

Damn the cabernet for her loose lips. Even so, she reached for her glass now and took a liberal sip while she waited for Simon's well-reasoned rebuttal.

It didn't come.

"So, are you going?" he asked.

"Am I going?" she repeated incredulously. She returned her wineglass to the table with a smart click. "You're kidding, right?" The question was rhetorical and they both knew it, so she plowed ahead. "You couldn't pay me enough to make so much as a token appearance at that thing. I'd rather give up ice cream for…for… *forever* than to step foot in the…" She craned her neck to read the invitation. The outrage whooshed out of her and she snorted. "The Tillman High gymnasium? Gee, that's classy. They couldn't spring for a banquet hall or something?"

"I don't know. I rather like the idea of seeing the old school again, even if I never spent much time in the gym."

Simon laughed then. He'd been a geek, not a jock. Chess club, computer club, debate team—those sorts of interests had been his thing. And Chloe's, too. His geek status had never bothered him as much as hers had bothered her.

Her gaze narrowed. "Wait a minute. Do you mean you're going to the reunion?"

Simon regarded her over his wineglass. Actually, he hadn't planned to attend until just that moment. Chloe needed to go. He'd never met anyone so haunted by high school. The invitation's crumpled appearance was a testament to that, as was her mac-and-cheese binge and wine indulgence.

She'd grown into a lovely, bright, funny and creative young woman. But then, he'd always found her lovely and funny, bright and creative. She, however, still entertained a ridiculously warped view of herself. It was time she exorcised her demons. To do that, she had to face the past. But he couldn't, wouldn't, send her into the lion's den alone.

"Sure. Why wouldn't I?" he asked.

"Did we or did we not attend the same high school?" Purple-hued lips turned down in a frown. He had to be crazy, but he still found those lips incredibly sexy.

And that was his problem. And the reason why women like Sara never lasted for very long. They simply couldn't measure up to Chloe.

"Those days are over," he told her, taking her hand in one of his. "Those girls have nothing on you, Chloe. They never did."

"They made my life hell!"

"They were cruel," he agreed in a tone more moderated than hers. "But they can't make your life hell now, unless you let them. Go back, face them and show them how far you've come since high school. You've got a lot to be proud of."

"Yeah, right." She pulled her hand free. "I'm twenty-eight years old, single, working part-time and living with an antisocial cat."

Simon waved hand. "All cats are antisocial. I told

you to get a dog if you wanted companionship from a pet."

She crossed her arms over her chest. "Must you lecture me now?"

"It seems so." He waited a beat before asking, "Are we going together? Or are you bringing a date?"

"A date." She frowned, apparently realizing what she'd said. Her hands fell to her sides. "How do you do that?"

"What?"

"Talk me into doing something that I absolutely don't want to do?"

"Years of practice," he replied.

"Okay. Since *you* think I need to do this, I will."

"Thanks."

"But only because I know you'll hold it over my head forever if I don't." She ended on a long-suffering sigh.

They both knew it was a cover and that she was grateful for the push.

"You'll thank me someday," he said.

"Or I'll blame you indefinitely for the years of therapy to follow."

"I'll take my chances." He shrugged and started in again on the mac and cheese. It was good, nearly as mouthwatering as Chloe's pout.

She was quiet while he finished off the last of the pasta, which was never a good sign. It meant she was thinking. More accurately, it meant she was plotting.

Sure enough, just as he blotted his mouth with a napkin, she said, "You don't mind if I go with someone else, do you? We can still sit together." Her expression brightened. "You can bring someone, too. We can double-date. That will be fun."

Simon ignored the twinge in his chest. He always felt it when Chloe talked about other men. In fact, one of the things Sara had flung in his face that evening during their breakup was what she termed his "unhealthy attachment to *that woman*."

Sara wasn't the first girlfriend to mention it. Nor, he suspected, would she be the last. He *was* attached to Chloe. How could he not be? They'd been close friends since before puberty and had seen one another through the good, the bad and the ugly of adolescence. They'd also been there for one another through high school and college and, now, the better part of their twenties. She was the only constant in his life.

"Well?" Chloe was frowning, and obviously waiting for his reply.

"Why would I mind?" Even to his ears, the words came out sounding hollow and defensive. He cleared his throat and shifted the conversation in a new direction. "I didn't know you were seeing someone."

"I'm not. But I plan to come up with the best-looking, most successful guy I can find, even if I have to pay him to attend with me."

Oh, yeah. Those wheels had been turning, all right.

"Chloe, really—"

She cut him off. "Yes, *really*. I want Natasha, Faith and Tamara to take one look at the hunk I'm with and drool an Olympic-size swimming pool."

"That'll show 'em," he drawled.

She nodded, oblivious to his sarcasm.

"Where do you plan to meet this Adonis?" God, please, tell him that she wasn't going to say the internet. He'd talked her out of cyberspace dating twice already.

Her smile was overly bright despite the fact that her teeth were tinted the same shade of purple as her lips. He knew he was in trouble even before she said, "I remember seeing a really attractive guy at your office the last time I stopped in to see you. Trevor something. I think you mentioned that he was a lawyer helping you with some of the details on your merger."

Uh-uh. No way was Simon going to set her up with Trevor, or, as the ladies at his company had dubbed him, "Mr. Hottie." He would be only too glad to have the merger behind him so he could cut the guy loose. Productivity among the women at Ford Technology Solutions came to a standstill whenever Trevor was around.

"No."

"Please." She clasped her hands in front of her. "Pretty please?"

Her smile, purple-tinted or not, was nearly Simon's undoing. God knew, as it was, he would do anything short of murder for the woman, and even that was negotiable. But, he managed to remain firm. "I'm sorry, Chloe, but no."

"All right." She nodded. "I understand. I mean, it's not as if I've *ever* done *you* a huge favor or anything."

It was all he could do to suppress a groan, because the list was long and, no doubt, Chloe planned to launch into it at any moment. Simon sighed and capitulated with the grace of a man being pushed to his death.

"Fine. All right."

"Thank you!"

"I make no promises."

"I know. I don't expect promises."

Which was exactly why Simon, to his everlasting regret, meant it when he said, "I'll see what I can do."

CHAPTER TWO

Cramming for Finals

THE FIRST THING Chloe did when she woke the next morning—after trying to rub off the worst of the wine stains from her lips—was to boot up her computer and make a list of all the things she needed to do before the reunion.

Six weeks.

That's all she had. It wasn't a lot of time…and she had a lot to do. Well, no problem. She was the queen of self-improvement. She'd had enough practice at it—she had an entire library of books in her apartment on the subject. More might be in order, she decided, thinking of a show she'd seen earlier in the week.

She prioritized her needs as she created the list.

First and foremost, she would whip herself into the best physical shape possible. Since this had been a regular New Year's resolution since her late teen years, she was familiar with the format. But rather than mere diet and exercise, the reunion timeframe called for a boot-camp mentality.

If she had to forgo ice cream, so be it. The same for her favorite bagels, pasta, comfort food and…food in general. She'd work out five—no, *seven*—days a week. And really work out. Not just don the outfits and sit in a smoothie bar, pretending to have just come from aerobics class. She'd even give in and accompany Simon on his morning runs in Central Park. He was always after her to join him.

Running. Hmm.

She tapped her bottom lip thoughtfully as she gazed at the computer screen. In parentheses next to the bit on exercise, she wrote: *Shape wear.*

She wasn't above a little cheating, as proved by the padded push-up bras she wore on a regular basis. As her mother was fond of saying, "What God has forgotten can be fixed up with cotton." Or synthetic filling, as the case may be. So why not reduce the appearance of a muffin top and jiggly bottom with a discreet foundation garment?

After all, realistically speaking, there was only so much one could do in six weeks. Chloe leaned back in the chair and folded her arms over her middle. She could feel the subtle roll just above the elastic waistband of her pajama bottoms. She straightened.

Shape wear, definitely.

Besides, celebrities and beauty-pageant contestants did it all the time. Heck, they did more than that to acquire their perky breasts and sag-free butts, so that everyone sighed with envy as they watched them strut the stage in Atlantic City or glide up the red carpet on premier night.

Which reminded Chloe. She needed a killer outfit to show off the killer curves she was planning to acquire through either sweat or spandex.

She typed, *Little black dress, emphasis on little.*

Smiling, she pictured it. Something sleek and cling-ing…okay, and with subtle ruching around the waist to distract from any flaws that remained despite the shape wear. Her legs, from mid-thigh down, would be the star of the show, which made sense since they remained her best attribute. Even when she gained weight, the extra pounds tended to collect at her hips and middle rather than on her thighs. And she had nice calves. They were shapely without looking like they belonged on a bicycle messenger. Put her in a pair of high heels and she could be a pinup…well, from mid-thigh down.

Heels. *Ooh.* She would have to practice walking in them. She'd never been very steady on anything higher than a couple of inches.

Stilettos, she typed.

That was what she had in mind to go with the sexy, stingy bit of black fabric that was going to pass for her dress.

Was black the best color for her? She studied her arms. Her skin was pale. Like most redheads, she had a tendency to freckle, which was why she stayed out of the sun whenever possible. Black brought out her most, well, *ghostly* hue. But if not black, then what?

Given her hair color, she generally steered clear of

reds and oranges. Pink was out, too. She didn't care for purple. It reminded her too much of eggplant, and she hated that vegetable on principle. She'd barfed up an entire plate-worth of eggplant parmesan in the cafeteria her freshman year, earning her the unfortunate nickname Yack-Attack.

Green would do in a pinch, though paired with her hair it made her feel a little too much like a pumpkin. As for blue...uh-uh.

She hated blue.

Any and all shades, but especially baby blue for reasons far more emotional than aesthetic. She'd worn a formal dress that color to her senior prom. Her mother had talked her into it, claiming it flattered her figure, when in fact the full skirt made it appear she was trying to smuggle someone into the dance.

She could still recall how humiliated she'd felt when Natasha and company had cornered her on the dance floor and pulled up her skirt to see if she was alone.

She'd been alone and wearing a pair of briefs the likes of which would have been right at home on her Nana.

Chloe shuddered now. Black it was. With thong panties. Under shape wear.

She'd compensate for her pale complexion with a salon-bought tan. Not the sort that involved lying on a bed under UV rays. That would only bring out her freckles, and Chloe hated her freckles, even if Simon had once commented that he found them adorable. She didn't believe him. After all, none of the women he'd ever dated had freckles. If he liked them as much as he claimed, the women in his life should have resembled leopards.

Chloe decided to go with a spray-on tan. Her sister had gotten such a treatment before her wedding the year before. Of course, Frannie was a brunette and her skin wasn't nearly as pale as Chloe's, but Frannie had come away with a nice, healthy glow. She was always after Chloe to try it.

The phone rang as she shot her sister an email asking for the name of her salon.

"Hello?"

"Good morning," Simon replied. "I'm going for coffee at the Filigree Café. Want to meet me there? I'll spring for the bagels."

The Filigree served some of the best coffee and homemade baked goods in Lower Manhattan. She and Simon met there on weekend mornings when neither of them had other plans. That was often the case for Chloe. Not so much lately for Simon, but then his dating status had changed.

Once again, she ignored jubilation, as well as the way her mouth watered at the mere thought of a toasted onion bagel with herbed cream cheese.

"Sorry. No bagels for me. I'm on a diet," she informed him.

"Since when?"

"Since when not?" she replied. "I'm always on a diet." Which, sadly enough, was all too true.

A wise man, Simon didn't point out that this had

never stopped her from joining him for a bagel in the past. Instead, he asked, "Is this about the reunion?"

"No."

They both knew she was lying.

"Come on, Chloe. Join me. What's the fun in eating alone?"

"Simon…"

"We'll go for a walk afterward," he promised. "A long, brisk one. It's a great morning for it. No humidity and the temperatures aren't supposed to reach into the eighties until this afternoon."

She pulled at her curly hair, and relented. "Okay. But I'm not having a bagel."

"Agreed. And I won't let you have so much as a bite of mine."

"You're humoring me," she accused.

"I'm dead serious. Meet you there in half an hour?"

The old Chloe would have said yes. The brand-new and improved Chloe knew that half an hour would barely give her enough time to brush her teeth and hair and throw on whatever clean clothes she could find hiding amid the heaps of laundry on her bedroom floor.

"Make it an hour. I'm not even dressed or any-thing."

"An hour?" Simon sounded surprised and no wonder given their long history as friends. "You *really* need an hour to get dressed?"

"I'm turning over a new leaf. I want to actually wear makeup and look presentable when I appear in public. Even if it's just with you," she replied drily.

"Okay, an hour." Rather than sounding irritated, he almost sounded intrigued. "I'll get our usual corner table. See you then."

Simon was on his third cup of coffee when Chloe finally arrived at the cafe. It was hard to be angry with her given the way she looked. She didn't primp often, but when she did... Wow! He sucked in a breath and reached for his cup, failing in his determination not to admire the way her jeans hugged her hips or the way the vee of her shirt offered the slightest hint of cleavage.

She thought she needed to lose weight. When she dressed like this, he thought he'd lose his mind.

She was wearing makeup, not a lot, but enough to enhance her long lashes and bring out the cool green in her eyes. And her hair. No quick and easy ponytail intended to disguise its lovely and natural waves. No. She'd left it down in a riot of curls that framed her face and fell past her shoulders.

It was wrong of him, Simon knew, but he almost wished she'd shown up in baggy sweats and a T-shirt, no makeup and that dreadful, all-purpose ponytail. Then, at least, he wouldn't feel so damned interested and, well, needy.

He chanced a glance around and regretted it. Sure enough, several of the other male patrons were checking her out. He didn't like their interested expressions. Not one damn bit. Before he could stop himself, he pushed to his feet. The legs of his chair scraped noisily over the tiled floor. They seemed to scream, "Back off! She's mine."

The attention was on him now. All of the attention, including Chloe's. Her face lit up when she spied him and a pair of full lips pulled into a smile that was sexy without trying to be. How was it possible, he wondered for the millionth time, that a woman as naturally lovely as she was had self-esteem issues?

He shot a smug look at each of the guys who'd been ogling her, and took his time kissing her cheek when she reached the table.

"Sorry I'm late," she said as she slid onto the chair opposite his.

Simon shrugged. "It was worth the wait. Look at you. The hair, the makeup, the cleav…clean clothes," he amended hastily, forcing his gaze back up to her face.

She grinned. "So, you like?"

"Of course I do. So do half the guys in here, judging from the way they were watching you."

"Yeah?" Her face brightened and she glanced around. "Which ones?"

He unclenched his teeth and forced out a laugh. "Forget it. I'm not going to stroke your ego any more than I already have."

"Spoilsport," she replied.

Her expression said she didn't believe him. He considered relenting. He should throw her a bone—or a whole roomful of them. But their waitress arrived then. She was a heavyset woman named Helga with a thick accent of Eastern European origin. The woman had been waiting on them for half a decade. Even so, she eyed Chloe curiously before asking, "Your usual today?"

Chloe's usual was a double mocha latte and toasted onion bagel slathered with enough melted butter and cream cheese that it should have come with an American Heart Association warning.

"Not today. I'll have coffee, black. Make it decaf."

"And to eat?"

"Nothing."

Helga's bushy eyebrows shot up at that. "You no want something to eat?"

"No. Nothing."

"You feel okay?"

"Fine. I'm on a diet," she confessed.

"Chloe's always on a diet," Simon inserted.

Helga made a rude sound. "Girls nowadays, they all want to be so skinny. Too skinny, I think. A stiff breeze, they blow over." She motioned with her notepad, before turning to Simon. "So, you think she need to lose weight?"

"No. Not a pound." She was perfect in his book. Always had been.

"See." Helga nodded vigorously. To Chloe, she said, "I bring you onion bagel just how you like."

Chloe's expression turned panicked, but before she could refuse, Simon said casually, "You don't have to eat all of it. Or any of it, Chloe. Consider it a test of your willpower."

"Fine." She straightened in her seat and squared her shoulders, making the display of her cleavage even harder for Simon to ignore. It was like a magnet, drawing his gaze.

"What will you have?" Helga asked.

Because he knew what he really wanted was off-limits, he wrapped both hands around his cup of coffee and forced his gaze to the stocky waitress. "Two slices of whole wheat toast and a fruit cup."

Helga pursed her lips in distaste as she jotted down his order. "Fruit cup," she muttered as she walked away. "Is whole world on diet?"

"I think we've ruined her day," Chloe said.

"We'll leave a big tip," Simon replied.

They always did, regardless of the amount they spent. The way Simon saw it, she deserved the tip. He and Chloe took up one of Helga's prime tables for at least a couple of hours on a Saturday without running up a sizable tab.

Chloe fussed with her hair, pulling it back behind her head. No doubt if she had a rubber band at her disposal, it would wind up in a ponytail.

"I like your hair down," he said.

On a sigh, she let it drop. "It's not even humid out and my hair is already going nuts. You wouldn't know I'd used this expensive new antifrizz stuff. I want my money back."

"I don't know. I think it looks nice. I like it when you leave it curly."

"I don't mind curly, but it's heading toward steel wool. For the reunion, I'm thinking of having it professionally straightened."

Don't! He wanted to shout. But he doubted she would follow his advice. So, instead he lifted his shoulders. "Whatever you think best."

Helga was back with Chloe's coffee and refilled Simon's cup.

"I'm considering dying it a different color, too." She smiled at their waitress. "What do you think? Should I attempt blond?"

Helga issued that rude sound again. Before stalking away, she said, "Keep what God gave you."

To Simon, Chloe said, "I think God could have been a little more generous in certain areas and, well, spread the wealth in others, if you know what I mean."

"You wouldn't look good as a blonde."

She frowned. "I thought you liked blondes? The last three women you dated all looked like they just stepped out of the California sun."

True enough, he realized, although it hadn't been intentional. They'd been available and interested and, well, since he'd been available… He didn't like how that made it seem, though he'd never pretended to have deep feelings for any of them. Nor had he made any promises.

He wasn't his father…a man who made promises, vows even, with the ease of a politician, only to break them, as wives one through five could attest.

"Simon?" Chloe was staring at him.

He pulled himself back to the present. "Your coloring is all wrong for blond hair. You're too fair."

"That can be changed, too."

He didn't like the glint in her eye. "Please tell me you're not thinking about tanning again. Remember what happened before senior pictures."

She shuddered, making him sorry to have brought it up. She'd gotten the bright idea to lie under the heat lamp her grandmother kept to warm new litters of Persian kittens, and had wound up burned to the point of blistering on her cheeks and the bridge of her nose.

"Not tanning per se," she murmured, but before he could question her further, she asked, "Will you be going for your usual run tomorrow morning?"

He frowned at the change in subject. "Why?"

"I was thinking of joining you."

He couldn't help it. His brows shot up. "Are you going to run?"

She wrinkled her nose, a sign she was insulted. "You don't need to look so shocked. Haven't you pestered me since Nana's heart attack to do more cardio conditioning?"

He had indeed, worried that Chloe's addiction to comfort food might take her down the same hardened-arteries path as her seventy-four-year-old grandmother. But he knew Chloe's sudden decision to listen had less to do with his persuasive abilities than their upcoming class reunion. He almost called her on it. But the truth was, he liked the idea of having company during the runs he took four mornings a week.

"We can meet in the park at eight," he said after a moment.

"Great."

Her smile lasted until Helga arrived with their food. The cream-cheese-laden bagel beckoned. The way she swallowed before sucking in her bottom lip told him as much. Whoever had been manning the knife in the kitchen had been generous with the topping.

"Anything else?" Helga asked, her meaty hands resting on a pair of what Simon remembered a great-aunt referring to as good child-bearing hips.

No way he was going to point out that his so-called fresh fruit cup looked suspiciously like the syrup-drenched cocktail variety that came in a can.

"No. We're good."

More than half of the bagel remained when Helga brought the check. Chloe considered that a victory of the highest order. She'd actually sat on her hands to keep from finishing it off. Whatever it took, she was willing to do it. She had her eye on the prize.

"You promised me a walk," she reminded Simon.

"So I did. And I never renege on my promises," he replied. He always looked surprisingly serious when he made comments such as that, and now was no exception. "Do you have a destination in mind?"

"How about that little bookstore just off Fifth? We haven't been there in a while."

It was one of the few independent shops of its kind left in the city. And while Chloe had nothing against the big stores that held every title and obscure periodical under the sun and housed trendy cafes where patrons could get a good, if pricey, cup of coffee and read their

purchases, she was especially fond of this place. It was
the clear underdog. Chloe knew how that felt.

"Sure."

CHAPTER THREE

The girl most likely to obsess…

IT TOOK FORTY-FIVE minutes to get to Bendle's Books, but only because Chloe stopped to do a little window shopping along the way.

"What do you think of that dress?" she asked, pointing to a clingy black number draping a mannequin that was wand-thin and eerily faceless. She turned to Simon expectantly, only to find him frowning.

"On you?"

"No. On the mannequin. I'll be sending it to the reunion in my place," she snapped, even though she was a little more wounded than irritated by his dubious tone. It didn't help that the dress undoubtedly did look better on the faceless and tummyless dummy.

He rubbed a hand over the back of his neck. "It's kind of…revealing."

"And you think I've got a little too much to reveal at this point, is that it?"

"No, Chloe—"

"I'll be thinner by then. The reunion is six weeks

away. If I lose two—okay, more like three—pounds a week, I'll be able to pull off that dress." Especially if she threw in regular toning workouts and shape wear. She mentioned the exercise to Simon, but not undergarments, adding, "You're always after me to get healthy."

"I want you to eat more balanced meals and exercise more often. I don't think you need to lose weight, at least not by going on some kooky crash diet."

She brushed off his reply and started walking. "It's not kooky."

He fell in step beside her. "Excuse me?"

"I'm not going on a kooky diet. I plan to eat sensibly, just smaller portions, and cut out comfort food entirely."

"Entirely?" Again the dubious tone.

"Last night was it. No more mac and cheese for me and no more ice cream."

"And bagels? What about those?"

"Today was an exception. What was I to do? Helga plopped that thing in front of me. I didn't eat it all," she reminded him.

"You showed admirable restraint."

"I thought so, too."

But her restraint took another beating when they passed a pizzeria and the smell of melted mozzarella cheese and spicy Italian sausage wafted out the door along with a satisfied-looking customer. She swallowed, not out of despair, but because her mouth had actually started to water. Why couldn't broccoli smell like that?

"Maybe at the bookstore I'll be able to find a cookbook

that includes some of my old favorites, just with a lot less fat and fewer calories and carbohydrates."

It was a tall order, to be sure. But hope sprang eternal.

"You could just log on to the internet, you know. A couple of keystrokes and thousands of recipes would be at your disposal."

He would know, tech geek that he was. Chloe shook her head. "I like books. I like holding them in my hands and flipping through the pages. Besides, when I download free recipes from the internet, I don't get to see Millicent."

Millicent Cox owned Bendle's. Although her daughter was largely in charge of the quaint little store these days, Millicent was a fixture behind the counter on weekend mornings.

"She's a character." He said it with fondness, rather than with the snarkiness that Chloe's last boyfriend had injected into the simple statement.

Millicent was pushing eighty and had as many stories to tell as she had obscure books to sell. Between her eclectic title selection, which included some rare editions that appealed to collectors, and a colorful past that allegedly included a turn as CIA mole, visiting her shop was always an adventure.

The older woman greeted them with a shaky wave when they entered to the jangle of cowbells.

"I haven't seen either of you in here in a while."

"Worried about us?" Simon asked on a smile.

"Not in the least." She cackled at his fallen expression,

before admitting, "Okay, maybe a little. You get to be my age and your social calendar tends to include a lot of funerals. It's easy to think the worst when you haven't heard from someone in a while."

Chloe forced a smile. Millicent didn't seem to notice.

"So, what have you kids been doing to keep yourselves busy?" the older woman asked.

"The usual," Simon replied on a shrug.

"That means he's working too many hours," Chloe clarified.

"And you?" Millicent asked.

"Not enough."

"Still part-time, hmm?"

Chloe nodded. She'd been part-time at the graphic-design company where she'd been working for the past three years, which meant she had to supplement her income by doing freelance work. It was far from ideal, but her boss kept assuring her she would become full-time soon.

"What about your love lives?" Millicent asked shamelessly. "Anything of interest to report in that area? And be generous with the details. I'm an old woman who spends all of her evenings alone. Vicarious living is the only thing I'm capable of at this point in my life."

"Sorry." Chloe shrugged. "I'm still dateless."

"Still? Heavens, it's been months," Millicent remarked, sounding horrified.

The older woman's tone, so similar to that of Chloe's mother's and the happily married Frannie, had her blurting out, "Well, Simon got dumped yesterday."

"I didn't get dumped." To Millicent, he said, "My girlfriend and I reached a mutual decision not to continue our relationship."

The older woman waved one thin, blue-veined hand in his direction. "It's the same thing, my dear."

When Chloe giggled, Simon shot her a black look.

Millicent was saying, "Workaholics make lousy mates, Simon. I found that out the hard way with husbands one through four."

He blinked in surprise. "You were married four times?"

"Five. Only the first four were workaholics. Unfortunately, I was a slow learner." She winked from behind a pair of thick bifocal lenses. "What can I say? I was a sucker for a pair of broad shoulders and a firm behind."

Chloe was past the point of being shocked by Millicent's unexpected bluntness. So was Simon.

"I'm not a workaholic," he protested.

Chloe disagreed silently. He spent too many hours at the office. It wasn't all the fault of the upcoming acquisition. He'd come far enough that he could give others in his employ more of the responsibility.

She couldn't help noticing that he also had a pair of broad shoulders and a rather fine backside.

He was saying, "As the head of the company I have a lot of responsibility, especially right now. There's a lot going on that requires my attention."

"Delegate, young man. Delegate."

Exactly, Chloe wanted to shout.

"The relationship wasn't going anywhere," he muttered. "It pretty much had run its course."

"Regardless, life is too short. It passes you by quickly. Believe me. Before you know it, you'll be worrying about hip fractures, misplacing your dentures and dozing off during the evening news." A sigh rattled out. But then Millicent offered a crafty smile. "Besides, you'll never turn the head of the girl of your dreams if you keep long hours at the office and spend your free time with women who are more interested in your title and looks than what's behind both."

Chloe felt her skin prickle.

Simon leaned one of his broad shoulders against the cash register. "You know, if you'd agree to marry me, Millicent, I'd agree to work reasonable hours, not to mention forsake all others."

"I'd be tempted to take you up on that, but I think all three of us would be disappointed." Her gaze shifted to Chloe and she smiled. "Don't you, Chloe?"

Chloe shook her head. No matter how many times they'd tried to tell Millicent that they weren't anything more than friends, the older woman kept insisting and insinuating they were or someday would become something more.

Silly, Chloe thought.

Surely, if Simon were interested in her as anything more than a pal, he would have made it clear by now. Not that she wanted him to. Or that she was interested back, despite those odd tingles she sometimes got when they were together. No. They were friends. Pals. Buds. BFFs.

She was as surprised as Millicent and Simon when a wistful sigh escaped.

Chloe cleared her throat. "I'm looking for a cookbook."

"Well, you know where to find them, my dear. The shelf by the window has some vintage ones."

"She wants one with low-carb, low-calorie recipes," he said, his bias obvious.

Millicent's mouth puckered in distaste. "The trendy ones are on the next shelf over."

Simon went with Chloe and helped her leaf through the limited selection. She settled on one that boasted nutritious meals in thirty-minutes or less. The pictures looked appetizing, the recipes didn't appear too difficult and the ingredients weren't something she'd have to hit specialty stores to find. Portion control would be the key, though. She'd learned that with the first batch of low-fat cookies she bought. Low-fat or not, it turned out that when a person ate the entire box in one sitting, the calories still wound up going straight to her hips.

"All set?" he asked.

"Just one more thing." She started for the back of the store and a section in which she had spent way too much time over the years.

"What are you doing in the self-help aisle?"

"Looking for, well, a way to help myself," she quipped.

"What book are the talk-show gurus pushing this week?" he asked in a weary tone.

"They aren't pushing anything."

One of Simon's eyebrows rose.

"Okay, so one of the guests on a show I caught last week mentioned a book that sounded sort of interesting."

"I'm almost afraid to ask, what's the title?"

She had to clear her throat before the words *The Best You, Ever* made it past her lips. She doubted he would care that the subtitle was "From the Inside Out." She couldn't be sure, but she thought she heard him swear. And his expression made his disdain plain.

"You're already the best you that you can be, Chloe."

Her heart did a funny somersault at his assessment, as off base as she knew it to be. She was a far cry from the person she wanted to be, especially physically, which was her main objective now with the reunion fast approaching.

"You're just saying that because you're my friend." *Pal. Bud. BFF.*

He folded his arms across his chest. "And if I wasn't your friend? Would you believe me then?"

"Simon," she began patiently.

But his tone was impatient and surprisingly irritated. "Answer me. What will it take for you to finally accept that you don't need improvement? If that last loser you dated had said so, would you have believed him?"

Whoa, whoa! Her mouth went slack.

Loser? That was cold. Okay, so she'd called Greg a loser, too, not to mention a couple dozen other choice names in the weeks following their breakup. But Simon hadn't seen the need to malign Greg's character then, other than to say the guy wasn't good enough for her. She'd been well into a pint of mint chocolate chip ice cream at the time. Simon had taken away her spoon, made her dress in something other than sweats and had taken her out to a fancy restaurant for dinner.

"This is how you deserve to be treated," he'd said at the end of the evening.

It dawned on Chloe then. Simon had never maligned the character of any of the guys she'd dated. Never... until just now.

He was joking. He had to be.

She waited for humor to leak into his expression, for the corners of his mouth to quirk in a well-remembered smile. But a full minute ticked past and Simon remained stoic, his countenance as unyielding as that of a tombstone.

"What do you want me to say?" she asked at last.

"I want you to say that you believe me when I tell you that you look fine just as you are."

"I do believe you," she assured him.

Well, sort of. Mostly. But he was her friend, her pal, her bud and BFF. People with those titles were known to lie. Which was why on days when Chloe was feeling particularly insecure about her body, she peppered Simon with questions such as, "Do these pants make my butt look big?"

No woman in her right mind asked that question of someone they thought might actually tell them the truth. Besides, the man regularly dated lingerie models.

He squinted sideways at her. "You do?"

She nodded to add emphasis. "Of course, I do." All the while, she was thinking, he had to be lying.

The rigid set of his shoulders relaxed fractionally. Simon really did have nice shoulders and the cotton pullover he was wearing did them justice. It was just snug enough to show off some of the definition that his regular workouts had created.

"Mmm."

His brows tugged together. "Chloe?"

Good God! What was she thinking? Bad, bad Chloe.

"Hmm. I said, hmm. You know, it's a kind of humming sound that can be taken for, um, well, an affirmation." Or the prelude to an orgasm. Though she was barely managing to tread water, she decided to dive in again. "As in, I believe you when you say that I look fine."

He exhaled and the beginning of a smile lit his face. "So, we can go now?" he asked.

"Yes. Right after I pick up that book."

Just that fast, he was frowning again. "But you just said that you believe me."

"And I do. I know I look fine." And, gee, could there be a more tepid word in the English language to describe one's looks? *Fine* made *plain* seem almost like a compliment by comparison. "For the reunion, I want to look spectacular."

She rolled the *R* at the end to give the word its due. His eyes pinched closed for a moment. When he spoke, his words came out clipped.

"You already do."

"No, Simon. You yourself just said I look *fine. Fine* is a far cry from spectacula*rrrrrr.*"

When she turned to browse the books, he exhaled sharply and she heard something extra slip out. This was no petty potty oath like the last time she'd thought she'd heard him cut loose. Nope, this was the mother of all bad words—the very one for which his own mom had washed out his mouth with a ghastly lavender-scented bar of soap when they were in fifth grade.

She turned back. "Did you just…swear?"

"Why would I swear? What reason, Chloe McDaniels, would I possibly have to swear?"

She knew a trap when she heard one. God knew, her mother had laid enough of them during her teen years.

"Simon?" She eyed him in confusion, not at all sure why he was suddenly so mad.

He presented her with his profile and the silence stretched. Just as it was becoming awkward, he plucked a book from the shelf and held it out to her. "*The Best You, Ever.* Knock yourself out."

His smile was forced, but she didn't comment on it. In truth, she wasn't sure what to say. Millicent was still perched on her high stool behind the counter.

"What's this?" the older woman asked as she rang up the sale. "Another self-help book? What did I tell you when you purchased the last one?"

"You, too?"

Millicent frowned.

"Chloe needs more improvement," Simon said. "She

wants to be spectacular*rrrrr* for our ten-year high school reunion."

Okay, the rolled *R* just sounded ridiculous when he did it.

"A class reunion, hmm?" Millicent's smile was both sad and knowing. "I've gone to every one and can tell you I don't know why I bother."

"Why do you say that?" Chloe asked.

"I don't care about any of those people, well, except for the friends I had, and I keep in touch with those on my own. The ones who are still living, anyway."

Simon grunted.

"The others," Millicent was saying. "They're still keeping score."

Simon was nodding, feeling validated, no doubt.

Don't ask. Don't ask. Don't ask. Chloe told herself. Out of her mouth came the words, "What do you mean?"

"Well, at the tenth, it was about being married. Not many of us were career women back then. Even if we went on to college, the goal was an *M-R-S* degree. I'd already walked down the aisle twice." Her lips pinched into a frown. "Didn't score me any points, believe me.

"At the twentieth, the gossip was over who was divorced or having an affair." Millicent cleared her throat. "My ears burned all night.

"At the twenty-fifth, the talk was all about what colleges our children had been accepted to or were attending, or who they were marrying. At the thirtieth, tongues were wagging over who still looked the best."

"It took till the thirtieth for that?" Chloe asked before she could think better of it.

"Actually, that was a recurring theme throughout my reunions, much as it was back in high school."

"Some things never change," Simon muttered.

"Let me guess," Millicent said. "There were some girls who made your life miserable and maybe a boy or two who failed to glance your way."

"Right on the girls, wrong on the boys." Chloe shrugged. "I didn't find any of them to be all that interesting," she admitted. "They were so boring and immature. Well, except for Simon."

"Ah. So, who did you go to parties and school dances with?"

"Simon, of course."

Millicent's smile turned canny. Chloe didn't trust it. Before the older woman could say anything, she thrust her charge card into Millicent's hand.

"Put it on this, okay?"

"Delaying the inevitable?"

Millicent's question, accompanied as it was by a sly wink in Simon's direction, left Chloe wondering if she was talking about paying the bill or something else.

CHAPTER FOUR

Prettiest Smile

"WOULD YOU BRING Chloe and me some coffee?" Simon said to his secretary just before she exited his office.

It was a Monday morning, his schedule had been power-packed with back-to-back meetings, but when Carla had buzzed a moment earlier to tell him Chloe was in the reception area wondering if he could spare a moment, he'd had no problem clearing out his office and his schedule.

He needed a break, a few minutes away from the buttoned-up stiffs, many of whom were far older than he was, and who either didn't get his offbeat sense of humor or, worse, pretended that they did and laughed out of obligation.

Chloe's impromptu visit offered him the perfect excuse to end one meeting early and delay by half an hour the next one.

At least, that's what he told himself, ignoring the little pop of excitement he always experienced when she sought his company out of the blue.

"No coffee for me, thanks," she said.

"Would you prefer tea?" Carla asked.

Chloe shook her head. "They both stain my teeth."

Last week, Chloe had shown up for one of their morning runs with dazzlingly white teeth. Her smile looked fantastic—as far as he was concerned, it always had been one of her best features—but now in addition to all of the other don'ts on her long list of ingestibles, she'd added beverages that could dim her newly brightened pearly whites.

"I suppose red wine is off your list, too," he said once they were alone.

"I switched to chardonnay," she admitted. "Which pairs better with salads anyway."

He squinted at her blinding smile.

Salads were pretty much all that she was eating these days, despite his regular lectures on the importance of protein and complex carbohydrates.

"The reunion can't come soon enough," he said on a sigh.

"It can for me. I have a lot left to do."

From his vantage point, she'd already made a lot of progress. She'd dropped a couple of pounds and was definitely taking more care with her appearance. Case in point, the outfit she had on today—a flattering printed blouse and pencil skirt paired with rounded-toe flats that had a flirty little bow stretching over the vamp. Her frumpy, figure-hiding days apparently were over. She shifted in her seat, tugging at the hem of her skirt. Standing, the garment fell just above her knees. Sitting, it pulled to midthigh and posed way too much of a distraction, which was why he regretted that he'd moved to the sitting area in his office rather than staying at his desk. With a wide expanse of polished cherry between them, he wouldn't have been able to see her gorgeous legs.

"I'm thinking of having the gap between my front teeth fixed. That's why I came by today. I wanted to get your opinion."

His gaze snapped from her thighs to her mouth. She offered a toothy smile. Even so, he was sure he'd heard her wrong. "What?"

"I asked the dentist about it when I was in for the whitening treatment," she said. "They got back to me today on costs and…and, well, payment plans. My insurance won't pick up anything, since it's considered cosmetic. Same for the whitening, but that cost considerably less."

"You're getting braces?"

"Don't be silly." Her lips pursed in exasperation. It was an expression he knew well and one he was perversely fond of. For that matter, he even found it a turn-on, which was not exactly what he needed at the moment.

She was saying, "It would take months for my smile to be corrected with traditional braces. The dentist suggested porcelain veneers. I may be able to get away with only a couple, and truthfully, even that is more than I can afford. But that would fix the gap, at least. With, say, half a dozen more, the dentist says I could have a Hollywood smile."

Just what she felt she needed, apparently. But Simon honed in on one word and snorted. "Corrected? There's nothing wrong with your smile."

She did the exasperated lip purse again before opening her mouth and pointing. "I can spit a watermelon seed through this gap."

"Stop exaggerating. A sunflower seed at most. But even if you could spit a watermelon seed, so what? Lauren Hutton has a much bigger gap between her front teeth and she was a successful model."

"I'm no Lauren Hutton."

"You're absolutely right on that score. You're way better looking."

"That's so sweet," she said. But he knew her too well. The words were code for, "Yeah, right."

So, he tried again. "Why would you want to look like everyone else? Your differences are what make you who you are. Hell, they're what make you so damned hot."

His face grew warm afterward. He imagined his cheeks were turning a blotchy shade of red as they always did when he was embarrassed. It was an inherited trait passed down from his father, yet another thing to hold against the old man.

"You think I'm hot?" Of course he would have Chloe's full attention now.

Simon shifted in his seat and affected a considering pose that allowed him to obscure the lower half of his face behind one hand. Over the years, he had called her pretty and attractive and a host of other complimentary adjectives, mostly in answer to her prodding question, "How do I look?"

After the "fine" debacle at the bookstore, he'd even added *spectacular* to his repertoire. But *hot?* Never. Somehow that description seemed more personal. It seemed *too* personal. It crossed the invisible line in their relationship that kept them just friends.

Lovers found one another hot. Friends didn't, or at least they shouldn't.

He cleared his throat. "I've overheard guys talking."

"What guys?"

His plan to redirect her interest had worked. That was the good news. But now he was at a loss. He couldn't exactly name names, although that was precisely what she was expecting.

"I...um..."

"Oh, my God! I know!" She clapped a hand over her mouth. A pair of rounded eyes studied him.

She's figured it out. Simon wasn't sure whether to be relieved or sick. *She knows I'm not only lying to her right now about other guys, but that I've secretly had a thing for her for years. She's...*

"It's Trevor!"

Clueless.

"Trevor?"

"He's the guy you overheard saying I'm hot."

"Chloe—"

"Oh, my God!" She slapped the hand over her mouth a second time. Simon wanted to slap his forehead.

"He hasn't said hot in so many words."

In fact, Chloe's name had never come up in any of their conversations, and why would it? Despite her recent nagging of Simon to introduce her and the lawyer who was helping handle the acquisition of a smaller competitor, he hadn't.

Trevor was a nice enough guy. He played a decent game of one-on-one basketball and could talk trash with the best of them. And he was good at his job. Top-notch, in fact. He'd come on the highest recommendation and with a boatload of experience and credentials, including a Harvard law degree and five years as a junior partner at one of Manhattan's biggest firms. But he was a player.

Simon had figured that out during their first lunch together, when the guy had flirted shamelessly with their waitress, gotten the young woman's telephone number, even though he'd told Simon he had a date that evening. Since then, he'd seen the guy leaving the building with half a dozen other women, each one more lovely than the last.

Player. Definitely.

No way was Simon going to introduce someone like him to a woman as sweet and trusting and terminally romantic as Chloe.

"But are you saying he's interested in me?"

"Chloe, he's interested in everything with two legs and a pair of breasts," Simon said in exasperation.

"You're just being overprotective."

Forget terminally romantic, the woman was terminally dense when it came to men who were all wrong for her.

"So, when are you going to introduce us?"

When hell freezes over. But Simon said, "He's been out of the office a lot lately. Off in a former Soviet country, doing some work for another client. I'm not sure when he'll be back. It could be weeks."

Carla came to the door then. His secretary had foul timing. "Trevor is here."

Simon worked up a smile. "Gee. Back from Uzbekistan already?"

Carla frowned in confusion, but didn't challenge him. Rather, she said, "Apparently he didn't get the email I sent about delaying the next meeting." She glanced in Chloe's direction. "Will you be much longer?"

"No."

"Actually, we're finished." Of course, Chloe would say that. Of course she would hop up with a smile on her face, all talk of veneers forgotten, when the man entered the office.

"Sorry," Trevor said when he spied Chloe. "I didn't realize I was interrupting something personal."

"Personal? No way." This from Chloe, whose whitened teeth were blinding now. "I just dropped in to chat with Simon. He and I are old friends." Was it his imagination, or did she place way too much emphasis on the words *old friends?* "I'm Chloe McDaniels."

She stuck out her hand, which Trevor shook, a smile

spreading across his face like an oil spill. "I'm Trevor Conrad. It's nice to meet you."

"Likewise. I'm sure I'll see you around."

"A man can hope."

Simon felt his blood pressure spike. His face probably was turning blotchy again, this time from irritation rather than embarrassment. Chloe's expression was rhapsodic. This was exactly what he didn't want to happen.

"I'll walk you to the elevator," he told her as he grabbed her arm just above the elbow. "Be back in a minute, Trevor. Have Carla get you a cup of coffee."

Wouldn't it just figure that the man said, "No, thanks. I'm cutting back on coffee. It stains my teeth."

In the hall, Chloe sighed. "Can you believe that? We have something in common."

Simon thought his head would explode. Before he could get a handle on either his emotions or his tone, he snapped, "You can't really be interested in him."

"I don't want to marry him and bear his children, but sure, I'm interested. A nun would be interested."

His heart sank, weighted down with an emotion he refused to admit might be jealousy let alone something more damning. "He's a player, Chloe."

"I know that."

"You do?"

"I'm not a complete idiot, Simon. But player or not, the girls at the reunion would eat their hearts out if I showed up with him."

His blood pressure dipped a little, although not nearly enough. "So, your intention is just to use him?"

"Don't worry." She patted Simon's cheek. "I promise I won't hurt him. I'll leave him heart-whole and capable of performing his job here for you."

Simon snagged the hand that had just patted his face and pressed it tight against his heart. "I'm not worried about Trevor. He can take care of himself. I'm worried about you. I don't want to see you hurt. By him. By anyone."

She blinked, swallowed. "You're serious."

"Never more so."

He leaned forward, intending to kiss her cheek, but his mouth came to rest against hers. He'd kissed her before, hundreds of times. On the cheek. On the forehead. He'd even kissed the back of her hand in a gallant gesture that had been completely wasted on her since she was still loopy from laughing gas after having her wisdom teeth pulled. But he'd been careful not to kiss her on the lips. For this very reason. They were way too tempting.

The moment lengthened.

The dinging from the elevator just before its doors opened was what snapped him back to his senses. He pulled away, but slowly. And he could have sworn Chloe leaned after him before righting herself and offering up an uncertain smile that showed that sexy little gap.

"Don't change that," he said softly. His raised one hand and cupped the side of her face. "Don't change anything."

* * *

Don't change anything.

Simon's words echoed in Chloe's head long after they parted ways. True, he'd said those words or ones with a similar meaning dozens of times, especially recently. But hearing them had never had quite the effect they'd had on her today. He'd sounded so adamant and sincere. He'd looked so…well, gorgeous. And when he'd kissed her…

It was just a kiss, she reminded herself. A friendly peck that she was blowing out of proportion. Except, friendly pecks were usually on the cheek and the giver didn't linger and pull back slowly, almost as if in regret. Nor did the receiver of such a peck lean forward, disappointed to find the contact ending and wishing, foolishly, that it could last and turn into something more.

"I'm making too much of it," she said aloud. "He didn't mean anything by it."

The suit-clad man seated across the aisle from her on the subway train didn't so much as bat an eye. This was New York, after all. People here were used to other passengers having conversations with themselves.

But Chloe still felt like an idiot. And not only because she had an audience. This was Simon she was thinking about.

Back at her apartment, she spent the better part of the afternoon pacing and fretting even though she had some freelance work to do. She couldn't concentrate. She couldn't think. Finally, she couldn't stand it. Just after six o'clock, she dialed Simon's number.

"It's me. Chloe," she added needlessly after he

answered. He had caller identification on his telephone. And it wasn't as if her voice had changed over the past several hours, even if it seemed something had.

"Hi. This is a surprise."

"Why is it a surprise? I call you all the time. Well, not all the time, but often. And you call me." Though he hadn't tonight, and, frankly, she'd expected him to. She'd expected some sort of explanation.

"I meant, a *pleasant* surprise."

Her pulse perked up a little, which she both anticipated and found ridiculous. "I hope I didn't throw your schedule off by stopping by your office earlier."

"Believe me, I welcomed the excuse to spend a few minutes not looking over documents."

"Oh. Good. And I appreciate your advice on the veneers."

"Does that mean you're going to follow it?"

"I'm still thinking."

He made a humming noise. "So, is that the only reason you called?"

"No." Her heart knocked out a couple of extra beats. "I was just wondering…" *Why did you kiss me like that? Why did you stop? Did you feel all woozy and confused afterward, too?* Since she couldn't bring herself to ask any of those questions, she finished with "—how your day went. The rest of it. You know, after the elevator when, um, when I left."

"The rest of my day." He sighed heavily. "In a word, *lousy.*"

"I'm sorry to hear that." And she meant it, even if misery did love company.

"Want to know why?" he asked. It was issued like a dare.

Chloe swallowed and in a voice barely above a whisper asked, "That kiss?"

"I didn't hear you."

She chickened out. "I said, merger giving you fits?"

"Yeah. The damned merger." His tone turned wry. "Among other things."

"Like who? Er, I mean, what?" She wasn't being nosy. They often traded bad-day stories. She reminded him, "I'm a good sounding board. You can tell me anything."

"I know I can." But she got the distinct impression that he was holding out on her now, even though he said, "You had it right the first time. It's more like who."

Chloe knew that tone. "A woman?"

"Got it in one."

An assortment of confusing emotions nibbled around the corners of her curiosity. The one that gave her pause was betrayal. "I didn't realize you were seeing someone again."

"We're not dating." He sounded weary.

"Yet?" Chloe prompted.

"Ever."

"Why? What's wrong with her?" she asked.

"Nothing's *wrong* with her."

Chloe didn't care for the way he leaped to the woman's defense.

"Something's got to be wrong with her if she's not interested in you."

"You think?" He sounded amused now.

"She must be an idiot."

"She can be a little clueless at times," he agreed on a laugh. "In an adorable sort of way."

Uh-oh. Adorable? Chloe didn't like the sound of that. He'd never been interested in a woman he'd considered adorable. Gorgeous, sexy, sophisticated and exotic… sure. "Have you two known each other long?"

He took his time answering. "Sometimes I think maybe too long."

"Then why is this the first I'm hearing of her?" she demanded.

That odd feeling of betrayal niggled again. This time, she told herself she understood its source. Simon had always been forthcoming about the women in his life. Not that he provided intimate details, but Chloe always knew when he was involved or interested in becoming involved. So, how had she missed this one?

"It doesn't matter. Forget I mentioned it. She's…not my type," he said.

"Okay. But you're interested?"

"Forget it, Chloe. Please."

Still, she couldn't resist saying, "A bad girl, huh? The kind who wears black leather, has major body art and piercings in places that make me shudder?"

"No." But he chuckled, letting her know that as off base as she might be, at least she'd lightened his mood.

Or she thought she had.

"Let's just drop it, okay?" She heard him sigh and imagined him sinking into the cushions of the supple leather recliner in his living room.

If he swiveled around in the chair, he had a stunning view of the city out the wall of windows that faced the park. He had a killer apartment. It was three times larger than hers was, and she didn't need to be an expert on Manhattan real estate to know it had cost him a pretty penny. It fit his success, as did his tailored suits, sports car and choice tables at the city's nicest and priciest establishments. Yet Simon didn't mind, indeed, he seemed almost to prefer, spending time in Chloe's dive of a walk-up eating pizzas or Chinese takeout.

Which gave her an idea.

"I'm thinking of calling Fuwang's to place an order for Happy Family." The seafood dish was a favorite of both of theirs. "You want to come over? My treat?"

It would give her an opportunity to grill him about this mystery woman and to, well, get over this latest silly bit of interest in him that she had going.

"What happened to your diet?" Simon asked.

"Oh. Yeah. That." Her stomach growled, and no wonder. Not only was she starving, Fuwang's made some of the best Chinese food in all of Manhattan. "I can afford to splurge a little. I've eaten light all day."

"How light? I'm telling you, Chloe, you'll keel over in a dead faint if you skimp too much. Remember what I said about healthy snacks."

Grazing, he called it. The idea was to eat several small servings of nutritious food throughout the day.

Unfortunately, the word *grazing* conjured up the image of a cow in Chloe's mind, and that was not exactly the kind of mascot a chronic dieter such as herself wanted to have.

Still, Simon's obvious concern for her well-being was touching. Her boss wouldn't have cared if her current diet regimen involved regular purging as long as it didn't interfere with her productivity. Helga at Filigree's was only interested in selling more bagels. Her parents just wanted her to catch a man's eye so that she could settle down and give them more grandchildren. And then there was Frannie.

Whenever Chloe talked to her sister these days, Frannie's only question was about the scale's reading. In truth, Chloe didn't know. For that matter, she didn't have the nerve to find out, since looking at a number on a scale was the kind of downer that typically sent her into binge-eating mode. So, she was going by how her clothes fit. And they were definitely hanging a little looser these days. Yesterday, for instance, she hadn't had to lie on her bed in order to get her favorite jeans over her hips. Now, that was measurable progress.

Frannie didn't see it that way. Chloe's slim-hipped, narrow-waisted sister never had experienced a weight problem. Even after popping out two perfect children, she'd returned to a lithe one hundred and twenty pounds within mere weeks. Frannie's secrets? In addition to being rather apathetic when it came to food, spinning class and yoga. A few years back, Chloe had tried yoga at her sister's insistence. It only took one downward dog for her to sustain a minor head injury and take out the woman on the mat next to her. The instructor had refunded Chloe's money in full and begged her not to return. When asked about their relationship, Frannie claimed they were distant cousins…several times removed. They might as well have been, given their different body shapes and metabolisms.

"So, Chinese?"

"It's tempting," he admitted.

"But?"

"I'm tired, Chloe."

"Oh." A curious ache formed in her chest. "Another time, then."

CHAPTER FIVE

Best Body

SIMON MANAGED TO avoid Chloe for the rest of the week. Not seeing her was torture, but then seeing her would have been, too…after that fleeting kiss.

He'd needed to be sure that the next time they were together all of the wayward emotions he'd been experiencing were corralled back in place. So, he'd canceled a couple of running dates, claiming his work schedule was the culprit.

But now it was the weekend, and his excuses had run dry. Besides, he missed her.

She was waiting for him at their rendezvous point in the park, already stretching when he arrived. Her pose nearly had him turning around. A pair of gray jersey cotton shorts were pulled snug across her rounded bottom as she loosened her muscles. Her backside was definitely more toned than it used to be.

It was his moan that caught her attention. She turned around and offered a tentative smile. A week ago, her face would have split into a wide grin. Now they stood at arm's length in awkward silence. This, Simon told himself, was exactly what he didn't want. He recalled how things had become between him and his stepmother after she'd announced plans to divorce his father.

"Nothing will change between us, Simon," she'd assured him.

But once the divorce was final, their relationship became more and more strained. She still loved his father and now that Sherman had moved on to the woman who would become the third Mrs. Ford, Clarissa gradually stopped coming around. Simon was practically an adult by then, but he'd missed her. He wouldn't let romance botch up things between him and Chloe.

"I was worried you weren't going to be able to make it again," she was saying.

"Running a little late this morning," he lied. "Sorry about that."

"It's okay. I've just been stretching."

"Yeah. I saw." He cleared his throat and said the first thing that came to mind. "Great weather for a run."

Her brows tugged together and no wonder. Though it was barely nine, it was already pushing eighty and the air was dense with humidity.

"Just kidding." He forced a laugh. "Ready?"

They started out at a leisurely pace. As always, they were in sync. She matched his strides perfectly, one long leg kicking out in unison to his.

"I've missed you," he said. To make the statement a little less damning, he added, "Our runs are a highlight of my day."

She glanced sideways. "I've missed you, too. And, I've been worried."

"About me?"

"I think that woman has gotten under your skin. You're not acting like yourself."

Understatement of the year. "I've been busy."

"Is that all?"

It was the perfect opportunity to mention that kiss and…what? Apologize? Explain? No, the less said on that subject the better.

"It's my dad," he told her. It wasn't a complete fabrication.

"Your dad? Is he okay?"

"Actually, he's lost his mind." At Chloe's puzzled expression, Simon clarified, "He's getting married again."

Her lips formed a silent O. Then, "Does this make number six or seven?"

"Six, I think. I've lost count."

Simon sped up. Chloe matched his stride. She had long legs and was putting them to good use. He heard her breath chuffing in and out, the sound rhythmic and, in a way, comforting. He liked having her beside him.

"Sorry." He knew that she meant it. She was the only one who understood how deeply the revolving door of stepmothers in his life had affected him. "Wh-when is the w-wedding?" she asked, getting winded.

"This afternoon."

He told himself to slow down, but the demons snapping at his heels had him surging ahead. He and Chloe were in a full run now on a path dotted with other joggers and walkers. They wove in and out of the pedestrian traffic. Talking was impossible. Chloe remained at his side for a good two minutes before starting to fall behind. Little by little, his lead lengthened. He could no longer see her from the corner of his eye. When he finally stopped, it took her a moment to catch up. They stood together, panting. Both of them were bent at the waist with their hands braced on their thighs.

When her breathing somewhat returned to normal, she asked, "Feel better?"

He knew what she meant. "Not really."

"So, back to your dad's wedding, did you just learn about it?"

He straightened and pushed the damp hair back from his forehead. "I've known for a few months."

"Why haven't you said something to me before now?" She looked hurt. "First you're keeping secrets about a woman and now this? And then that—"

"That what?"

"Never mind." But he knew she was thinking about the kiss. "You're not acting like yourself, Simon."

He ignored the comment. "I figured she'd bail on my father before now. If she's smart, she'll leave him at the altar before saying 'I do.'"

"Are you going?"

He shrugged. "I thought about skipping it, but Dad asked me to pick up the ring from the jewelers, so I'll be there."

"Alone?"

"Are you offering to go with me?"

Simon hadn't planned to invite anyone. The event was akin to a dental visit, uncomfortable but necessary. But he wouldn't mind the company. Especially Chloe's.

"Of course, I'll go with you."

"Thanks."

Perspiration dotted her skin and her hair was staging an all-out revolt. He wanted to kiss her again, maybe even up the ante from the last time.

Which was why he said, "You know, I've been thinking that I'd like to host a small cocktail party at my apartment next weekend, mostly people from the office but a few friends, as well."

He'd come up with the idea the night after the kiss while he'd lain awake feeling restless and desperate. A cocktail party would allow Simon to fulfill his promise to Chloe regarding Trevor, and as such it might help restore to normal his and Chloe's just-friends status.

Two birds, one stone and the only casualty would be Simon.

"Such as me?" she asked.

He forced a smile. "It will give you an opportunity to talk to Trevor and you might consider it a dress rehearsal of sorts for the reunion, since some of the people from the office can be every bit as snobby and boorish as the Unholy Trinity."

"You'd do that for me?"

"You'll have to help Mrs. Benson with the planning," he said of his housekeeper.

"Thank you, Simon. I can't tell you how much I appreciate it."

Yeah? So why was she frowning? Sometimes he thought there was no figuring out the woman.

They finished their circuit of the park on a leisurely jog. Chloe was grateful for the less hectic pace, even if she understood why Simon had sped up. And she ached for him. As annoying as her family could be, at least they stuck around, unlike Simon's mother and favorite stepmother. And while Chloe's parents' marriage was far from ideal, beneath the nitpicking and bickering, she knew her mother and father would stick together till the end.

Perhaps because of Simon's experience, she'd never taken that kind of permanence for granted.

They arrived at the same park entrance where they'd started an hour earlier. She couldn't wait to peel off her damp clothes and stand under the cool spray of her shower.

"I think I lost five pounds in water weight," she commented.

"Same here."

Beside her, Simon tugged his drenched T-shirt over his head, exposing the kind of physical perfection his clothes only hinted at. Chloe swallowed a wolf whistle before it could escape.

Check out those abs!

How was a woman not supposed to gawk? She tried

her best to look elsewhere, but time and again her gaze returned to his defined chest and chiseled abdomen.

"You're so…"

His brows rose as he waited for her to continue.

"Lucky." She managed after clearing her throat. "You can take off your sweaty shirt in public and no one cares."

"If you want to lose yours, you won't hear me complaining." He'd said similar stuff to her before, but this time, even though he'd grinned afterward, her pulse began to rev like it had during their run. She blamed that kiss, chaste as it had been. It had her mind wandering to places where she'd previously never let it go.

"Well, I'd better head home," she said. "I have to turn from a pumpkin into something presentable for your father's wedding."

"I'll pick you up at noon."

CHAPTER SIX

Most Graceful

SIMON WAS WEARING a tuxedo when he came to collect Chloe later that day. And he arrived in a limousine rather than in his own car. The overall effect was fairy-tale-esque. No one did traditional black-and-white attire better than Simon. He had the build for it—long limbs, slim hips and broad shoulders. And he had the attitude—confident without coming off as cocky.

Indeed, he was as comfortable in formal garb as he was wearing faded jeans and a sweatshirt bearing the logo of his college alma mater. Whereas Chloe was already reminding herself to keep her shoulders back and stomach sucked in, and looking forward to the point in the evening when she could kick off her shoes. The ones she had on now were new. Already, they were killing her.

She'd never been good at walking in heels higher than an inch, but as the saying went, practice made perfect. So, she'd been wobbling about her apartment in a pair of the three-inch-high, peep-toe pumps since shortly after her shower. She'd already had to apply bandages to the back of her heels. Other blisters were forming on her toes. But she was determined to suck it up. No pain no gain and all that.

"Are you taking that, too?" He pointed to the top of her head.

With a sheepish smile she pulled the book off. It was the self-improvement one she'd purchased with him when they were at Bendle's.

"Reading by osmosis?" His lips quirked.

Actually, she hadn't gotten past the introduction, but she was determined to get her money's worth.

"Very funny. I've been practicing walking more gracefully." No small task wearing torture chambers that masqueraded as shoes.

"And the book helps?" He looked doubtful.

"If it stays on my head it means that my movements are more fluid and refined. I'm not flailing or stomping about."

"Ah. So, how many times have you dropped it?" Again his lips quirked.

"That's not the point."

The answer was seventeen, but who was counting? Well, other than her downstairs neighbor. Mrs. McNally had started banging on the ceiling with a broom handle after the fourth thud. The woman had become a bear to live above ever since she'd gotten her hearing aids fixed.

"All set?" Simon asked, consulting his watch. He

didn't look eager to be off, as much as he looked eager to have the day behind him. She understood completely.

The wedding was at a church in Connecticut with the reception to follow at a nearby banquet hall. It might be wedding number six or seven for Simon's father, but it was the first for the bride and she'd invited half the state's population. At least that's what Simon said his father had claimed.

"Just let me get my bag."

The purse was new, too, a stylish little clutch with a silver buckle. Unlike the shoes, the only pain it inflicted had been on her bank account. Forcing herself not to limp, Chloe followed Simon outside to the limo. Its uniformed driver stood at the ready with the rear door open for them.

"Thanks. I've got this," Simon told the man.

As the driver headed around to the front of the limo, Chloe said, "Wow, you went all out."

Simon sometimes relied on hired vehicles, but generally he preferred getting behind the wheel of his Mercedes.

"Actually, my father did." Simon's expression turned grim. "I think he was worried I wouldn't show up if he didn't take care of my transportation." He plucked at his tie then. "Dad paid for the tux, too."

"You look very handsome in it."

Indeed, he looked perfect. Even so, she couldn't resist fussing with his bow tie. Afterward, she glanced up and offered an embarrassed smile.

"Your tie was a crooked." By about a millimeter.

The disturbing fact was, Chloe had been looking for an excuse to touch him.

"Thanks."

"What would you do without me?" she asked on a laugh.

Despite his wry smile, he seemed utterly serious when he replied, "I hope I never find out."

Her entrance through the limousine's rear door wasn't exactly graceful or modest given the way her skirt hiked up. She tugged at the hem after settling onto the seat. Simon joined her.

"I meant to tell you earlier that your workouts are paying off."

Chloe was pleased he'd noticed, if a little embarrassed. She also felt guilty. The shape wear she'd purchased to help suck in her waist was worth every penny.

"Thanks."

"Don't mention it." He pulled at the tie she'd just straightened and his face reddened.

"Tie too tight?" she asked.

"Something's too tight," it sounded like he muttered.

Under his gaze, she started to feel warm, too. She cast about for something to say. "So, um, what's your new stepmother's name again?"

It was the wrong thing to ask. His lips curled from smile to snarl. "I think this one is Brittany, but since Dad has called them all 'Sweetheart' I'm not quite sure myself."

Chloe tipped her head to one side, but before she could say anything, he said, "Don't."

"Don't what?"

"Don't tell me to try to be happy for him."

Okay, that had been her advice the past several marriages, which might help to explain why he hadn't mentioned this one till the last possible moment. It struck Chloe then that even when Simon was in a relationship, he had always taken Chloe with him to his father's weddings.

"Maybe she's the one, Simon. Have you considered that?"

He snorted. "Please, she's twelve."

Chloe rolled her eyes.

"Okay, so she's not twelve, but damned close. She's younger than I am by a few years. It's…disturbing."

There was a definite *ick* factor there, she would admit.

"Sorry."

She reached for his hand. Simon's fingers wove through hers and their palms pressed together. Once again, she found it difficult to breathe. She forced herself to concentrate on what he was saying.

"At some point, you'd think my father would learn."

"Maybe he's a hopeless romantic," she replied, trying to be diplomatic.

"More like just hopeless." A muscle ticked in Simon's jaw, a sign that he wasn't only mad but hurt.

She couldn't blame him. His parents had divorced not long after he'd moved into her apartment building when they were kids. His mother had been the bad guy, or so Simon had thought since she'd been the one to move out and later hadn't fought for custody of her son.

"He looks too much like you," he'd overheard his mother say to his father during one of their many heated arguments before the divorce was final. "And I want no reminders of you."

That had been the first time Chloe ever saw Simon cry. He'd come to her apartment, his face ashen, his eyes swollen and red. After throwing up, he'd told her about the exchange. Then he'd fallen asleep on the beanbag chair in her bedroom.

Chloe's parents had let him stay the night.

The second and last time she saw him cry had been when his father divorced wife number two.

Clarissa had been Simon's babysitter since shortly before his mother left, which, looking back later, explained a lot of things to Chloe and shed light on the whispered conversations of some of the neighbors. But Simon had loved the woman and she'd loved him back, treating him, finally, like a child deserved to be treated by a mother. Clarissa had gone to his school functions, made a fuss over his accomplishments, arranged fun if sparsely attended birthday parties. Simon was a nerd, after all.

Clarissa had promised him that, no matter what happened between her and his father, she would always—*always*—be there for him. That's not quite how it had worked out, though.

"It's just too painful," she told him after Christmas

during his sophomore year of high school. By then, Simon's father had married wife number three.

Simon had come to Chloe's apartment once again. Sobbed as he'd sat in her bedroom. The beanbag chair was long gone, but he'd fallen asleep on the rug next to her bed. Despite the fact that Chloe and Simon were teenagers, her parents once again let him stay over. They'd been less worried about their daughter's virtue than the emotional well-being of the boy they'd long considered a son.

Recalling his pain now, Chloe asked, "I know you've said in the past that his multiple marriages aren't the reason you've never settled down, but…but don't you think they might have something to do with it?"

"Analyzing me?"

Another person might have been put off by his flinty expression. Indeed, adversaries in business probably cringed when they saw it. Chloe had grown up around it and so was immune. "Yes. So?"

"I don't want to make his mistakes," he admitted after a moment.

"You wouldn't."

"You say that with such confidence."

"And yet you don't believe me."

His response was surprisingly candid. "I'd like to."

"Simon—"

"Have I mentioned that you look lovely?"

He was trying to change the subject, but she decided to let him.

"Only once." That had been when she'd opened her

apartment door. His appreciative smile had caused her flesh to prickle. It was nice to be complimented. That was the reason behind the reaction. Which was why she said now, "Feel free to say it again."

"You do look incredible, Chloe. An absolute vision."

"What? In this old thing?" She plucked at that fabric of her new dress, but she couldn't keep a straight face.

As the car made its way through traffic, he poured two glasses of champagne and handed one to her. "Did you buy it for the reunion?"

"Our class reunion?"

"Is there another one I don't know about?"

He had her there. "No. And not exactly. I've got three contenders so far. Two still have the price tags on, so I can return them if need be."

His lips quirked. She remembered how they'd felt pressed to hers.

"Hedging your bets?" he asked before taking a sip of bubbly.

"More like my bank account," she admitted ruefully.

By the time it was all said and done, between clothes and the dentist, special diet foods and God only knew what else, Chloe was going to be out several hundred dollars.

Or more.

None of which she could afford on her current salary. Her credit cards had been inching toward their limits even before that cursed reunion invitation arrived. Her boss kept promising her a full-time position with better benefits and paid vacations, the date for which she could never pin down.

"It's the economy, Chloe," Mr. Thompson pointed out whenever she asked. "The company's bottom line has taken a real beating."

After saying this, he would grimace and turn slightly pale, making her regret having confronted him. So, she freelanced when and where she could. Even so, she never broke even, especially since her landlord had raised her rent yet again.

Simon would be appalled if he knew her true financial state. He was always after her about being prudent with her money and offering insight on smart investment opportunities. She appreciated his advice. Truly she did. And she would take it, too. Except that she never seemed to have the extra cash to spare.

Still, she considered the dresses and all of the other things for the reunion to be as smart an investment as the ones Simon had noted in the past. To her way of thinking, they would be worth the cost and then some, even if they never paid off monetarily.

Chloe needed to make a stand.

She was determined to show those horrid girls from high school that despite their nasty treatment of her, she'd turned out to be a successful, desired and appreciated adult.

Which was why it almost pained her to admit to Simon, "You'll be happy to know that I've opted not to have my teeth fixed."

To the outside observer Simon wouldn't have appeared affected by the news. Chloe knew him too well. She caught the glimmer in his eyes just before he sipped his champagne. He was delighted.

"Cloned, you mean," he said afterward.

She frowned. "Excuse me?"

"Nothing about your teeth needs to be fixed, Chloe." He shrugged. "That's why I say you were going to have them *cloned,* to look like some Hollywood starlet's."

"Whatever." She took a sip of her own beverage, not quite willing to agree with him.

"So, sanity prevailed. I hope something I said made a difference in your decision."

He could be boorish when he thought himself in the right. Still, recalling his argument now—and the kiss that followed it—warmth shimmied up her spine, every bit as effervescent as the champagne's bubbles. It caught her off guard, so much so that she spoke the truth.

"Actually, it had more to do with my bank account. Even if all I do these days is eat lettuce, I still couldn't afford it."

She laughed afterward, trying to turn her words into a joke. Simon, however, didn't share her humor. He stared straight ahead in stony silence before turning to face her.

"If you really want to have veneers put on your teeth, I'll pay for them."

Her mouth gaped open, no doubt giving him a good look at all of the dental wizardry that would be involved. "Oh, that's not necessary. I mean, I can pay for it myself."

It was a bald-faced lie and they both knew it.

"What's the latest word on your promotion to full-time?"

"Oh, you know. The economy." She shrugged her shoulders.

"I know you like your job, Chloe. And I admire your loyalty, as you know. But you need to either become more assertive or start sending out your resume. He's taking advantage of you."

"I know." She sighed.

"I'll pay for it," he said again. "If you really want those veneers, go for it."

A lump formed in her throat. It was a moment before she managed to say around it, "Why?"

"If it's important to you, it's important to me."

"After the comment you just made about cloning, you'd do that?"

"I just said I would."

"I...I don't know what to say." It was rare Chloe was struck speechless. But this was one of those occasions. Simon had been so vocal in his opposition to her getting veneers, yet now he was offering to pay for the dentist's services.

"It can be an outright gift," he was saying. "Your birthday is just around the corner." Actually, it was seven months away, but who was counting? Not Simon apparently. "Or it can be an interest-free loan if you prefer."

He'd covered all of his bases. He'd made sure that

she could choose an option that left her pride intact. Emotions swelled inside her so intense that for just a moment she had to turn her head, look out the window and battle back tears.

"Chloe?"

"The bubbles from this champagne, they're making my eyes water," she lied. She gazed into the face she knew almost as well as she knew her own. "Thank you for your kind offer, but my answer is no."

"No?" He seemed surprised.

Oddly, she wasn't, even though mere days ago she would have considered selling her soul to the devil to swing the cost of those veneers. "I've reconsidered."

"Yeah?"

"Yeah." She nodded. "You know, you're right."

How perverse, but she loved the sound of his dry chuckle just before he said, "I don't hear that often enough from you."

"Do you want to hear this or not?" she challenged.

"Oh, definitely. Go on."

"I rather like my unconventional smile. It's got... character."

"I like it, too."

He reached for her chin and pretended to examine the smile in question. She nearly started to laugh, but quickly sobered when he leaned toward her. For just a moment she thought... Nah. Ridiculous, she chided when he pulled away. He hadn't been going to kiss her.

* * *

Damn. He'd come close to kissing her again. It was going to be a very long day if every time he turned around he found himself tempted to pull her into his arms and bare his soul.

He needed her in his life too much to ever risk losing her. Friends stayed friends. Lovers…even the best of them parted ways eventually. And, when their feelings ran deep, they parted with enough acrimony to keep them from ever speaking again.

If it had been up to him, Simon would have made a perfunctory visit at the wedding reception and called it good. As far as he was concerned, his father's multiple marriages made a mockery of the institution.

But his father had ensured he would be there for the duration by tapping Simon as his best man, a fact Simon didn't know until he showed up at the church, ostensibly to deliver the ring his father had asked him to collect from the jewelers the week before.

He walked out of the back room the groomsmen were using to prepare for the ceremony and sighed with relief when he spied Chloe. She was standing next to a large potted palm tree, looking furtively about as she divested herself of her heels. He'd wondered how long she would last in them. In the choppy wake of his father's emotional ambush, the usual humor Simon would have found in the situation was lacking.

When he reached her, she asked, "What's wrong?"

He unclenched his jaw. The words that spilled out of his mouth were no less bitter. "You know how my dad asked me to pick up the ring for him?"

"Uh-huh. Saved him a drive into the city you said."

"Yeah. That's what I thought when I agreed to do it."
He plucked at his pleated shirtfront. "And this tuxedo
and the stretch limo…"

"Hedging his bets," she said slowly.

"Exactly. He wanted to be sure I'd be here today. On
time and dressed the part."

She frowned. "The part? What do you mean?"

"I'm the best man." Simon swore afterward, soft
enough that he couldn't be overheard by anyone but
Chloe.

And God.

He scrubbed a hand over his face. Here he was, in
church of all places, and he'd let loose with a prime
curse. It just went to show that, as always, Sherman
Ford had a knack for bringing out the worst in his only
child.

"Best man, hmm." Chloe whistled through the slim
gap in her teeth. "I guess he really was hedging his
bets."

"He set me up."

"Yes."

"He manipulated me."

"He was worried you would say no," she said softly.

"That's because I would have. I've told him no ever
since I was the best man at his second wedding." Simon
had been a boy then, still wounded from his mother's
abandonment and so damned idealistic that he'd actually believed his father's second stab at "until death do
us part" would hit the mark.

"So, what are you going to do?"

He wasn't one to make snap decisions, but he made one now, eschewing manners or protocol or whatever else a situation such as this demanded in favor of righteous indignation. "I'm going to leave. Put your shoes back on. We're out of here."

She slipped her feet back into the pumps, not quite able to camouflage her wince as she did so. And, yes, he'd noticed the bandages she'd applied where blisters had started to form. Another time he would have teased her about them. Right now, he was too focused on his anger.

"You can't just leave."

"Watch me. To hel…" He glanced around, half expecting to catch the glint of a lightning bolt. Hastily, he amended, "To heck with him. I didn't want to come today anyway, at least to the ceremony. It's a farce."

Simon folded his arms over his chest. He was being belligerent, borderline petulant, and he knew it. Hated it. But damn if he didn't feel like a child again, one told how to act and how to react to being manipulated by the adults in his life.

Chloe, now as back then, was the voice of calm and reason. "You're here. You're wearing the tux he paid for." She ran her fingers under the edge of the lapels. The gesture had Simon forgetting his irritation with his father for a moment. "What will it hurt to do this for him, Simon?"

He bent closer, lowered his voice, though his words came out no less vehemently. "I hate being a party to

it, Chloe. Even if I'm an adult now, I hate getting to
know someone, maybe even starting to like her, and
then—bam! Dad or his new wife moves on to greener
pastures."

He swallowed. It was a truth he wouldn't have spoken
to anyone else.

Her hands were now resting on his chest. Her cheek
mere inches from his mouth. A stray curl tickled his
jaw and the simple scent she'd worn since high school
twined around him. To anyone watching, they would
appear to be a couple, lovers lost in an intimate moment.
Only part of that was true. They weren't lovers, but he'd
never achieved the same level of intimacy with another
woman, even those women with whom he'd made love.
Chloe pulled him into a hug, pressing her lips against
his cheek.

Afterward, she told him, "As I said in the car, you
have to go in hoping for the best. Maybe this marriage
will work." She coughed delicately. "The vast differences in their ages notwithstanding."

"You don't honestly believe that?"

"For their sake, yes." She smiled. The arms that were
still encircling his shoulders tightened. "You can do this.
You can get through this."

The words she spoke were familiar, he realized. She'd
told him the very same thing on occasions in the past
when he'd found himself facing something seemingly
insurmountable, whether it was finishing up an award-
winning project for the annual science fair or getting

his IT business off the ground on a shoestring budget just after college graduation.

"You always have faith in me."

"Of course I do." She grinned. "And, I'll be right here the whole time for support. Or to supply liquor."

Of course she would.

"You know what you are, Chloe?"

"A good friend," she replied.

She was much more than that, but he nodded. "The very best. And always grace under pressure."

She snorted at the compliment. "Don't expect any grace out of me. You'll probably have to carry me at some point. As it is, I'm already all but maimed from these shoes. And the night is young."

A moment ago Simon had longed for the day to be over. He'd wished himself to be anywhere but in this quaint church in rural Connecticut about to witness his father's latest attempt at matrimony.

But now, with Chloe at his side, the night stretching out in front of him seemed to hold much more promise.

CHAPTER SEVEN

Best Dancer

"I CAN'T SIT at the head table," Chloe hissed through a brittle smile as Simon guided her from a seat at the rear of the banquet hall to the long table at the front.

The bride didn't look happy about the arrangement, and no wonder. The symmetry of the head table was off now that the waitstaff had hastily added a place setting next to Simon's on the groomsmen's side.

"Sure you can," he told her.

"I'm not a member of the bridal party."

"I'm making you an honorary one. I have that power as the best man, you know." They reached their destination and he pulled out a chair for her. "It's one of the perks."

"It is not." But she was hard-pressed to keep a straight face.

"Sure it is. At least in my case. See, when I agreed to do this after talking to you, Dad said he owed me." Simon settled into the seat next to hers. "Well, I called in the debt."

Chloe glanced down the table and intercepted twin death stares from the young woman wearing white and the chartreuse taffeta-clad maid of honor. "The bride is not very happy."

"She'll have to get used to it. It won't be the first time she's unhappy while married to my father," he said.

"Simon, this is her day."

"I'll make it up to her with the toast," he said. "It will be inspired."

That caught her off guard. She blinked, impressed. "When did you have time to write a toast?"

Every second between the ceremony and the limousine ride to the banquet hall had been taken up by the photographer, a demanding perfectionist of a man who'd insisted on every possible shot. Bride holding flowers in front of her. Bride holding flowers slightly offside. Bride smelling flowers. Bride balancing bouquet on her nose and clapping like a seal. Well, maybe not that one, but the session had taken forever. Thank goodness Chloe had been able to sit in a church pew and remove her shoes for the duration, although it had been all the harder to stuff her feet back inside afterward. The pumps now felt about two sizes too small.

Of his toast, Simon was saying, "I haven't actually written one. But I remember bits and pieces from the ones that Dad's other best men have given over the years." He shrugged and reached for his water glass. "Change a couple of names and dates, add in a personal story or two that she probably hasn't heard and, *voila*. It will be as sweet as saccharine."

"Simon, I meant it when I said this is…um…" Bethany? Brittany? Brandie? "What's her name's day."

"Call her sweetheart," he suggested with a wink. "Or baby will do."

His sarcasm in this case was understandable. The woman was very young. In fact, Chloe wasn't sure the bride was of the legal age to indulge in the champagne she was sipping. "She's the bride. She's in love. She's dreamed of this day for a long time, making plans, picking out colors and cake designs. Under her bed, she's probably got half a dozen scrapbooks filled with pictures of wedding dresses that she's collected over the years."

Simon's brows puckered at that.

"Never mind. What I'm saying is, don't spoil this moment or this memory for her just because you're ticked off at your father."

"He'll ruin it. Maybe not today, but eventually. He always does."

"Then let him be the jerk. You don't need to be one."

Simon didn't say anything. Rather, he fiddled with the handle of his soup spoon for a moment before tapping the end against the side of his water goblet. The clanging caught the attention of the other guests. Conversations quieted as they picked up their own utensils and joined in the quaint tradition.

Simon nodded to Chloe before glancing down the table at his father.

"Hey, Dad, in case you've forgotten, this means you're supposed to kiss your bride."

Afterward, Chloe leaned over and said, "Now, *that* is true grace under pressure."

"That's only because you bring out the best in me."

A little while later, Simon gave his toast. It was simple and eloquent if not completely sincere. Only Chloe, of course, recognized the latter.

Rather than plagiarize the toasts of his father's previous best men, he said, "Someone once told me that love is a gift to be cherished. I was a kid at the time and I don't think I gave the words much thought. But as an adult, I know them to be true." He raised his glass then. "To the bride and groom and a gift to be cherished."

The room echoed with "hear, hears" and the sound of glasses clinking together.

"I'm proud of you," Chloe whispered when Simon returned to his seat.

"You should be. And thanks for the inspiration."

She frowned.

"You were the one who told me that. It was just after Clarissa left."

Ah. His first stepmother and the only real mother he'd ever known. She remembered now. Simon had vowed that he would never love or trust anyone again. Chloe had told him he wasn't being fair to himself or the other people in his life. She hadn't been quite as eloquent as he'd been just now.

As she recalled, she'd said, "It's like chocolate. I love chocolate. Last year, when I got the stomach flu, I barfed up the candy bar I'd just eaten. Now, if I'd given up chocolate after that bad experience, I would be depriving myself."

"Gee, you should work for a greeting card company," he'd replied drily.

But they'd both laughed.

"I'm glad you didn't use my analogy," she told him now.

"I thought it best not to given that we're about to eat."

"Do...do you really believe love is a gift to be cherished?"

"Yes."

"Have you ever been in love?"

He twisted the stem of his glass between his fingers. "Yes."

This was news to her and an even bigger surprise than his revelation of a mystery woman. Were they one and the same? Perhaps not since he said they'd never dated and never would. Her mind flipped through the mental index of his past girlfriends. "Who?"

"Someone really special."

He was being evasive. And she was being nosy. Even so, another question popped out. "Does she have a name?"

"Let's just call her sweetheart."

She folded her arms over her chest. "That is so unfair."

"What?"

"You know the vital statistics of every guy I've ever

fallen for, not to mention the kind and quantity of ice cream I ate after the breakup."

"You're an open book."

And he was being way too closemouthed, which wasn't like him. "A little *quid pro quo,* please."

But he sipped his champagne and remained silent.

"God! Please tell me it wasn't that horrible Daphne Norton woman."

"What did you have against Daphne?"

"She was rude, self-centered and…and a lingerie model."

Simon chuckled. "I fail to see how her being a lingerie model made her horrible."

"You wouldn't," Chloe grumbled, and since her glass was empty, she reached for his champagne. After taking a sip, she said, "Not Gabriella."

"Ah, Gabriella." He made a humming sound of appreciation. "We had some good times."

"No doubt. The woman was capable of putting both of her legs behind her head."

"Very flexible," Simon agreed with a fond smile. "She was a former gymnast, you know. Went to college on a scholarship and nearly secured a spot on the U.S. Olympic team."

Chloe's lips curled. "I didn't want to mention this, but she hit on me once."

"She did not." He took back his champagne.

"Well, not overtly, but I sensed some…vibes. I think she was only using you to get to me."

He laughed. "It's a good thing I didn't love her, then."

"So, who? It's not like you to hold out on me."

"Someone who hasn't got a clue," he said softly.

"Unrequited love," she murmured on a sigh. As romantic as she found such things in novels, she ached for her friend. At least that's what she told herself caused the twinge in the region of her heart. "I'm sorry, Simon."

"It's okay." He handed his glass back to her. "Actually, it's for the best."

"How can you say that?"

"We'll never have a chance to hurt or disappoint one another."

Over the next couple hours, dinner was served and the dishes cleared away. The cake was cut and the bouquet tossed. Chloe managed to be elsewhere during the last event. As far as she was concerned, nothing shouted desperation more than a gaggle of single women jockeying for position behind a bride, so eager to catch a bunch of wilted blooms that they would mow down anyone who stood in their way.

Chloe should know. She'd sustained bruised ribs at her sister, Frannie's, wedding after their cousin Marilyn had launched herself over the competition like a heat-seeking missile. Marilyn caught the bouquet and was spared injury thanks to a soft landing...on Chloe.

The incident was family lore now and preserved for succeeding generations thanks to the video taken on a cell phone camera and uploaded to the internet. Last time Chloe had checked, it had been viewed four hundred and seventy five thousand times. She'd even been recognized on the street once by a teenage tourist, who'd pointed to Chloe and hollered excitedly to her friends, "Oh, my God! It's the woman from the Battle of the Bridesmaids video!"

The girls had actually asked for her autograph. More mortified than flattered, Chloe had signed their I Love New York T-shirts with an alias.

As she returned to the head table from her hiding spot in the restroom, the lights were lowered and the disc jockey announced the bridal dance would soon commence.

"Duty calls," Simon said, resigned.

"Where's your better half?" Chloe looked around for the maid of honor.

"Probably texting the pimply-faced kid who caught the garter to see if he wants to take her to the prom."

"She's not *that* young." Chloe slipped off her shoes on a groan. "And we're not *that* old."

"Says the woman with the arthritic feet."

She reached over and punched his arm. "They're not arthritic. They're blistered. Big difference."

He pretended to rub his biceps. "Does that mean you won't be able to dance with me tonight?"

"I can still dance."

"That's the spirit."

"Nothing fast, though," she said. Just the thought had her wincing.

"Perfect. You know me. I don't do fast. Nor does any other man who is sober and prefers not to make a fool of himself."

She laughed until she spotted a blur of chartreuse. "Uh-oh. Maid-of-honor closing in at three o'clock."

"Damn. I thought for a moment that I might be off the hook. Save me the next slow one?" he asked.

Just the thought of squeezing her sore feet back into her pumps had Chloe wincing anew. "Can I leave off my shoes?"

"Sorry." Simon's expression turned appropriately rueful. "It's the bride's wedding day. What's Her Name has been dreaming of this day for years. Everything must be perfect. Barefooted guests? That's not so perfect."

"It's all right. I know the best man." She winked. "I hear he has pull."

"Okay, but it will cost you."

"What's the going rate for a shoeless dance?" she asked.

"I'll let you know," he replied just as the maid-of-honor reached them.

He pushed to his feet and buttoned his jacket, looking handsome and sophisticated and miserable, though the latter was only obvious to Chloe. She knew that polite smile to be a fake, his polished manners a facade behind which he hid his true feelings. What's Her Name and What's Her Name's Friend, had no idea what this was costing him. But Chloe knew. And so did his father.

Sherman stopped behind her chair on his way to the dance floor. He was a big man, his build leaning more toward stocky than muscular. But he had a charming smile—it was where Simon got his—and a way with women. Another trait his son had inherited. It was hard not to like him, even if he had a lot of qualities that made him a bad father and a lousy role model.

"I wanted to thank you, Chloe."

"For what, Mr. Ford?"

"For getting Simon to do this for me today. I know he wasn't happy when I approached him about being my best man before the ceremony."

That was because he'd felt trapped and played, but Chloe kept those thoughts to herself. "Oh, I had nothing to do with it. He might have been a little upset at first." Total understatement of the year. "But you're his dad. He wanted to do this for you. He was actually looking forward to the toast," she embellished.

"You're a rotten liar, kiddo." His face split into a wide grin that took the sting out of his words.

"Okay, maybe not looking forward to it, but he… um…rose to the occasion."

Sherman sobered at that. "He certainly did. Surprised me, I have to say. I was prepared for him to launch a verbal grenade or two."

"I'm sure that never crossed his mind."

"I'm sure it did." Sherman laughed again before leaning down to kiss her cheek. "So, thanks for talking him out of it." Before she could deny it, he added, "We both know you're the only person in the world my son listens to."

"Would you listen to me, already? I'm telling you, Burton Cummings was no longer with The Guess Who when he recorded 'I Will Play a Rhapsody.'"

But Simon was shaking his head before she finished. "You're wrong."

The pair of them had become fans of the Canadian singer/songwriter in high school after some students lip-synched the words to "American Woman" during a mock rock competition. They both were partial to the stuff he'd recorded as a solo artist.

"I'm not wrong," she insisted. "I can't believe the DJ has that one in his collection."

"Actually, he doesn't. But he did have another one of Cummings's songs."

Chloe's eyes narrowed. "Which…" The music started and she had her answer: "Stand Tall," a ballad about a man pining for his lost love. Cummings voice was flawless, the melody moving, but the song wasn't exactly standard wedding fare. In fact, it was downright inappropriate.

"Simon, you didn't."

"What?" He shrugged innocently. "I like this song. You like this song."

"I wouldn't say I like it," Chloe muttered. The truth was, she only played it after breakups, singing into an empty spoon between mouthfuls of ice cream.

"And it's slow," he was saying. "You said you'd dance with me. I'm even willing to protect you from the bride, since you don't want to wear your shoes."

He put out his hand. His smile was devilish, but engaging. It said, I've behaved myself enough for one night. How was she to resist? Interestingly, dancing to music more suited to a wake than a wedding wasn't the only thing Chloe found tempting once she and Simon were on the dance floor and he took her into his arms. Their bodies brushed, bumped together. They both pulled back, far enough at first that Orson Welles could have stood comfortably between them. Slowly they came back together, though a gap remained.

Her sister referred to this as the chastity gap. Frannie claimed that if a man was interested in a woman in a romantic or sexual way, he breached that gap, leaving no doubt as to his intentions for later in the evening. Of course, Frannie had been the queen of dirty dancing back in her pre-marriage days. Still, she had a point. If a man wanted a woman, he held her close. She wasn't thinking of Simon now, but the guy she'd dated three boyfriends ago. The chastity gap had showed no signs of closing the entire four months of their relationship.

"Maybe he respects you too much," had been Simon's take.

She liked that explanation far better than Frannie's, which was that the only reason he was dating Chloe was for all of the free design help she was giving him with his start-up business. She'd mocked up a few—okay, seven—promotional brochures and fliers for him. And had created a company logo and slogan. And had gotten him a deep discount at the local print shop she used. And had hooked him up with an up-and-coming webpage designer whose prices were really affordable given the quality of his work. Hmm. Now that Chloe thought about it, he'd bailed on her just after the site went live.

"You're frowning," Simon remarked. "How are your feet feeling?"

Better than her ego at the moment. She smiled. "Better now that I'm not wearing shoes."

Without the heels, her eyes were level with Simon's chin. She spied the scar just below it. A sixth-grade science experiment gone awry was responsible. He'd been lucky that the volatile mixture he'd accidentally concocted hadn't resulted in more damage to either him or his apartment when the beaker exploded. The scar was visible only at certain angles and his eyebrows had grown back nicely.

"I think my dad just saluted me." Simon was the one frowning now.

"What?" She glanced around. Mr. Ford was at the head table, grinning broadly as he sat next to his none-too-happy bride. He raised his hand to his brow again, this time apparently for Chloe's benefit. "I think he appreciates how long you've managed to behave yourself."

The song ended and another slow one began. They stayed on the floor. Most of the other young people cleared off. This song was an oldie, dating back to the days of crooners such as Bing Crosby and Frank Sinatra.

It got Chloe thinking.

"How many weeks of ballroom dancing lessons do you think it would take to have the basics down?" she asked Simon.

"I don't know. Why?"

"For the reunion, I think it would be really nice to be able to do more than turn in a circle like a drill bit."

His brows shot up. "Is that a stab at my dancing?"

"Not at all. Besides, you're not going to be my date."

The corners of Simon's mouth pulled down. "You don't know that Trevor will go or, assuming he does, that he knows how to ballroom dance."

"Good point."

"I'm still offended, by the way." He grunted. "Drill bit."

"I wasn't talking about you." She coughed. "Not directly, anyway."

"That's it." The arm around her waist tightened.

"What?"

It sounded like he said, "Prepare to be dazzled," before the hand on her hip pushed her away. She stumbled a few steps out only to find herself reeled back to him with the hand holding hers.

"Simon?"

"Shut up and follow."

No drill-bit dancing now. The style wasn't quite ballroom and definitely not salsa, but his moves were choreographed rather than random. And he executed every one of them flawlessly, even as Chloe shuffled around after him. And forget that so-called chastity gap. He'd breached it half a dozen times already, each time a little more erotically than the last.

"You've been holding out on me. When did you learn how to do this?" she asked as he guided her through a turn. It wasn't the moves that left her breathless.

"A while ago. Margo was fond of dancing."

Margo. Tall, thin, with jet-black hair and a pair of exotic green eyes. She'd been the understudy in a Broadway musical when she and Simon dated two years earlier. In addition to having the sinewy body of a ballerina, the woman sang like an angel. Chloe still wasn't sure why she'd hated her. Or, for that matter, why it had been mutual. But they'd disliked one another from the start.

"Get ready." Simon was wearing that charming, devilish grin again.

"For wha*aaaaaat?*" The word stretched until it became shrill. She couldn't help it.

One minute, Chloe was upright. The next, she was tilted back over one of his arms, far enough back that she could see the silver disco ball rotating overhead. And then Simon's face appeared mere inches from her own. They were both out of breath. From the dancing? She couldn't be sure. He wasn't smiling. Not really, even though one side of his mouth was lifted smugly. She knew he was pleased with himself. Which was why the rest of his expression was so out of place. His brows were gathered together so that a line formed between them. He seemed disoriented, as if he were the one whose world had been turned on its axis.

The song was over. An up-tempo one now played in its place. Slowly, he returned her upright. Chloe became aware of the floor filling up again around them with young people, mostly women dancing with their girlfriends. Simon was right, she thought idly. Most guys didn't like to dance fast unless they were either really good at it or really drunk. Since he was neither, it was even stranger then that they were still on the dance floor.

But, of course, they weren't dancing.

A woman bumped into Chloe from behind, causing her to stumble forward. She tried to catch herself before she could crash into Simon's chest, but she couldn't quite manage it. That chastity gap was a goner. What Chloe discovered in its place when their bodies pressed together was disconcerting.

"We probably should sit down. I don't think my bare feet are safe out here amid all these spiked heels," she told him on a forced laugh.

But it wasn't only her feet that felt vulnerable.

CHAPTER EIGHT

Most Naive

CHLOE WAS MEETING Simon for dinner. It had been his idea, but she had been planning to call him anyway and see if he wanted to cash in on that rain check for Chinese. The reason she gave was that they could go over plans for his upcoming cocktail party. Actually, she just wanted to see him. Even though only a few days had passed since his father's wedding, it felt way too long.

They'd left the reception half an hour after their dance. She'd felt light-headed, which she'd blamed on the champagne. Simon walked her to her door, as he always did. Every step of the way, her pulse had revved. Would he kiss her? Did she want him to? But he was a perfect gentleman, even if he'd hesitated for just a moment before bussing her cheek.

She went to bed that night confused and needy and a little lost. He wanted her. At least his body had told her so after their dance. What was happening between them? In the past, she would have called Simon to discuss her feelings. But how could she do that now when he was the source of them?

She took an unexpected detour on the way to the restaurant, stopping in at Bendle's Books after spying Millicent through the window. It wasn't like the older woman to work a weeknight.

"What are you doing here?"

"My daughter had a hot date and we're short-staffed tonight. So, I offered to man the counter."

"That's nice of you."

"More like crafty. She was going to cancel on him. At her age, she can't afford to be canceling dates." Millicent's eyebrows rose then and her gaze skimmed Chloe's attire. "Speaking of hot dates, where's yours?"

Knowing that Simon would be dressed in a suit since he was coming right from the office and that the restaurant required men to wear jackets, Chloe had gone with another of the dresses in the running for the reunion. It was sleeveless and black, but with a subtle print in charcoal around the hem. It looked best with the fun red stilettos she'd bought, but since the blisters on her feet hadn't had a chance to heal, she'd gone with black kitten heels.

"Oh, I'm not going on a date." Chloe waved her hand. "I'm just having dinner with Simon."

"Oh?" The older woman smiled knowingly.

"Come on, Millicent," she chided out of habit. "You know that he and I are just friends."

"I never could figure that one out." The older woman leaned over the counter. "It's just the two of us here now. You can tell me. Haven't you ever wondered what it would be like if you and Simon were more than friends?"

"No."

"So, he's like a brother to you?"

"No!" Chloe coughed.

Millicent grinned. "I thought so."

"We're just friends," she stressed.

The older woman's eyes narrowed. "Are you telling me that, in all the time you've known one another, he's never kissed you?"

"Well, sure, he's kissed me."

"I mean, the way a man kisses a woman he'd like to take to bed."

Chloe's skin prickled and the sensation was not completely unpleasant. "Millicent!"

"Oh, don't sound so shocked. I'm old, not dead. Well?"

"No. Not really." Given the gleam in the older woman's eye, Chloe regretted her slip immediately. She only succeeded in making it worse, however, when she added, "It wasn't a major kiss."

"What constitutes minor these days?" Millicent wanted to know.

Chloe had put her foot in it now, so she said drily, "The same as what did in your day, I'd imagine. This was a peck, really."

"Was it recently?"

"Last week."

"Where were you when he gave you this *peck?*"

"At his office, waiting for the elevator. I was just leaving."

Millicent looked crestfallen. "When you said minor, you weren't kidding."

"It's just that he's never kissed me on the mouth before." Nor had he ever danced with Chloe quite as he had at his father's wedding. She'd woken up more than once the past few nights, thinking of the way their bodies had fit together and the awareness that she'd felt simmering just beneath the surface. And then there was the telltale hardness she'd felt when they'd been pressed together.

It was wrong. It had to be. Yet, in so many ways, it felt so right.

"On the mouth, you say?" Millicent perked up upon hearing that.

Chloe wanted to groan. It was for her own benefit that she said, "You're making too much of this. Nothing Simon did or said was over the line. And, ultimately, the kiss was very platonic."

"You sound almost disappointed," Millicent remarked.

Was she?

"Oh, no. Why would I be disappointed? Simon and I have been friends forever. If he were interested in me that way, he would have said something long before now. Besides, the women he dates are, like, supermodels."

"So, what does that mean? You're not his type?"

She's not my type. A warning bell went off in Chloe's head. Simon had made that very comment regarding his mystery woman when the two of them had talked on the telephone the night of their kiss.

"Are you interested in him that way?" Millicent was asking.

"I never really let myself be."

"That's a curious answer. Why ever not?"

"He's my best friend. If I'm wrong, I risk not only making a fool of myself, I risk losing him."

"And if you're right?"

It was a lot to think about, unfortunately a glance at her watch revealed that she didn't have time.

When Chloe arrived at the restaurant fifteen minutes later, Simon was already seated at a table. The restaurant was a new, upscale eatery in the theater district that both of them had expressed an interest in trying. They'd sampled lots of new Manhattan restaurants together during the past decade. She'd never felt awkward about their quasi-couplehood until now. Tonight, she weighed his every gesture and expression.

He stood when she reached the table. If the maître d' hadn't pulled out her chair, she knew Simon would have performed that simple courtesy for her.

"I took the liberty of ordering an appetizer and a couple of glasses of wine. White," he said before she could protest. "And don't worry about blowing your diet. A little tomato and basil bruschetta won't kill you."

"Thanks."

"Another reunion contender?" he asked, his gaze skimming her dress.

She nodded. "What do you think?"

"I think you'd look great wearing a burlap sack, but this beats burlap hands down."

It was the sort of compliment she usually dismissed with a laugh. Tonight, her heart actually fluttered and her mouth went dry.

He apparently noticed. "I like this."

"What?"

"Your quiet acceptance of the truth for once. No arguing or brushing my words aside." He nodded. "Yeah. I definitely like this."

The waiter arrived then with their wine, which was just as well. Chloe wasn't sure how to respond without making a fool of herself.

The food didn't disappoint and neither did the ambience. Chloe couldn't help noticing that the secluded tables and low lighting were perfect for intimate conversation. As usual, she and Simon never ran out of things to say, though every now and then one or the other of them seemed to lose their train of thought. The pauses weren't unpleasant exactly, but they seemed pregnant with meaning.

The evening ended on an awkward note, too. Outside the restaurant, after he'd hailed a cab for her, he leaned in to kiss her on the cheek. They both moved in the same direction, before both moving in the other direction. Finally, he cupped her face between her hands and turned it to the side so he could buss her cheek.

They both laughed afterward. But something between them was off-kilter.

* * *

The following afternoon, Simon made it to Chloe's apartment in record time. He'd defied death and the speed limit after his secretary gave him the message that Chloe needed to see him. It was a matter of life and death.

He should have remembered Chloe's gift for hyperbole.

Still, he was enjoying the show. She was stalking around her tiny living room, an enraged goddess, with one fist raised and shaking.

"I can't believe I didn't get the mailing from the reunion committee about sending in a biography for our class booklet until today! When did you get yours again?"

"It came with the invitation."

"Which you received an entire week before I did."

"I'm sure it was an oversight."

She stopped pacing. "Oversight my… It was intentional. And now I only have one day to get it in before the deadline. How convenient is that?"

"You still have time. You can send it to them via email. The booklet doesn't go to the printer's until tomorrow."

"I need more time."

"For what? It's a biography. No more than three hundred and fifty words."

"It's our yearbook all over again."

"No."

But silently, he had to admit it was. For their yearbook, Chloe's senior portrait had mysteriously gone missing. They'd plugged in a cropped down shot of her from Spirit Week when she'd painted her face the school's colors. It wasn't her most flattering look. Under her name, in the spot used to list the accomplishments of the high school seniors, hers was left blank. No mention of her involvement in several school clubs or her honor roll ranking.

"Well, I'm not going to let them make assumptions about me. I'm going to email them a biography, and they're going to weep when they read it." She booted up her laptop, looking determined, looking lovely.

It was after ten when she finally stood and arched her back. Several vertebrae cracked. Simon, who'd drifted off to sleep, stirred. He pushed her cat off his chest and sat up.

"Are you done?"

"I am. And it's a masterpiece."

He didn't trust her smile. "Mind if I read it?"

"Sure. If you see any typos, let me know. I'm going to jump in the shower."

It was free of typos, but full of…embellishment. Heck, Donald Trump was a piker in comparison. She hadn't been commissioned to design the invitations for the mayor's inaugural ball. Nor was she responsible for new tourism brochures for Ellis Island. For that matter, she hadn't done most of the stuff she'd listed in her biography. But Simon could think of dozens of things that Chloe had left off. Things that she didn't think made her sound successful, but that in his mind spoke to her character.

Such as the pro-bono work she'd done for her favorite bookstore and the internet blog she'd set up for Helga so the woman could keep in touch with family members who were spread around remote parts of Europe.

Chloe still didn't get it. She was measuring herself by some faulty past standard, unable to see her own worth. He started typing. He finished just as he heard the shower switch off, and he was quite pleased with the result. In his mind, it truly reflected the remarkable woman she was.

He did a quick copy and paste of his version of her biography into the body of an email and sent it off to the address the reunion committee had supplied. When Chloe joined him a couple minutes later, her version was back up on the desktop.

Her hair was wet and she'd pulled on a pair of sweats he'd seen her wear a million times. She smelled of soap and inexpensive shampoo, but expensive perfumes were no more enticing. The way his body reacted upon seeing her, she might as well have been wearing lingerie.

As she dried the ends of her hair with a towel, she asked, "So, what did you think?"

His mouth went dry before it dawned on him that she was referring to the biography.

"I didn't realize you were so talented," he replied drily.

She cleared her throat. "Everybody embellishes when it comes to these sorts of things, Simon. Well, unless they're like you and have practically conquered the world before age thirty."

"You've done plenty to be proud of." He shrugged. "But I know better than to argue with you. So, I sent it."

"You did? As is?"

"As is."

He refused to feel the least bit guilty about lying.

CHAPTER NINE

Easiest to Talk To

SIMON GRUMBLED AN oath as he reached for his tie.
What on earth had possessed him to offer to host a party
at his apartment so Chloe could chat up Trevor with the
goal of getting him to take her to the reunion?

"Because I'm insane," he told his reflection in the
mirror.

He also was jealous.

He wasn't willing to admit that character defect out
loud. It was hard enough to admit it to himself. He'd
thought he'd dealt with his attraction to Chloe a long
time ago and accepted the necessary limits that he'd im-
posed on their relationship. He loved her, but he would
never make love to her. Or act as anything other than
her longtime friend. But lately he was having a hard
time not trespassing on territory that he'd deemed out
of bounds.

It didn't help that Simon was between girlfriends or
that ever since the invitation to their reunion had ar-

rived, he and Chloe had been spending more time in one another's company.

Being with her was proving to be hell on his self-control. The other night was a prime example. He'd left her apartment not long after sending her biography into cyberspace. But he'd wanted to stay, and not just to watch the old Hitchcock movie she found playing on cable.

But what really concerned Simon was the way she was letting their damned reunion take over her life.

If she were anyone else, he would suggest she seek therapy or, at the very least, urge her to take up a hobby. But since Simon had been present for Chloe's high school years, with an up close and personal view of the bullying and abuse she'd endured at the hands of that brazen trio of girls, he understood what drove her. And he understood that going back, rubbing their faces in her current success, *was* her therapy.

That's exactly why he'd talked her into attending in the first place.

In that regard, he was proud of her. She was standing up for herself and willingly facing her demons. He'd always known she didn't lack nerve. Or smarts. Or anything else. She was the one with doubts.

But he wished that she would face her past just as she was, comfortable with herself, proud of the girl she'd been and the woman she had become. She didn't need to change, let alone improve. Sure, he was happy to see her eating healthier and getting more exercise. It was her motives for doing so that troubled Simon.

Just as it was his motives for throwing this party that troubled him. He was doing it for Chloe, because he was her *friend,* and yet hoping desperately that nothing would come of any flirtation that might occur between her and Trevor. That didn't exactly make him the friend he professed to be.

Simon's tie was a mess. He pulled it loose and started over.

"He's not that good looking," he grumbled.

Who was he kidding? Trevor was a god. Adonis dressed in Armani.

"I don't want to see her get hurt," he told his reflection.

And he was worried that she would despite her assurances that she had no real interest in Trevor beyond thinking he was hot and wanting him to take her to the reunion so that the other women there, especially a certain three, would turn green with envy. He pictured Chloe and Trevor walking into the old gym, the guy's hands resting in places that, while respectable, still held an overtone of intimacy. They'd share a dance. A laugh. Maybe steal a kiss or two. Chloe would get that dreamy look on her face and the other women would sigh, imagining the hot sex to come.

When he mangled the knot a second time, he decided to give up. After tossing the tie aside, he unbuttoned his collar.

He sighed heavily. "This is going to be a very long night."

* * *

The bell rang just as he came out of the bedroom. His housekeeper went to answer it.

It was Chloe. She was wearing a damp trench coat and water dripped from the tip of her closed umbrella onto the foyer floor before Mrs. Benson took both it and the coat.

"It's raining buckets out there," Chloe said. "I thought I'd need a rowboat to get here."

Simon glanced at the rain-splattered windows. According to the forecast, the worst of the storm was supposed to have subsided by now, but it was showing no signs of letting up. Surely that was an omen of some sort. Whether good or bad, though, he didn't know.

"The party doesn't start for another hour," he reminded her.

"I know, but I thought I'd come early." She pointed to her hair. "I straightened it for the occasion. Can you tell?"

It was a mess of corkscrews. In other words, adorable. He loved it this way, but he knew better than to say so. He knew better than to say *anything*. So, he kept his expression neutral and offered nothing more than a grunt that could be interpreted a number of different ways.

"I brought my flat iron, just in case." She'd brought more than that judging from the small suitcase she'd wheeled in behind her.

"You know, you could have gotten ready here and saved yourself the hassle of doing your hair twice."

"Next time."

Two words that caused an inappropriate amount of interest to lick up his spine like flames. To douse them, he crossed to the makeshift bar that had been set up in the corner and helped himself to a gin and tonic.

Chloe joined him there. "What do you think of my outfit?"

He took a liberal swig of his drink. She'd gone for understated with a copper-colored, cotton dress that she'd paired with wedge sandals. She wasn't limping… yet. In fact, given the graceful way she'd just crossed the room, he'd say the hours she'd been spending walking around her apartment in high heels with a book on her head were paying off. He focused on her toenails. They were painted a hue similar to that of the dress.

His gaze traveled back up her legs and stopped at the hem. Just what did she wear with her heels when she walked around her apartment with that book on her head? A dress such as this one? Or maybe shorts and a T-shirt. Or…or…

"I'm a dead man."

"What?"

He coughed. "That dress. It's killer. Hence my…um deadness." He coughed again.

Chloe frowned. "Are you all right? You're not coming down with something I hope."

He nearly laughed at that. Coming down with something? Hardly. He had a full-blown case and he'd probably suffer from it for the rest of his life.

"I'm fine." He gave his chest a couple of thumps. "My

drink went down the wrong pipe is all. Getting back to your outfit, is it new?"

"Sort of."

"How can something be sort of new?"

"I went to a secondhand shop in the Village that my sister told me about. It carries mostly designer label stuff, castoffs from the well-to-do." She plucked at the fabric and grinned in triumph. "This retailed for three times what I paid for it."

"Is it another contender for the reunion?"

"No, but I felt it an essential investment in my pre-reunion preparations."

"Like the whitened teeth."

"Exactly. As for the reunion, I've decided to go with black."

"The color of mourning." He sipped his drink again.

"It's also a power color. And classic for formal occasions," she replied primly.

"The reunion is in the old high school gym. How formal will it be? I'm thinking of wearing my workout clothes."

"You are not."

He shrugged. "Fine, but I'm not wearing a tux."

"But you'll put on a suit, right?"

"I'm thinking sport coat and maybe no tie. Kind of like what I'm wearing tonight." He pushed away thoughts of the mangled length of silk he'd tossed in his closet.

Chloe was frowning. "Do you think Trevor will wear a suit?"

Already she was banking on the man as her date. Simon's grip tightened on the tumbler in his hand.

"I'm not a mind reader. You'll have to ask him." The words came out harsh, so he moderated his tone and changed the subject. "Getting back to your dress, non-power-color that it is, you still look amazing."

She smiled shyly and her gaze slid to the side. Just as she had the other night, she didn't try to brush off the compliment.

"That looks good on you."

"What?" She looked confused.

"Confidence."

She eyed him a moment, obviously searching for a response. He figured she couldn't find one, because what she said was, "Do you mind if I use the bathroom in your room to revisit my hair? More room to spread out my stuff."

He glanced at the suitcase again. "Not at all."

"Thanks. It won't take me long. When I'm done, I can help you set up."

"Don't worry. I have a staff for that," he said. "And I hired some extra people to help out this evening."

The added help arrived about the time Chloe began obliterating her curls with a flat iron, and included a caterer, a bartender and some waitstaff to see to his guests' needs. Simon needed the extra hands now that his small soiree had ballooned to more than three dozen people.

He blamed Chloe for that. He'd tried to keep it small, no more than a handful of guests, but she'd insisted that if it were too intimate a gathering, Trevor might suspect a setup.

When Trevor arrived fashionably late more than an hour into the party, it became clear he'd been none the wiser. He brought a date, a lithe and leggy young woman who dwarfed every female in the room and quite a few of the men. Including Trevor. She even had an inch or two on Simon. And she was wearing flats.

"Who is the Amazon?" Chloe wanted to know.

"No idea."

Chloe crossed her arms over her chest and tapped her nearly empty glass of white wine against one biceps. "God, this is just great. Did you know he was seeing someone?"

"He's *always* seeing someone, Chloe. I told you that. The guy is a serial dater."

"Like you?" she asked with a subtle arch of one brow.

Since he couldn't argue the accuracy of her assessment, he didn't try, but he pointed out their differences. "Worse. He moves on to his next victim before he's finished with his current one."

"Yeah, she looks like a victim," Chloe muttered. "All six-plus feet of her."

"She's crying on the inside. She just doesn't know it yet," Simon said, earning a half-hearted chuckle.

Chloe's laughter stopped abruptly. "Oh, my God! They're coming this way."

"Of course they are. I'm the host."

"And I'm out of here."

"Too late." He put a hand on her arm. "Stay. Face them." When she continued to edge away, Simon pulled out his trump card. "Consider it good practice for the reunion."

He wasn't sure whether to laugh or groan when Chloe squared her shoulders and her face brightened with a smile.

"Simon, great party," Trevor said. The two men clasped hands.

"Glad you could make it."

"Yeah. Sorry we're late."

"The weather is horrible," Chloe commiserated.

Trevor nodded, but his smile turned carnal when he added, "We decided to wait out the worst of it in my apartment."

The Amazon issued a smoky laugh that could have served as foreplay.

"This is Shauna Ferrone," Trevor was saying. "Shauna, this is Simon Ford and, I'm sorry, I can't quite remember your name."

Ouch. Simon nearly winced on Chloe's behalf, though part of him was overjoyed that his oversexed colleague apparently hadn't catalogued her in his mental black book.

"Chloe McDaniels."

"Chloe. Right. Simon's friend." Trevor nodded, his expression turning speculative again as his gaze traveled south.

His date seemed to notice. "My Pomapoo is named Chloe," she said.

"Pomapoo?" Simon asked.

"She's half Pomeranian and half toy poodle."

One of those trendy little designer dogs for which an entire industry of clothing and accessories had been born. Next to him, Chloe was poised like a pit bull ready to attack.

"It's nice to meet you, Shauna. So, are you a lawyer like Trevor?" he asked.

The woman looked insulted. "You don't know who I am?"

"I'm…afraid not." Simon glanced at Chloe for support. She gave an imperceptible lift of her shoulders.

"I design jewelry," the woman said. "Celebrities clamor to wear my pieces on the red carpet."

"Shauna crafted the necklace the first lady wore at the inaugural ball," Trevor supplied. Simon doubted he cared in the least who the woman had designed jewelry for, but Trevor was a man hoping to get lucky, so he had to look suitably impressed.

"I can't believe you didn't know that, Simon." This from Chloe, whose eyes shimmered with amusement. To Shauna, she said, "You'll have to forgive him. You know how men can be. They don't pay attention to such things."

Shauna tossed her mane of perfect waves. She was a beautiful woman, if self-centered. Standing next to her, Chloe looked simple, but in the best possible way. Even wearing more makeup than normal and dressed über-fashionably she exuded an authenticity that the Shaunas of the world couldn't match.

"Is this piece one of yours?" Chloe pointed to the gemstone necklace that fell into Shauna's décolletage.

"Yes. It's one of my favorites."

"I can see why. Can I get you a drink?" she asked, steering the woman toward the bar.

That was Chloe. She might not like someone, but she would always be polite and find common ground for conversation. She was so easy to talk to.

"I can't believe your friend's name slipped my mind," Trevor said. "I hope I didn't offend her."

"She'll get over it."

"Is she…seeing anyone?"

Simon's hand froze halfway to bringing his drink to his mouth. Here was the moment Chloe was hoping for.

"No. She's not seeing anyone." Only, that wasn't what made it past Simon's lips. Rather, he said, "Yeah. She's involved."

"Oh. Is it serious?"

Take a hint, dude, he wanted to say. Instead, he nodded. "I think so. Maybe even heading-to-the-altar serious."

"Really." Trevor rocked back on his heels. "I got a totally different vibe from her the other day in your office."

"Cold feet." He shrugged. "She told me tonight she's pretty sure he's about to pop the question."

Trevor glanced around. "Is he here?"

"No. He's…away on business. He travels a lot. He's a…a…an archaeologist." Simon was astounded at the lies popping out of his mouth. And ashamed, of course. Really ashamed.

"No kidding."

Ashamed or not, they just kept coming. "Seriously. He digs up dinosaur fossils and…and stuff like that for a living. He's on a big dig now. It could change the theory of evolution."

Trevor looked impressed. Hell, Simon was impressed. But then, no one was too good for Chloe.

Neanderthal that Trevor was, he honed in on only one detail. "So, he's gone a lot?"

Uh-oh. "Yeah. But he'll be cutting back on travel soon. You know, with their wedding right around the corner."

"Too bad. She looks like she'd be a lot of fun," Trevor said.

Fun. That was code for a good romp, in Trevor-speak. Simon gritted his teeth. No doubt Trevor was already considering offering to be a last fling.

"Yeah. Chloe's really great. Smart, funny." He sipped his drink. "She has a black belt in jujitsu, you know."

"Jujitsu?"

Simon made a chopping motion with his hand. "She could probably kick your ass."

Trevor frowned. Simon held back a smile. Judging from the women his colleague had dated, it was clear he preferred strong females, but probably not the kind who could flip him over one shoulder and then crush his larynx with their bare hands.

"Is that how she keeps in shape?"

Great, now he was checking out her body. What was with this guy?

"Nah. Weight lifting. She can bench press almost as much as I can. It might not be obvious now, but she considered going into professional body building at one time."

Trevor grimaced. "Those chicks are scary. Arnold Schwarzenegger in a bikini." It was exactly what Simon wanted to hear. Until the other man added, "I'm glad she changed her mind. She's not all grossly sinewy now and she has a really nice…upper body."

"They're fake."

"How do you…?" Trevor's eyes narrowed. "Have you guys ever dated?"

"Me and Chloe?" He laughed. Maybe a little too loudly and a little too long. He reeled in his manufactured mirth. "Nah. We're just friends."

Trevor's eyebrows bobbed. Like the rest of the man, they were a little too perfect. Simon suspected waxing. "Friends with benefits?"

Simon wanted to punch him. One solid jab to that Brad Pitt-like jaw.

"It's not like that. Chloe and I have known one another since we were kids." Across the room, he saw her laugh at something Shauna said. She was a good listener. Even when she was bored, she always gave the appearance of hanging on the speaker's every word. As he watched, she reached up to push a straightened bunch of hair behind one ear. A flash of silver caught his eye. The small hoop earrings had been a gift from him for her twenty-first birthday. All these years later, she still wore them, even though they weren't especially flashy or expensive. He hadn't been able to afford expensive back then. "She's like my sister."

Trevor's laughter could be heard over the music and conversation. "Just a heads up, friend. Society frowns on guys looking at their sisters the way you're looking at Chloe right now."

"I'm not looking—"

Trevor cut him off. "It must really suck that she's seeing someone else."

No, what sucked was that she didn't *see* Simon.

Not that he wanted her to, he amended quickly. That unspoken lie, unlike the whoppers he'd just told Trevor, left a nasty taste in his mouth.

"Want a drink?" God knew Simon could use a refill.

"Sure."

It was closing in on two in the morning. The party was on its last leg and so was Simon. Most of the guests already had left, including Trevor and Shauna. In fact, they were among the first to leave. With the food nearly gone and the bar running low, the last of the holdouts finally staggered toward the exit and the cabs Simon had called to ferry them home.

He'd dismissed his housekeeper early in the evening and then the waitstaff and bartender just before one o'clock. He'd seen no need for them to hang around for the handful of his colleagues who'd remained. Now, finally, he was alone.

Except for Chloe.

He found her in the kitchen, standing next to a platter of cold *hors d'oeuvres* and staring at them with a covetous expression.

"Step away from the stuffed mushrooms," he commanded in an appropriately stern voice.

She actually jumped.

"I've only had one. Okay, two, but I dropped half of the second one on the floor, so it doesn't count."

"How much have you had to drink?" He'd counted at least three glasses of wine, but then he hadn't been with her every moment of the evening. She could have slipped in a fourth. Maybe even a fifth.

"Not nearly enough." She sighed and levered herself up onto the granite countertop. One wedge sandal hit the floor, followed by the other. She wiggled her toes and sighed again.

"I'm sorry the night didn't turn out how you'd hoped."

Guilt nipped at him after he said it, since Trevor had expressed interest in her and might very well have approached her if not for Simon's comments. He shouldn't have lied and said she was involved with someone. As for the jujitsu and power-lifting comments, they weren't completely baseless. She'd taken an aerobic kickboxing class last summer, and when they went for their morning jogs, she often carried hand weights.

"He asked me out."

"Wh-wh-what?" he sputtered. "Who?"

"Trevor."

That son of a… "Even after I…"

"Even after you what?"

"Nothing." He popped a cold stuffed mushroom into his mouth, stalling as he searched for a plausible response. It turned out he didn't need one.

"You were right about him, Simon. He's a serial dater of the worst sort. Here he is out with a beautiful and interesting—if totally self-absorbed—woman, and the moment she excuses herself to go to the restroom, he comes on to me. Me!" She frowned. "For some reason, he asked me to show him some martial arts moves."

Simon swallowed. "Kinky."

"A guy like that is a snake, no matter how gorgeous."

"So, you said no?"

"I'll probably regret this for the rest of my life, but yes. I said no. My luck, if he'd gone with me to the reunion he would have hit on my archrival."

Whatever the reason, Simon wasn't going to quibble. "I'm glad."

"Yeah, and I'm dateless for the reunion." She fussed with her hair, pulling it into a ponytail at the back of her head before letting it fall free. It spread around her shoulders in a fiery cascade. He jerked his gaze away before a full-fledged fantasy could form and focused on her bare feet instead.

"You kept your shoes on until the guests left. That's a record."

She smiled and stretched out her legs. Copper-tipped toes wiggled again. He swallowed. Damn those fantasies. They just kept coming.

"I'm paying for it now," she was saying.

"Here, let me." It was pure folly and he would regret it later. But he pulled a chair in front of her and sat down. Taking one slender foot in his hands, he began to massage the arch. Her eyelids slid shut and her expression turned rhapsodic. The moan that escaped was nearly his undoing.

"You've got great hands," she said.

"This isn't even my best work."

Her eyes opened. Neither of them said anything as the moment stretched. All the while, he continued his ministrations on her instep.

"Don't…don't neglect the other one," she whispered when his hands finally stilled.

He did as instructed.

"You've got such soft skin." He was no longer rubbing her foot. He'd worked his way up to her calf. "It feels like silk."

"I…I…always apply lotion right after I get out of the shower," she told him. Simon didn't think he'd ever heard her sound quite so breathless. Unless it was after a run. "It locks in mmm-moisture."

"I'll have to remember that." It was his voice that sounded breathless now. He started to work on the other leg from ankle to knee. "Do you…apply it all over?"

"On every inch of me."

"That must take a while."

"Uh-huh. If you do it right." The knuckles on the hands wrapped around the edge of the countertop turned white, telling Simon that he was doing something right.

"Anything worth doing is worth doing right."

He rose from his chair. His hands caressed the backs of her knees, finding a sensitive spot that caused her to moan. He knew he should stop. He was flirting with disaster. He never should have let it get this far. He wanted to blame his lapse in control on the beverages he'd consumed. But he'd cut himself off over two hours earlier, and even then after only three relatively diluted gin and tonics. No, what had him intoxicated now was the woman before him. The woman whose legs he was literally standing between.

"I...I must have had more to drink than I thought," Chloe said. She pulled her legs free, swiveled to the side and hopped down.

So, she was going to use the excuse he'd already discarded. He would let her.

"Light-headed?"

"Out of my mind," it sounded like she muttered. Or maybe he just needed her to say something to that effect. He didn't want to be the only one who felt so desperate and disturbed.

"Maybe you should stay here. I hate the thought of you going home at this hour, especially if you're a little drunk."

"I'm not drunk."

"You just said—"

"Light-headed. Which could be attributed to not eating more than a few appetizers all evening."

"I've got leftover pizza in the fridge. It's from our favorite place."

"At this time of night? Too many calories and fat grams. That kind of indulgence requires a strenuous workout afterward to keep the guilt at bay."

"I can think of a strenuous workout."

She blinked at that, but was the color rising in her cheeks from surprise or interest? He decided not to find out. Too much was at stake to change the rules of their relationship now. "We're going running in the morning, aren't we?"

Chloe nodded vigorously. "Of course. Exactly. I knew that was what you meant."

"Does that mean you'll have some pizza?"

"It means you'd better call me a cab before I make a huge mistake."

He nodded. He knew exactly what she meant.

CHAPTER TEN

Best Complexion

PANIC BUILT AS the taxi Chloe had splurged on crawled through midday Manhattan traffic.

What was she going to do?

Well, besides lock herself in her apartment and live like a hermit until several layers of her epidermis had sloughed off.

How come she had to get the one person at the tanning salon who was new and, well, stupid? These kinds of mistakes had a way of finding Chloe. It was as if she'd been born as the test subject for practical jokes and laughable mishaps.

Only, she wasn't laughing.

She was hiding.

And probably looking like a wannabe celebrity with a scarf pulled over her hair and a pair of oversized sunglasses covering much of her face. She'd bought both from a street vendor outside the salon who'd been so preoccupied with her appearance that he hadn't even bothered to try to sell her any of the knockoff designer watches strapped to his arms.

The cabdriver was eyeing her in the rearview mirror. Since she was talking to herself, she understood why.

"It's going to be okay. It's going to be okay." She'd been chanting those words since leaving the salon.

"I've changed my mind," she said. When the driver didn't respond, she leaned forward and tapped the Plexiglas partition. "I've changed my mind."

"It's not going to be okay?" he asked warily.

Chloe cleared her throat. "No. I mean, yes. It's going to be…forget it. I've changed my mind about where I want you to take me."

She rattled off a new address and leaned back in her seat, where she continued her chant. Fifteen minutes later, the taxi driver pulled his cab to a stop outside Ford Technology Solutions, where Chloe quickly dashed inside, slipped into the first available elevator and rudely closed the door on the man rushing toward it, calling, "Hold, please!"

It was lunchtime, so Simon's secretary wasn't manning her usual guard post outside his office. But he was there. He'd mentioned during an earlier phone conversation that he was going to eat a sandwich at his desk while preparing for an afternoon meeting. She nearly went limp with relief when she spied him. Lunch and a sheaf of papers were spread out in front of him. His tie was askew, his shirtsleeves rolled nearly to his elbows. His thick and usually neatly combed hair was mussed, probably from running his fingers through it. She liked it better this way. She found it sexy.

More and more lately, Chloe was finding things about Simon to be sexy. The way he'd rubbed her feet the other night definitely qualified. She'd engaged in foreplay that hadn't left her that breathless and keyed up.

A warning bell went off in her head. She'd done her damnedest not to recall that night or her reaction. She concentrated on the attributes that had brought her here today. Simon was dependable, level-headed and pragmatic. He would know what to do.

Apparently that was to choke on a mouthful of smoked turkey on whole wheat and spill his opened bottle of water on his desktop.

"Chloe?" He thumped his chest and reached for a napkin to blot the soggy papers. "I can't believe you got past security wearing that outfit. Are you impersonating a celebrity or something?"

"Something," she replied on a sigh and pulled off the sunglasses and scarf.

His eyes widened. "Good God! You're—"

"Don't say it," she warned. Actually, the words came out more as a plea.

But Simon apparently couldn't stop himself from stating the obvious: "You're orange."

She wanted to cry. In fact, she already had cried in the salon's changing room. The only thing a good bout of tears had accomplished, however, was to make her eyes puffy and red-rimmed. Now they clashed with her new complexion.

Simon tossed the wet napkins into the trash. "Actually, you're more tangerine than orange."

She nodded, as if the distinction made a bit of difference. The fact remained that Chloe looked as if she had escaped from a box of crayons.

"Mind telling me what happened?"

"I went to a tanning salon. Frannie suggested—"

"Why do you listen to her?"

She ignored him and went on. "Frannie suggested I get a faux tan and gave me the name of the place where she goes. Well, they were busy today. One of the sprayer thingies was broken, and someone had called in sick. The girl who'd just been hired last week to staff the reception desk was pitching in." Chloe worked up a smile. No doubt her whitened teeth gleamed against her new skin tone. "On the bright side, I didn't have to pay for my session."

"I should hope not."

Her bottom lip wobbled. "Is it as bad as I think?"

"No. Uh-uh." The fierce way he shook his head was overkill. "The, um, lighting in here is horrible. It gives everything an orange, er, tangerine tint."

He was lying and badly, but she loved him for it. She collapsed into one of the chairs that faced his desk.

"All I wanted was a nice glow, something to tone down my fish-belly whiteness."

"Your skin color is called alabaster."

"I was just going for off-white," she cried. "I wanted to camouflage my freckles."

"I like your freckles."

She scrunched her eyes closed. "My freckles are the least of my problems now."

"So, exactly what happened?"

"I got a teeny-bopper named Cinnamon—"

"Cinnamon? Are you kidding? Her parents actually named her after a spice?"

"It happens. Think Rosemary or Sage."

Simon nodded in consideration. "Now that you mention it, I went to college with a guy called Basil, and my cousin named her first-born Dill." He shook his head. "Scratch that. I think his full name is Dillon."

Chloe snapped her fingers. "Can I get back to my story, please?"

"Sure. Sorry." He picked up his sandwich and motioned for her to continue.

"So, this Cinnamon girl apparently failed the remedial reading class at her school and…" Chloe's words trailed off and she let her head fall back on an exasperated shriek. Studying the ceiling tiles, she asked, "Why do the cosmos hate me?"

Simon didn't bother trying to answer the unanswerable. He was too practical for that, which was precisely why she'd hightailed it to his office when any sane person would have gone home and begun scrubbing with a loofah.

"It's a fake tan, right?"

A grunt served as her reply.

"It will fade long before the reunion, which isn't for three weeks."

"Two weeks and four days." But she straightened in her chair.

"That's plenty of time."

Chloe sniffled. "Do you really think so?"

"I know so. You'll be back to alabaster in no time."

"Alabaster. You know, that does have a better ring to it than fish-belly white," she conceded.

"You have lovely skin, Chloe. And, as I discovered the other night, incredibly soft."

Her hands stilled. Her pulse, meanwhile, took off like a thoroughbred coming out of the chute on race day. She'd replayed every second of their encounter in his kitchen a dozen times since then, wondering what might have happened if she'd stayed. Wishing…

She realized she was staring at him. He was staring at her, too, his expression indecipherable, which was odd. She'd known him so long that she felt she could read him like a book. Well, if he were a book now, he was written in hieroglyphics.

"What are you thinking, Simon?"

Why had she asked him that? Not that she wasn't curious, but she was in the middle of a crisis and… and…and there had to be some other reason the topic was off-limits.

"What am I thinking?"

Here was her opportunity to back away. But did she take it? "What's on your mind?"

He put down what remained of his sandwich and wiped his hands on a napkin. "The same thing that's been on my mind for quite a while."

Oh, that was helpful. He could be referring to base-ball or work or—and she'd kill him for this—that hot new girl at the lobby's reception desk that Chloe had spied on her mad dash to the elevators.

Let it go, she told herself. She asked, "Does it have anything to do with…me?"

God! She wanted to slap a hand over her mouth, maybe follow it up with several layers of duct tape. The question hung in the air between them. His expression remained unreadable.

Finally, he said, "It does."

Two simple words and her breath hitched. It actually *hitched*.

Chloe tried to remember another time in the com-pany of another man when her breath had caught in her throat before shuddering out. The best she could come up with was Justin Timberlake back when he was part of *NSYNC and she'd saved up her allowance for a whole month to buy a ticket to the group's upcoming con-cert. For weeks beforehand, she'd listened to the band's latest CD, singing into her hairbrush and dancing in front of the mirror in her bedroom, all the while dreaming of catching Justin's eye at the upcoming concert.

She hadn't. No big surprise there since her seat had been about three miles from the stage.

Other than that, even the men she'd dated post-college, the very ones she'd claimed had stomped all over her heart and prompted her to overindulge in ice cream, had never caused her respiratory tract to go all wonky like this.

"H-h-how?"

He expelled a breath and then said her name.

Suddenly, she didn't want to know. She was misreading signals and being foolish. If Simon were interested in her that way, he would have said something. As it was, since he hadn't, she'd been content with his friendship. Well, maybe not completely content, but she'd accepted it since she didn't want to lose him.

"Getting back to my situation, I guess I can be thankful I went for a trial run."

His brow crinkled.

"At the tanning salon," she clarified. "Can you imagine if the reunion were this weekend?"

She wasn't acting when she shuddered.

"Would you have gone?" he asked.

"What? And give those girls another reason to tease me? Not a chance. It's bad enough I'll be showing up dateless."

"You could go with me, you know."

He was being practical. After all, he and Chloe would wind up sitting together anyway. Just as whoever they brought with them would wind up being bored.

"Aren't you bringing a date?"

He shrugged. "I'm not seeing anyone."

But he could find a date if he wanted. Someone totally hot and drool-worthy. Simon had long ago outgrown his geekiness. Well, what other people considered geekiness. Add in a successful career and a touch of standoffishness that women couldn't resist, and members of the opposite sex were all but lined up outside his door.

Chloe swallowed. "It's all right, you know."

"What's all right?"

"You don't have to take pity on me. Bring someone to the reunion if you'd like." She nodded and worked up a smile, hoping to seem more convincing. "That model you dated awhile ago would probably go with you. You parted on good terms. If you bring her, every guy in the place would drool."

"That's the thing, Chloe, I don't see the need to make them drool."

She tilted her head. "You don't harbor just a little resentment toward them for the way they treated you?"

"If I did, it's long over. They didn't like me because they didn't understand me. I was…weird."

"You were not."

"Mature, then."

"I'll give you that," she agreed.

"Whatever. It was a long time ago. I turned out okay."

Chloe laughed. "That's a total understatement and we both know it. You're company will make the Fortune 500 within the next couple of years."

"Assuming we continue the current level of growth," he added, matter-of-fact. No braggadocio was required when you had the business community's respect to back it up.

"Have I ever told you how proud I am of you?"

He glanced away. "A time or twelve."

"That's because I am. You are amazing, Simon. Not just because you're smart and a whiz at what you do professionally. But because even when you're supposed to be going over notes for a meeting, you make time for a friend who's in the midst of a crisis."

"You're orange," he said deadpan. "What was I supposed to do?"

She laughed. "This is exactly what I'm talking about. You can make me see the humor in this."

"You would have eventually."

"Eventually," she agreed. Ten or twenty years from now, she probably would laugh like a loon. "But thanks for helping me see it now."

"You're amazing, too, you know. I'm proud of you, Chloe."

"But I haven't—"

"Haven't what?" he demanded almost angrily. "You graduated with honors from high school despite constant bullying and an older sister who was only too happy to keep you in her shadow. You graduated from college in four years, paying for a good chunk of it yourself."

"You did the same."

"I had a full-ride scholarship."

"Because you're so stinking smart."

He rose abruptly to his feet. "Don't do that."

"What?"

"I'm sick of you taking shots at yourself. It's bad enough you had to endure them from Natasha and company during high school. And your sister certainly doesn't help your self-esteem."

"Frannie?"

"She's jealous of you. Always has been. Always will be."

She gaped at him and said again, "Frannie?"

Simon waved a hand. "I'm not going to sit here and listen to you denigrate yourself."

"Actually, you're standing."

"I'm…" He put his hands on his waist. His tone was impatient when he asked, "Is that all you're taking away from this conversation?"

Chloe blinked. "I…don't know."

"Then, let me clarify it for you." He stalked around the desk, grabbed her by the arms and hauled her to her feet. "You're a good person, Chloe. You're kind and funny and plenty smart. You're also beautiful and…and as sexy as hell!"

"You're yelling."

"Yes, I'm yelling. Because I'm mad."

"Why?"

"Because you keep settling for less. You settle for idiots who say the right things but never follow through on the promises they make. You settle for a part-time position because your boss claims that's all that is available when you have the skills and credentials to go elsewhere."

"Mr. Thompson—"

"Is taking gross advantage of you. Again, because you let him. You're a doormat. For your boss, for your sister, for the men you date. For that matter, when are you going to stop letting a bunch of jealous and insecure girls you haven't seen in a decade dictate your life?"

"They're not dictating my life."

He snorted. "Chloe, you're contorting yourself to fit their idea of perfect."

"I wouldn't say that."

"You're orange! Orange!"

"We agreed on tangerine. And it was a mistake on the salon's part."

"The only mistake was that you were at the salon—Frannie's suggestion, by the way—in the first place."

"What do you want from me, Simon?"

"I want…I want…" The hands gripping her shoulders tightened before dropping away. "I just want you to be happy. I want you to look in the mirror and be pleased with the woman who's looking back at you."

"I like myself."

"I want you to love yourself."

"I do."

"Do you?"

"Of course. Well, most of the time. I'm not perfect, but I'm getting there."

"See, I don't agree. I think you've been perfect all along."

"That's because you're my friend." The words were automatic. His scowl told her how off the mark he found them. Once again, her breath hitched.

"Your friend." He scrubbed a hand over his jaw and glanced away.

"Sim—"

He hauled her into his arms. Her breath and the rest of his name whooshed out when she came into contact with the solid expanse of his chest. His face was so close to hers that she could see the flecks of gold in his brown eyes. Odd, she'd never noticed the intricacies of his eye color. Before she could comment on it, his mouth lowered to hers.

Chloe told herself it was surprise that kept her from pulling back. Just as it was surprise that had her opening her lips and granting him access. Good heavens, the man could kiss even better than she'd been expecting. And, oh yeah, she could admit she'd been anticipating this moment. Eager for it in the way one is eager for the plunge before cresting the highest peak of a roller coaster.

"Friends don't kiss like this." The words followed her ragged sigh when the kiss ended.

His eyes were pinched closed. "I know. Should I apologize?"

"No, but…"

"But?"

"I don't know."

He blew out a breath and nodded. "Well, I do know."

"What?"

"I need to apologize. I was trying to get you to see yourself through a pair of objective eyes. I went too far."

"So the kiss…" She swallowed around the lump that had formed in her throat. "It was like a life lesson?"

Say no. Say no. Say no.

Simon had always seemed able to read her mind in the past. Now, it was painfully clear he was not telepathic. "Yes. I'm sorry. It was wrong of me."

"I…well…" She settled a hand on one hip. Between

that damned lump and confusion, she wasn't sure what to say.

"Mr. Ford… Oh, Chloe." His secretary glanced between the two of them. Whatever she thought of the situation—or Chloe's orange skin tone—she was too professional to let it show. "Those other charts you wanted were faxed over while I was at lunch."

Simon backed away, nodded. "Terrific. Great. I'll have a look at them now."

"I was just leaving," Chloe said.

His secretary withdrew.

"Chloe, you…"

"I have to go." She pulled the scarf back into place and plopped the glasses on the bridge of her nose. "Sorry to have bothered you."

"You know better than that."

She didn't know anything at the moment, except that if she stayed much longer, she was going to cry.

She backed out the door, nodded. "And thanks."

"For…?"

Good thing for the dark glasses. Despite her best efforts, her eyes were filling. "The life lesson."

It wasn't one she would soon forget.

Simon had screwed up royally.

He knew that even before he watched Chloe dash away. Sunglasses or not, she'd been on the verge of crying.

Go after her, he told himself. Apologize and explain. But he returned to the chair behind his desk instead. An apology was what had caused her hurt feelings.

Another one would only make matters worse. As for an explanation, he didn't have one. Not one she would understand.

"I love you" weren't words he used often or, when it came to women, ever. But he knew without a doubt that he loved Chloe. He'd always loved her.

The only thing more painful than being in love with her was hurting her.

And now he'd done just that.

CHAPTER ELEVEN

Most Focused

CHLOE COULDN'T THINK straight.

She soaked in the tub, catching the drips from the leaky faucet with the tip of one prunelike toe and trying to wrap her mind around what had happened.

And she wasn't talking about her skin tone, even though this was her third bath in two hours. The first two had been as hot as she could stand. She'd gone through an entire bottle of body scrub and two loofah sponges. She couldn't tell if her skin was less orange since it was now red and irritated. Which is why she'd opted for a third bath. This one had started out tepid and had since grown cold. She was too preoccupied to care.

Simon had kissed her. He had *really* kissed her. With passion and purpose and, for a moment she'd thought, promise. The earth had moved. Maybe that was being a bit dramatic, but Chloe definitely had felt off-kilter afterward.

And ridiculously hopeful until he'd apologized

and chalked it up to a life lesson. She hadn't seen that coming.

She would be the first to admit that she wasn't good at reading men. She had a hard time assessing their true feelings and their level of interest in her—well, beyond sex. It had led to a lot of heartache over the years, as well as one particularly embarrassing situation involving a guy from her political-science class who had flirted outrageously with her. On Frannie's advice, Chloe had gone to his dorm room after finals armed with a bottle of wine and a box of pizza. (It was college and pizza was all she could afford, especially since she'd splurged on the wine. No twist-off cap this time. Nope. She'd gone for a bottle with a bona fide cork.)

She'd felt like one of the cast from *Sex and the City* until a beautiful young woman answered the door. Mortified to discover that Mr. Flirtatious was all but engaged, she'd handed over the wine and pizza, and pretended to have been paid to deliver both. The night wasn't a total bust. She'd made back five bucks in a tip. But it was yet more proof of her ineptness when it came to reading men.

Still, she'd always thought she understood Simon. He said what he meant. He was up front. No subterfuge. No game playing. Straightforward.

Until lately.

Right now, thanks to that amazing kiss, Chloe found him to be a full-blown enigma.

A life lesson? Seriously? He'd kissed her in his office to *teach* her something? That wasn't like him. Oh, Simon had given her plenty of advice and instruction over the years, but it had been constructive and helpful. It had never caused her to question…everything.

The phone rang. By the time Chloe toweled off and pulled on a robe, the call had already gone to voice mail. It was her sister. Frannie had heard from a friend about what happened at the tanning salon and was calling to see if there was anything she could do.

Chloe dialed Frannie's number and waited for her sister to answer. Children's shrieks could be heard before a woman's weary-sounding hello made it through.

"Hey, it's me. Sorry I missed your call. I was in the tub when you called."

"Chloe, hey. Just a minute, okay?" Muffled threats followed. And then there was silence. Frannie's children had either obeyed her commands or had been bought off with cookies.

"I'm back. How are you? Or, I should ask, how is your skin? According to Melanie Lester, the people at the salon said you were all but glowing when you left."

"Did they?" And here they'd assured Chloe that the orange tint was barely noticeable.

"How did the bath work?" Frannie wanted to know. "Did some of it come off?"

Chloe studied the backs of her hands. "It's hard to say, since I'm red from all the scrubbing. I think I sloughed off several layers of skin."

On the other end of the line, Frannie sighed. "I'm sorry, Chloe. I know you wanted to look your absolute best for the reunion. On the bright side, your freckles won't be so noticeable now."

Simon was right, she realized. Her sister always did this. Whenever something bad or disappointing happened in Chloe's life, Frannie was the first to commiserate with her. There was nothing wrong with that, except that Frannie, who'd always been popular and pretty, never encouraged her younger sister to keep trying. Indeed, she often accepted defeat long before Chloe did. And sometimes had a hand in talking Chloe into accepting it, as well.

She recalled some of those incidents now.

In middle school:

Chloe, hon, you're just not cut out to be a cheerleader. You're too uncoordinated. But don't worry. You can always cheer from the stands with your friends.

In high school:

So what if you can't fit in the dress I wore to my prom? You need to accept that you'll always be a little chubby. We can't all be a size four or even a ten. Besides, you have pretty eyes.

And most recently:

If you were passed up for that promotion to full-time again, it's probably because Mr. Thompson doesn't think you're ready for it. Whatever you do, don't rock the boat. You'll find yourself out of a job. Do you know how hard it will be to find another one without a good recommendation from your former employer and an impressive resume?

Time and again, Frannie had encouraged her to

embrace the status quo, to settle for less, all the while implying that was all Chloe deserved.

"I'm not giving up," Chloe said now.

"What? What are you talking about?"

I'm talking about being happy. About being satisfied with myself and fulfilled in all aspects of my life.

"I'm talking about the reunion, of course. I'm going and I'll look spectacular. I've got some time yet. Nearly three weeks." Surely she would experience some more epidermal turnover by then. "Simon said it will fade."

"Simon? When did you see Simon?"

"I went to his office after leaving the salon."

"That was brave of you," Frannie murmured. "I would have hurried home and barricaded myself in my bedroom."

That had been Chloe's first inclination. She wondered now if she should have heeded it. Her life certainly wouldn't have been turned upside down.

"So, did Simon make you feel better?"

"He put things into perspective." Yep. They were clear as mud now.

"He's good at that."

Chloe frowned. "Frannie, what do you think of him?"

"Of Simon?" She sounded surprised and no wonder. It was like asking, what do you think of breathing? He was a constant in their lives. "What do you mean? As a man?"

"Yes." She hurried ahead with, "I'm thinking of fixing him up with a colleague from work. She's been in some bad relationships and she's, um, got a knack for picking some real losers."

"It sounds like the two of you should form a support group," Frannie remarked.

"Thanks." Between gritted teeth, Chloe said, "Could you just answer the question?"

"Simon's great. But you know that. The man is smart, good-looking and very successful. Given all of the women who have thrown themselves at him in recent years, I can't believe he's still single. For that matter, I'm a little surprised the two of you never… Forget it."

"Never what?"

"You know, got together. You get along better than most married couples. God knows, you're together as much as most married couples."

A ripple of excitement worked its way up Chloe's spine, but she forced herself to keep her sister's words in perspective. "We enjoy one another's company."

"Probably because you like the same weird things," Frannie said.

Chloe sniffed. "We have eclectic tastes."

"Weird. Eclectic. Same difference," Frannie said on a laugh. "You're the only two people I know who regularly flock to midnight showings of *The Rocky Horror Picture Show*."

"It's a pop-culture phenomenon and your friends are boring."

"You know all of the songs by heart. You quote the lyrics in ordinary conversation. Time warps and what-not. People who aren't familiar with the movie probably think you're insane."

"I don't care what other people think." She frowned and realized that, when she was with Simon, having a good time, she really *didn't* care.

"And Sudoku puzzles," Frannie was saying.

"A lot of people like Sudoku puzzles. Where have you been? They're hugely popular and considered a good way to keep a person's mind sharp."

"Okay, but what about *Guess*. Honestly, who our age listens to *Guess?*"

"It's not *Guess*. It's *The Guess Who*. And we're not as much fans of the original group from the 1960s and '70s as we are of its former lead singer, especially the stuff he recorded after going solo." She hummed a few bars from "You Saved My Soul." "It's from 1981. Classic. And for the record, he's still around."

On the other end of the line, Frannie exhaled dramatically. "This is my point exactly. It's really too bad that you and Simon don't have any chemistry."

Chloe plucked at the lapels of her robe and felt her cheeks grow warm. If her face hadn't already been in the red-orange color family, it probably would be now. "Wh-what do you mean by that?"

"Well, for a while when you guys were in middle school and high school, I thought maybe Simon was interested in you. In fact, I thought Mom and Dad were nuts for letting him spend the night in your bedroom."

"He was upset and he slept on the floor."

"Still. He was a teenager. You were a teenager. Raging hormones and all. Kids nowadays hook up for kicks."

"You sound like Mom."

"That's because I'm *a* mom." She huffed. "My children aren't going to be left alone with members of the opposite sex until they're, like, thirty."

"Good luck with that."

Frannie ignored her and, unfortunately, got back to the subject that was making Chloe increasingly uncomfortable. "About you and Simon, every now and then when the two of you were in college, I thought I saw a glimmer of something pass between you. A look, a smile. But—" she sighed "—nothing ever came of it. Didn't you ever think about him in that way?"

"No! Never." A time or two. Maybe more. And too many times to count lately.

Frannie's laughter halted Chloe's musings. "Your long-term platonic relationship completely disproved my husband's theory, by the way."

Chloe was probably going to regret this, but she asked, "What's his theory?"

"That a man and a woman can't be just friends unless, well, either the guy is gay or the woman is really ugly."

"Simon's not gay!" Chloe shouted, incensed on his behalf. Then, incensed on her own, she added, "And I'm not ugly."

"Which is why it shot Matt's theory all to hell."

It was time to change the subject. She worked up a wounded tone, hoping to put Frannie on the offensive.

"You guys talk about me? Thanks. It's so nice to know my life is fodder for conversation in your home."

"We don't talk about you in a mean way," her sister soothed. But like a dog with a bone, Frannie wasn't letting go. "It's just that we do find it odd, Chloe. You date loser after loser and, in the meantime, you and Simon are both single and, well, the guy is hot."

Red alert! Red alert! Change the subject fast!

Unfortunately, Chloe's mouth ignored her brain's request. "You think Simon's hot?"

"You don't?"

"I…I…he kissed me," she blurted out. She reached for a throw pillow and whacked herself on the side of the head with it.

"Oh, my God! When did this happen?"

She decided to go with their most recent lip lock. "Today. In his office."

"Let me get this straight. You went to see him for reassurance after the salon fiasco and there you were, all neon orange and everything, and he…he *kissed* you?"

"That about sums it up. Yes."

"Describe the kiss."

Chloe held the phone away and pressed her face in the pillow so she could scream. To describe the kiss, she would have to think about it. And she'd been doing her damnedest not to.

"Chloe? Are you there?"

She lowered the pillow and returned the phone to her ear. "It was a kiss, Frannie. Surely, you've engaged in a few of those over the years."

Her sister wasn't dissuaded. "There are kisses and there are kisses." And wasn't *that* an understatement? "Describe it. In detail."

"He, um, came around his desk and…and he, um, pulled me in his arms."

"Where were his hands?"

Not where Chloe wanted them, she thought now. A moment ago, she'd been freezing. Now, she tossed off the throw and began fanning herself. "They were on my upper arms."

"Mmm. Sounds forceful. Like he meant business."

I think you've been perfect all along.

The words that had preceded the kiss echoed in Chloe's head now, throwing off her heart's steady rhythm.

"Did this kiss involve tongues?"

"God. I mean, what are we? Twelve?"

"I have two pre-schoolers and a husband whose idea of foreplay is to give them Popsicles and lock our bedroom door. Indulge me and answer the question."

It was the first inkling she had that her perfect sister's life wasn't as perfect as she'd always assumed.

"Fine. Yes. It involved tongues, Frannie," she said impatiently. "It was an adult-variety kiss."

"How was it?"

Friends don't kiss like that.

"It was…it was…"

Before she could finish, a crash sounded in the background, followed by a child's shrill scream. "How in the heck did you get up on the refrigerator?" Chloe heard

Frannie holler. Then, "I've got to go. I'll call you back after Matt gets home. I want to hear everything!"

She hung up even before Chloe could say goodbye.

Just after six that evening, the bell rang. All Chloe could see when she glanced through the peephole were flowers. Her heart did a funny flip and roll, only to drop into her stomach when she opened the door and found it was a deliveryman holding the bouquet.

The young man's eyes widened and he did a double-take. She could guess why. "Uh, Chloe McDaniels?"

"That's me."

"These are for you." He all but thrust the roses into her hands and then backed away. "Hope you're feeling better soon."

At least he hadn't said rest in peace, she decided as she closed the door. The roses were white and smelled as lush and gorgeous as they looked. The card tucked inside the blooms included two words and no signature. But she knew who'd sent them.

Forgive me?

Of course Chloe forgave Simon. She just needed to figure out for what. That was why she didn't call him that night. She didn't know what to say.

She was at work the next day when a second bouquet of flowers arrived. Another dozen, long-stem white roses bearing the same two-word question on the card. She couldn't continue to ignore Simon. So, she picked up the phone and dialed his office. His secretary put her through immediately.

"Hi. How are you?"

"Okay." How odd it was to feel tongue-tied and awkward around Simon.

"I'm glad you called. I was getting worried." He cleared his throat then. "Should I be worried?"

"No. But I am a little confused. What exactly do you want me to forgive you for?"

"I overstepped the bounds of our friendship."

"Uh-huh."

"And I lied to you."

"About?"

"It wasn't a damned life lesson. I mean, I wanted you to start seeing yourself as others see you, but that wasn't the reason I kissed you."

She pressed the receiver closer to her ear and wished for some privacy. Even a damned cubicle would be better than the open office she shared with three other graphic artists.

"Why did you?" she asked in a voice just above a whisper.

He was silent a moment. Then, "Can we just forget it ever happened?"

She wasn't sure whether to be insulted, hurt, relieved or mad. "That's not exactly an answer to my question."

"I don't want anything to change between us."

That wasn't really an answer, either, but she let it go. She had to since, when she glanced up, she spied Mr. Thompson making a beeline for her desk. "I've got to hang up."

"You're upset."

"Yes. Um, no. We'll talk another time, promise. But I can't right now. My boss is heading my way."

"Dinner tonight?" Simon pressed.

"Sorry. I'm working late. We have a big project that just came in requiring a quick turnaround."

"Please tell me you'll at least be getting paid overtime."

It was put a little more nicely than his earlier assertion that she was letting Mr. Thompson treat her as a doormat.

"I'm being a team player," she whispered into the phone. "Rumor has it there may be another full-time position opening up."

"That rumor always starts circulating when Mr. Thompson needs you to do him a favor."

He was right, of course. "I've gotta go." She slammed down the phone and beamed a grin at her portly boss. "I'm nearly done with the mock-up of that menu you wanted."

"Terrific." He nodded a moment before frowning. "Are you feeling okay, McDaniels? Your color is a little…off."

Chloe nearly laughed. *Off* was a compliment at this point after the rigorous scrubbings she'd endured during the past twenty-four hours. That morning, after another go at it with a loofah, she'd opted for long sleeves and pants despite the ninety-degree temperature outside. And she'd slathered a heavy layer of foundation over the raw skin of her face with the end result being a complexion that was more tomato than orange.

"I'm fine, Mr. Thompson. Just hard at work."

"Pace yourself. It's going to be a long day and an even longer evening."

"I thought you said we'd be out of here by seven?"

"That was before I remembered that my wife has a dinner party planned. I've got to leave by four. Stevens and Fournier," they were two of the other full-time graphic artists, "will be here until five."

"Five?" That was their normal quitting time.

"They have family obligations."

"That just leaves me and…" She glanced across her desk at the pasty-faced guy who'd beaten her out for the last full-time spot. "Gallagher."

"You can handle it. You're both hard workers."

The only difference being that, as a full-timer, Gallagher had better benefits and paid vacations.

"I don't know what I'd do without you, McDaniels."

"Offer me a full-time job and you may never have to find out."

She'd said the words so often in her head it took her a moment to realize she'd said them out loud. Instead of being mortified or unsettled, she felt empowered.

"You're such a kidder, McDaniels." He laughed so hard his jowls shook.

This was her chance. She could join in and pretend it had been a joke rather than a quasi-threat. *Doormat.* Or she could hold firm.

"Actually, I'm serious. You keep promising me full-time and telling me I've earned it."

"You have. You have. But no positions are available. I want to expand, but, right now, with the economy…" He lifted his shoulders. "You know how it is."

What she knew was that she was no longer willing to settle for the status quo. "But I've heard talk there would be a full-time position opening up if you sign this new account."

"I don't know how those crazy rumors start."

Simon's words came back to her. "I think I do."

"Hmm?"

"Nothing." She pushed her chair back from her desk and rose to her feet. "I can't stay, Mr. Thompson."

He blinked. "You can't…you have to!"

Across from her, Gallagher's pasty face turned a ghastly shade of green that almost made Chloe's tomato complexion attractive.

"I'm just a part-timer. I've already hit my quota of hours for the week."

"Fine. I'll pay you overtime."

His offer represented a victory. Oddly, it was no longer enough. "No."

She bent over to switch off her computer and then gathered up her purse.

"I'll give you a dollar an hour raise."

Another victory. Yet it too fell short. "Thanks. But no."

"You can't just walk out." He cleared his throat and his tone turned stern. "I'll fire you if you leave."

"There's no need for that."

"I'm glad you're seeing reason."

His smile was smug, making it all the easier for Chloe to inform him, "I quit."

CHAPTER TWELVE

Most Likely to Succeed

CHLOE DIDN'T HAVE much to take with her, which made clearing out her desk easy. One box of miscellaneous junk, a half-dead potted ivy and the flowers Simon had sent and she was ready to go. A sputtering Mr. Thompson followed her all the way downstairs to the door that led to the street.

"You're going to regret this," he warned.

"Perhaps. But I think I'd regret staying even more."

It was an exit made for Hollywood. She swore she heard music swell in the background as she turned and walked away with her head held high, her face aglow with as much dignity as manufactured melanin. When she reached the entrance for the subway, however, reality set in. As much as Chloe had wanted to pump her fists in the air like Rocky Balboa a few moments earlier, now she wanted to curl into a fetal position and begin sucking her thumb.

Oh, my God! What have I done?

She pulled out her cell phone. The first person she

thought to call was Simon. She went with Plan B and dialed Frannie instead. She knew it was a mistake even before her sister launched into lecture mode.

"You didn't!" Frannie didn't say it with "you go, girl!" admiration, either. Rather, her tone asked "Are you crazy?"

Chloe went on the defensive. "Mr. Thompson takes advantage of me on a regular basis. And I let him. Until today." She balanced the box on one hip and shifted the phone to her other ear as people streamed around her to go down the steps to the subway platform. "Well, I've had enough of it."

"Fine. Fine. Meanwhile, a few dozen other graphic designers will have their resumes on his desk by this time tomorrow, all of them eager to be *taken advantage of*."

Chloe pictured Frannie using her fingers to make annoying imaginary quote marks.

She was saying, "What are you going to do now? Hmm? How are you going to pay your bills?"

"The same way I was paying them before. Just barely."

"That's not funny."

"Nor is your appalling lack of support."

"Well, excuse me for being a realist." Frannie's sigh was both exaggerated and dramatic. "Mom and Dad are going to be so disappointed in you."

Chloe sucked in a deep breath and let it out slowly. Frannie always did this. Whenever she wanted Chloe to toe the line, she played the "parental disappointment card." Damn her. It always worked. Fear and a good dose of guilt already were making Chloe's stomach churn like a blender.

She fought back a wave of nausea.

"I'll have a job before they find out. Unless you tell them, that is."

"I won't lie to them."

"How is it lying when they don't know?"

"They're our parents." Frannie's tone turned self-righteous when she demanded, "Do you have any idea of the sacrifices they've made?"

What that had to do with Chloe quitting her job, she wasn't sure. It's not like she was planning to move back to Jersey and take up residence in her old bedroom. Her stomach did a slippery turn and roll anyway.

"I'll have a full-time job soon enough, one where I'm compensated appropriately for my skills and where my work ethic will be appreciated rather than exploited."

A passerby overheard her comment and gave Chloe a thumbs-up.

The theme from *Rocky* echoed in her head only to come to a screeching halt when her sister said, "That's a fine speech, Chloe. Tell it to your landlord when you can't scrape together the rent."

Suddenly, Chloe could picture herself back in her old bedroom, not only as a twenty-eight-year-old screw-up returning to the nest, but as a dried-up old spinster, the highlight of whose week was a new booklet of Sudoku puzzles.

"God, help me," she mumbled.

"What?"

Instead of replying, Chloe hung up. The move wasn't so much one of defiance as practicality. She was going to be sick.

On the bright side, she was eating light these days. On the not-so-bright side, she was standing on the street and the only thing to retch in was the box from her office. She was able to spare the bouquet of flowers. But both the box and the sorry-looking plant were dumped in the next garbage can Chloe found after she bypassed the subway entrance.

Instead of heading going home, she hailed a cab and gave the driver directions to Simon's apartment.

She needed him.

She told herself she was being foolish. She'd already told him that she would be working late. He probably was out with other friends for dinner or flying solo. Guys could do that without looking either desperate or pathetic. A woman seated alone in a restaurant? Whether or not it was the case, she might as well be holding a sign that read "I've been stood up."

Or he could be out with a woman. Worse, he could be *in* with one. The perky new receptionist from his office building came to mind. Chloe thought she might hurl again.

"I should call him."

"Did you say something, miss?" The cabdriver asked in a heavy Indian accent.

"No. Well, yes." She waved a hand. "But I'm talking to myself. I'm not crazy," she hastened to assure him. "I'm just…never mind."

"Okay." The once-over he gave her in the rearview mirror told her he wasn't quite convinced.

Two blocks later, she was talking to herself again. "I'm leaving it to fate."

"Fate, miss?"

"Yes." She nodded. "If he's not in, I'll simply have you take me to my apartment, where I'll pass the evening. Alone. With my cat."

"Very good."

Easy for the cabby to say. He didn't know her cat. *Please, God! Let Simon be home.*

Mrs. Benson answered the door. The older woman was holding her purse, clearly ready to call it a day. Even so, her smile remained in place at Chloe's unexpected intrusion. And, if she noticed Chloe's unnatural color, she didn't let it show.

"Good evening, Miss McDaniels. Mr. Ford didn't tell me you would be dropping by."

"I…I didn't know myself. I was just…in the neighborhood and thought I'd take a chance." She waved the bouquet. "Is he in?"

"He just arrived a few minutes ago."

"Fate," Chloe whispered.

"Excuse me?"

"Nothing."

"Come in and make yourself at home. Can I get you a cocktail?"

She probably shouldn't. Her stomach had only just settled. "I would love one." She smiled. "And a breath mint if you have one."

Simon paced the expanse of his bedroom. According to Mrs. Benson, Chloe was seated on his couch enjoying a drink. He shouldn't be nervous. After all, he'd called her at her workplace earlier and had asked her to dinner with the very hope of seeing her tonight. He'd wanted to be sure that he hadn't done anything to permanently damage a friendship that he cherished beyond all others. He'd felt disappointed when she'd declined his invitation. Nervous and a little sick at heart. But he'd also been relieved. As much as he needed to talk to her, he wasn't ready to face her.

The kiss he'd already apologized for was front and center on his mind. He wanted to do it again. More thoroughly. He felt like a starving man who'd been given a glimpse of a grand buffet. One brief taste of her was hardly enough.

He'd never met another woman who could inspire, excite or, for that matter, exasperate him more. She was the standard by which he measured other women, and even before college he'd figured out no one else would ever come close. He'd given up trying to find someone like her. He'd settled for women who, in many ways, were her polar opposite. In a weird way, he'd hoped they would prove to be the antidote to whatever spell she'd cast over him.

A decade later, he knew. It was no spell. His feelings

for her were the real thing. Chloe meant everything to him. Which was why he felt so nervous now. What would he do if he lost her?

In the living room, one look at her face and he forgot all about his problems. She looked…shell-shocked.

"My God, Chloe. Is everything all right?"

"Do you mean beyond the fact that I'm orange, date-less for our upcoming reunion and now unemployed?" She sipped her drink. The hand holding the glass tumbler wasn't quite steady.

"Unemployed?"

"Yes."

Outrage had Simon's hands curling into fists at his sides. "That son of… He fired you?"

She sipped her drink again and was shaking her head even before she swallowed. "No, no, no. See, if I'd been fired, I would be able to file for unemployment benefits." Hysterical laughter followed. "Gee, Frannie didn't even think to rub *that* in my face."

Simon settled onto the cushion next to her. He needed a road map to follow this conversation. "When did you speak to Frannie?"

"Before I came here. I threw up in the box of my personal effects afterward." She made a face, but then shrugged philosophically. "It didn't really matter. It was no great loss. I mean, for the most part it was just a nameplate, business cards and some outdated floppy discs. Who uses floppies anymore?"

"Exactly."

"And that plant, it was a goner anyway."

He wasn't going to ask.

"The flowers you sent me were spared. They're lovely, by the way. And so was the bouquet you sent to my apartment last night. Thank you."

He acknowledged her gratitude with a nod. "So, you quit your job?"

"I did." She smiled in an overly bright fashion before taking another liberal swig of her drink, which was nearly gone by this point. "No more Miss Nice Gal. I told Mr. Thompson that I was through being taken for granted. Only one of his full-time people could work tonight, despite the importance of the account. But good old Chloe...." She wagged the glass in front of Simon's nose. Ice cubes clinked together. "It was just like you said. He was taking advantage of me."

Of all the days to listen to him, Chloe *would* pick today. Well, he'd be supportive. She needed him. That's why she was here. She was looking for a shoulder to lean on. He scooted over on the couch and put his arm around her, not as the man who wanted to make love with her, but as the man who loved her. Who would *always* love her. And he offered her that very shoulder.

"You're going to be fine."

"Of course I am." Her head came to rest in the crook of his neck.

"Your talents are in demand."

"Yep. High demand. Regardless of the lousy economy." She nodded vigorously. Her hair tickled his nose and smelled phenomenal.

"Regardless," he agreed, inhaling deeply a second time.

"You believe in me." She angled her head and smiled at him.

"Always."

Chloe moistened her lips and her gaze strayed to his mouth. He recognized interest when he saw it. Panic built right along with desire. All it would take was a simple pivoting of their positions and she would be beneath him on the couch. Then he could lose himself in her soft curves as he had so many times in his fantasies.

He straightened, forcing her to, as well.

"D-do you want to work on your resume?" he asked.

"Not right now."

"That's right. You're still in the wallowing stage."

He knew the stages Chloe went through after life handed her a lemon as well as he knew the back of his hand. Wallowing came first and involved food and three-hanky movies. She'd be hitting him up for ice cream any minute and wanting to know what was playing on cable.

"I was wallowing. That's one of the reasons I came here." Her expression remained sober. "But I just realized it wasn't the only reason."

"No?"

"I can count on you."

He relaxed a little. "Always."

"Simon, do you…do you think I'm adorable?"

It was an odd question, but he didn't think twice before answering. "Of course I do."

"But I'm not your type, am I?"

"Um…" Again, a map would have come in handy to follow the direction of the conversation.

That's when Chloe took him over the cliff. "Simon, why did you kiss me?"

"I shouldn't have."

She finished off her drink, setting the tumbler aside afterward. He waited for her to rise, expected her to leave, and prayed that she would do so without crying.

Her eyes weren't the least bit moist when she demanded, "Why? Aren't you interested in me?"

"We're friends, Chloe." He stood.

"That's not an answer." She shot to her feet, as well.

"What's gotten into you?" He forced out a laugh.

She wasn't put off. She poked his chest with her index finger. Another time, he would admire her tenacity and spirit. "Don't you dare. If anyone around here is entitled to ask that question, it's me. You've been sending me all sorts of mixed signals these past several weeks."

She had him there. "Okay, okay." He sucked in a breath, exhaled. "I find you…attractive." What a pathetic understatement that was.

"Is that supposed to be some sort of revelation?" He blanched when she added, "I figured that out for myself when we danced at your father's wedding."

He spat out an oath and scrubbed a hand over his face, but it wasn't only embarrassment he felt. At the moment, he was every bit as hard and tempted as he'd been that night.

Chloe nearly let the matter drop. His expression told her she was playing with fire. And, God help her, she'd never been more turned on in her life. Her hormones were humming in a way she'd never experienced even during foreplay.

A moment ago, Simon had asked what had gotten into her. She wasn't sure. She only knew she was sick of the status quo. She was taking charge of her life. She wanted to be in control of her destiny. It was what had prompted her to quit her job earlier. And what drove her now.

She pushed aside the recollection of barfing not long after drawing a line in the sand with Mr. Thompson.

"I have another question for you, Simon."

Here it was. The point of no return. Ask this question and nothing would ever be the same between them, assuming he answered honestly. And even if he lied, their relationship would shift.

"Do you think you'll ever kiss me again the way you did in your office?"

His brows tugged together, but before he could say anything, Chloe forged ahead. This was like her workouts. No pain, no gain. "I'm asking, because I liked it. A lot. And I've been thinking about it. A lot. I've been thinking about *you* a lot, for that matter. Even before that kiss, I was…curious."

"Curious about what?"

She took the fact that his voice cracked as a good sign.

"You. I've always admired your hands. I've wondered what they would feel like. On me. And I'm not talking about a mere foot massage, however delicious I found the one you gave me after the party."

"Chloe—"

"Getting back to that kiss. Will you?"

The gauntlet had been tossed down. Would he pick it up?

"No."

Her lungs deflated to the point she wasn't sure she would be capable of sucking in breath again. Since a graceful exit was out of the question, she was determined to at least wait till she made it to the elevator before she fell apart completely. Simon grabbed her arm before she could brush past him.

"I'm going to kiss you like this."

What she'd experienced that day in his office was tepid in comparison. His mouth was hot and demanding. The hands she'd complimented earlier were fisted in her hair. He tilted her head to one side and began to kiss and nip his way down her neck.

"I love your skin," he murmured.

"I love your mouth."

The mouth in question came back to hers. His hands were no longer in her hair, but at the front of her blouse, working the buttons free. She decided to return the favor, eager to revel in that first touch of skin to skin.

His hands fumbled at the back of her bra.

"The clasp is in the front," she whispered.

Need like she'd never known built as he brought his hands around and his fingers traced the V of her cleavage. The underwire had been a good call today. And fate had been looking out for her when she'd gone with lace panties, even though they had a tendency to ride up. It was then she realized, Simon had stopped caressing her.

"We can't do this, Chloe. As much as I want to, we can't."

A bucket of ice water wouldn't have been as effective. He'd better have a good reason for stopping, like they were related by blood. What he said floored her. Not so much the words as his doomed expression.

"I love you, Chloe." He plucked her blouse off the floor and put it around her shoulders.

She swallowed. "Just to clarify, when you say you love me, are you talking love with a capital *L* or love with a small *l?*"

"Capital *L.*"

Go figure. The only man who'd ever said that to her and he was using the words to talk her *out* of sleeping with him. She didn't know whether to laugh or cry. She did neither.

She got mad.

"Why haven't you said something?"

"I don't want things between us to change."

"They already have! They've been changing." She blinked, shook her head. "You've lied to me, Simon. I can't believe you, of all people, lied to me."

"I haven't lied."

"Well, you haven't been honest." She pushed her arms into the sleeves of her blouse and wrapped it over her chest. "I don't understand. You're interested in me and you date…everybody but me."

"You haven't exactly lived like a nun."

"No. And you've always been there for the breakups. A perfect friend. But you were glad, weren't you?"

"I won't pretend I was sorry. None of them was good enough for you."

"Who is good enough for me, Simon? Hmm?"

He snagged his own shirt off the floor and said nothing as he shoved his arms into it.

"Or maybe I'm getting ahead of myself. Maybe you don't think I'm good enough for you," she pressed.

He flung the shirt aside, grabbed her by the arms and gave her a little shake. Relief and a wave of love flooded through her at his outraged expression.

"Don't say that! Don't even think it! That's not the reason I've kept my feelings to myself."

"Then what is?"

"I need you in my life."

"I'm not going anywhere."

His hands dropped away. "Clarissa said that, too. She promised. But being around my father after their divorce was just too painful because she still loved him. As much as love can bind people together, it can drive them apart, too. If we become lovers, we won't be able to go back to being just friends. That's why I've always been so careful with you, Chloe."

"Oh, Simon."

She reached for him, but he backed away, shaking his head. His throat worked spasmodically.

"None of the women I've ever dated has mattered to me. But you… I can't risk losing you. I won't."

She swallowed. No man had ever said anything half as romantic. Or half as heartbreaking.

She buttoned her blouse and gathered up her things. "You're risking that now."

Then she walked out the door.

CHAPTER THIRTEEN

Cutest Couple

CHLOE'S COMPLEXION WAS nearly back to normal by the day of reunion. Funny, but she didn't care. The reunion was no longer such a big deal.

Oh, she was still attending. She needed to exorcise some demons and come to terms with her past. She'd never truly move on otherwise. Simon's struggle with his past made that crystal clear. He was willing to deny himself a romantic relationship with Chloe as a result of the hurt he'd felt as a child.

So, yes, she was attending, but she was going as herself. She canceled the appointment to have her hair professionally straightened, and she'd returned the third little black dress, since it still had the tags on it. Instead of the color of mourning, she decided to wear the copper-hued number she'd worn to Simon's cocktail party.

Simon. She had no doubt the man loved her. He'd arranged a party at his apartment so she could try to get Trevor's attention. It must have killed him.

Chloe knew she wanted to kill him.

But mostly, she just wanted him back. Even if friendship was all he could ever offer her.

She hadn't told him that, though. In fact, they hadn't spoken since that evening in his apartment. He hadn't called her and she couldn't bring herself to call him. How could she? The ball was in his court.

She wanted to burn with embarrassment when she thought of what had transpired between them, mostly at her urging. She burned, all right. But it had little to do with embarrassment.

And so she dressed for the reunion not with a sense of anticipation or triumph, despite her newly toned figure, but eager to have the evening behind her.

The old gym was nearly unrecognizable when Chloe arrived, as were many of her former classmates. She glanced around the sea of faces, hoping to spy a familiar one. Wouldn't it just figure her gaze landed on Tamara, Faith and Natasha?

Oh, they'd changed a little. They'd somehow managed to become more beautiful. And each was as thin and shapely as they'd been in their cheerleading days. The men they were with were gorgeous, even by Trevor standards. No doubt they all had successful careers going while Chloe remained unemployed.

Her newfound confidence began to wilt. She was sixteen again, frizzy-haired, freckled and bespectacled, standing in the middle of Tillman High's cafeteria with a tray of food and nowhere to sit. The exit beckoned, but she squared her shoulders.

She felt a hand at the small of her back then and glanced to the side to find Simon there. The man she loved. Just as importantly, the friend she needed.

She hadn't allowed herself to cry since the night she'd left his apartment. Her eyes filled now.

"I didn't think—"

"That I would come?"

"After what happened, what I said."

"You spoke your mind."

"I didn't mean it."

"No?"

"You aren't risking anything. I don't want things between us to change, either, if it means not having you in my life at all. I've been miserable these past couple of weeks. We've always been friends. Let's keep it that way."

"So, you want things to go back to the way they were between us before?"

"Yes. No… It depends on what you want."

"I vote for before." But he was grinning. "As in before I got stupid and made you put your shirt back on."

She blinked. Could she have heard him right? The pull low in her belly suggested yes, but she asked, "Can you repeat that?"

"How about I repeat this—I love you, Chloe. I always have. I always will."

The tears broke free, no doubt taking some of her mascara with them. "Just to clarify, you're not talking as a friend? Right?"

"How about if I kiss you and leave it to you to decide?"

He left no room for doubt as to his interest or intentions for later that evening. In fact, she didn't want to wait.

"I think we should leave."

Simon grinned. "So soon?"

"I came. I saw. I conquered."

She waved at Natasha, Faith and Tamara, who now were staring at them slack-jawed, apparently having witnessed the kiss. The good-looking men they were with had nothing on Simon. And the unholy trinity had nothing on Chloe. Simon had said so all along. Her champion and protector and dearest friend. The man she wanted to spend the rest of her life with…he'd been right there all along.

"How ironic."

"What?" Simon asked.

"It took until our ten-year reunion for me to figure out that you were my high school sweetheart."

He kissed her quick and hard. Her heart bucked and that was before he said, "As long as it doesn't take you until our twentieth to figure out a date for our wedding."

* * * * *

MILLS & BOON®

Want to get more from Mills & Boon?

Here's what's available to you if you join the exclusive **Mills & Boon eBook Club** today:

✦ *Convenience – choose your books each month*
✦ *Exclusive – receive your books a month before anywhere else*
✦ *Flexibility – change your subscription at any time*
✦ *Variety – gain access to eBook-only series*
✦ *Value – subscriptions from just £1.99 a month*

So visit **www.millsandboon.co.uk/esubs** today to be a part of this exclusive eBook Club!

MILLS & BOON®
By Request

RELIVE THE ROMANCE WITH THE BEST OF THE BEST

A sneak peek at next month's titles...

In stores from 20th March 2015:

- **One Wild Night** – Kimberly Lang, Natalie Anderson and Heidi Rice

- **Claimed by the Millionaire** – Katherine Garbera, Michelle Celmer and Metsy Hingle

In stores from 3rd April 2015:

- **His Temporary Cinderella** – Jessica Hart, Cara Colter and Christine Rimmer

- **His Secret Baby** – Marie Ferrarella, Carla Cassidy and Cindy Dees

Available at WHSmith, Tesco, Asda, Eason, Amazon and Apple

Just can't wait?
Buy our books online a month before they hit the shops!
visit www.millsandboon.co.uk

These books are also available in eBook format!

0315/05